1300 Moons

David D Plain

Art Work by Ferguson Plain
Medicine Bear Art Studios
www.nativeexpress.ca

Printed in the United States of America.

ISBN: 978-1-4269-9597-2 (sc)

Trafford rev. 09/26/2011

   www.trafford.com

North America & international
toll-free: 1 888 232 4444 (USA & Canada)
fax: 812 355 4082

Contents

The Early Years

Chapter 1

Chapter 2

A Time of Turmoil

Chapter 3

Chapter 4

To the citizens of Aamjiwnaang First Nation

ACKNOWLEDGMENTS

I wish to thank all the historians who came before me. Because of their hard work I was able to write this story. I also wish to thank the native writers from the nineteenth century who lived the traditional life then became literate and wrote about our culture and traditions. People such as Peter Jones and David Sawyer from the Credit, George Copway from Georgian Bay, Andrew Blackbird from Michigan and William W. Warren from Minnesota.

I also found the Wisconsin Historical Society's treatment of the French régime in North America and the Michigan Pioneer Historical Society Collection invaluable as a resource.

I particularly wish to thank my parents as well who provided me with so much by way of traditional oral stories. Lastly, I wish to thank my great, great, great grandfather, Young Gull, for living the events reproduced in 1300 Moons.

The Early Years

Chapter 1

Arrival of Mr. Nanabush—Introduction to Young Gull—Atironto addresses the Council—Young Gull prepares for his Vision Quest—The Vision Quest—Young Gull visits the Black Robes

1

Bang! The aged window slammed down with a start.

"Darn that window!" Karen muttered under her breath. "It would be nice if they would renovate this office," she thought angrily. No sooner had that thought popped into her mind then her psyche received another shock. As she lifted her head to look at the window that had fallen, he stood there in front of her, an elderly man and definitely native.

"Yes—who are you?" she sputtered.

"I'm sorry I startled you. I didn't mean to, the window slammed just as I came in".

"Whew," Karen gasped as she relaxed back into the huge, black leather, executive chair. It almost seemed to swallow her. "Can I help you?" she inquired.

"The Assembly of First Nations sent me—he hesitated as the young Cayuga woman stared at him with a blank look—in response to Mr. Blackman's letter. Is he in?"

"No, he's off on leave, but I am his assistant. Is this regarding the storyteller's position?"

"Yes," he answered.

"Have you filled out an employment application?"

"No, I came here".

"Well, you need to fill one out. Go down to the inquiry desk on the first floor and they will direct you to the human resources department. Fill one out and return it to me." He left the office to follow her instructions.

Karen Blackbird was doing a field credit at the Royal Ontario Museum. She was working toward her master degree in sociology at the University of Toronto. Little did Karen know that it was her boss, the Curator of Ethnology, who wanted his office décor left Victorian. He found old things nostalgic and very pleasing to the senses and this was why it had not been renovated. Karen determined to bring in a stick to hold the window in place and to bring it in the very next day.

Thirty minutes had passed and the old man returned with application in hand. He handed it to Karen and she motioned him to sit in one of the smaller leather chairs that adorned the front of the huge oaken desk. She quickly perused the single sheet, and then looked up.

"Mr. Nanabush?"

"En," he replied in Ojibwa, meaning yes.

"Where are you from originally?"

"Michipicoten Island" the old man replied.

"Can you tell me a little about your experience at storytelling?" she asked.

"I am the official storyteller of my band. I have been telling traditional Ojibwa stories for many, many years. We have a tradition of telling stories around the fireside in the council hall during winter. I have been known to tell a different story each night from November to April. I have much experience at telling all Ojibwa legends."

"You realize that this is a temporary position lasting only four weeks, beginning in July?" Karen said, half asking, half telling. "You would be required to tell Ojibwa stories to our patrons here at the museum for two hours each Friday afternoon. You would begin the first Friday in July and work each consecutive Friday for three weeks. The pay is minimum wage. Is this acceptable?" Karen liked the elder and had already decided to accept him.

"Yes," Mr. Nanabush replied, this time in English. "I would like to tell the Ojibwa story of a certain Ojibwa chief. He was a war chief of great renown who led his band south to a new home over three hundred years ago."

Karen's first thought was negative, thinking this would not relate the traditions and legends of the Ojibwa people. After all, this was the purpose of the project. She explained her concerns to Mr. Nanabush.

"Traditions and legends are only a part of the Ojibwa story," he replied. "All these will be told with the telling of the history."

"One other thing," Karen said. "We would want to tape your sessions. You could have a copy of the tapes, but you would have to sign a form relinquishing ownership of the contents to ROM. Is this acceptable?

"En."

"Excellent. Then you will start, um, lets see," Karen hesitated as she looked at her calendar, "that would be, July 5th, at 2 o'clock. Come an hour early the first day." She held out her hand to Mr. Nanabush who looked at it intently. He didn't seem to quite understand the gesture at first, but then he took her hand in his and she shook it. Then he left.

It was almost lunchtime and she thought that she should inform her temporary supervisor what has taken place. His name was Brad White and he was Curator of Egyptian Antiquities. Mr. White was only supervising Karen because of Todd Blackman's leave of absence. Karen liked Brad. She thought, "He is a handsome man, older than me, but nevertheless, handsome". She gathered up the application and her interview notes, left the antique office of Mr. Blackman and headed down the long, narrow corridor toward Brad's office.

Brad White was a strikingly handsome man, fortyish, but trim. His hair was just beginning to announce the aging process with slightly graying temples. His smile was pristine. He was also a bachelor.

"Come in Karen" Brad said as she approached his office door.

She entered, envying the modern decor of Brad's office. Karen much preferred the contemporary style of Brad's to the stuffiness of

Mr. Blackman's. "The storyteller from the Assembly of First Nations came in to see me this morning," Karen said. "I have his application here and I have asked him to start—um—" she hesitated, looking through her notes, "July 5th." He did seem to have some strange mannerisms but I attribute these to his being a native elder from the north. I liked him and I'm sure he will do a good job."

"That's fine. I trust your judgment" Brad said. "It's lunch time— would you join me?" Karen was delighted. Little did she know that mutual feelings of attraction and admiration were stirring in Brad as well.

Four weeks passed and July the fifth arrived. Mr. Nanabush appeared right on time, one o'clock. Karen sensing a presence looked up to see the octogenarian figure standing in the doorway. The light behind him made his silhouette more pronounced accenting his slightly stooped shoulders and heavily bowed legs, features that were telltale signs of his arthritic condition.

"Boozhoo," the old man said meaning "good day".

"Come in" said Karen while rising to greet him. "It's good to see you again." Karen's broad smile confirmed her feelings for Mr. Nanabush. They approached each other and shook hands. "I want to give you an orientation tour before you start."

The Elder looked at her quizzically.

"So you know where things are," Karen explained.

"Oh, I see," replied Mr. Nanabush.

"First I want you to meet my supervisor, Mr. White". They left the office together and she led him to Brad's office. After introducing him to Mr. White she finished the orientation tour and they arrived at the lecture hall.

"This is it, the place you will tell your stories," Karen said. "Signs have been posted advertising this location throughout ROM and people should be arriving anytime now. I have to return to my office, so if you need anything you know where I am. OK?" she asked.

"Things are fine" he replied.

Karen left the old man in the lecture room and returned to her work. The hall soon began to fill up as the clock on the wall approached two. When the flow of people seemed to subside he began.

"About the year 1640 the great Algonquian nations spread across the center of the continent from the east coast to the Rocky Mountains. The greatest of these nations were the Anishnaabek— inhabitants of the upper Great Lakes region. At that time their territory encircled Lake Superior. Today they are known as Ojibwa or Chippewa people. In the land called by them Saganan lived the Ouendat. Today we call Saganan Southern Ontario and the Ouendat we call the Huron or Wyandotte. South of Lake Ontario and the St. Lawrence River lived the Nahduwa or Iroquois people.

The Iroquois were at war with the Huron and had determined to drive them out of their territory. They wanted the rich hunting and trapping grounds for themselves. The Huron were being wiped out. The Iroquois traded freely for guns from the Dutch at Beverwyck, the site of present day Albany, and they had many. The Jesuits would only allow the Christian Huron, and only those who had been Christian for a very long time, to trade for guns, so they had few. Also, the smallpox disease brought by the Black Robes killed many Huron and the Iroquois overcame them. Before this happened there were many thousands of Huron but after this war there were only hundreds left. They were completely overrun and were escaping Southern Ontario for their lives. Some returned to Montreal with the Black Robes and some sought shelter with the Ojibwa."

2

Mr. Nanabush continued his story speaking in his slow, deliberate style. "Now I want to tell you of a great Ojibwa chief and how he led his people through a great war then led them south to a new home at the foot of Lake Huron. His name was Kioscance which means Young Gull." The old man hesitated and looked off into the distance, as if collecting his thoughts, then proceeded with his story.

Kioscance was about twelve years of age and the son of an Ojibwa, chief. One day Young Gull was alone in the forest. He was on his "first hunt" a tradition that required him to hunt and kill either a game bird or animal alone. This was the Ojibwa way for a boy to move toward manhood. It was always so. The forest was a formidable place for a young boy, full of dark corners in which lurked the wiindgookwe. They were mischievous fairies that would play tricks on the Ojibwa, especially young boys.

"Today will be the day I will earn my first-kill feast!" thought Young Gull. "I have thanked The Great Mystery for the day and have sent my prayers to him by the tobacco offering at this day's break. Surely He will bless my hunt and protect me from the tricks of the wiindgookwe."

Suddenly his thoughts were broken. There was a noise behind him—a noise ever so slight—a rustle of leaves on the forest floor. Was he being watched by the wiindgookwe or no, perhaps a deer! The young boy turned, slowly, quietly, so as not to frighten the animal that was behind him. Suddenly, he stood face to face with a full-grown Ouendat, or Huron, warrior. He towered over Young Gull. His body was muscular, his stomach flat. His hair was cut the Ouendat way with the sides plucked leaving only a strip down the center, combed about four inches high. The fierce looking Ouendat's face was painted with the war colors of black and red.

Young Gull was frozen. Another twenty-five Huron stepped out of the forest surrounding the frightened boy. They were all painted for war. Questions raced through the young boy's mind.

"Will they kill me right here? Will they take me captive for torture? What are they doing in Ojibwa country? The Ouendat never made war on us before, what are they doing? Where is my blessing from The Master of Life?" Young Gull had a sick feeling deep in the pit of his stomach. He felt faint.

"My nephew, I am Atironto; Ouendat War Chief." the warrior said in broken Ojibwa. "My nephew, take Atironto to your village."

"Does he wish to put himself in my care?" thought the young boy. He looked at the Grand Chief questioningly.

The Ouendat repeated, "My nephew, do not despair. Take Atironto to your village".

"My village is not far" said Young Gull. "Leave your weapons here or our warriors will fight you." The Huron warriors piled their weapons in a large heap.

The sun shone brightly on the village of Young Gull that day. He strode into the center of it followed by Atironto. Each Huron warrior followed them single file. The whole village came out, surrounding the young Ojibwa and his Huron "captives," all shouting whoops of praise for their chief's young son. A Grand-Council was called. Runners were sent to all the surrounding Ojibwa villages inviting the chiefs and principal ones to attend. They would hear the words of Atironto. Young Gull was invited to attend. It was a great honor to sit in council with chiefs and elders, much better than a first-kill feast. This was the blessing that Young Gull had prayed for that day and the beginning of the greatness he was born to.

3

It took several days for guests to arrive so the Grand-Council was held about ten days later. When it was convened Young Gull was given a prominent place beside his father.

Atironto rose to speak.

"My Ojibwa brothers—Iroquois kill many Huron. Many die of strange plague. We have no food left. No time to hunt. Iroquois overrun us. Attack, burn our castles. Kill our women, children. Take our wives, sons, our daughters. Torture them to death before us. Make us eat the flesh of loved ones.

My brothers—some Huron go with Black Robes to Montreal. Ask French for help. Iroquois are enemies with French. French will help. Atironto escapes to your country. Atironto begs for Ojibwa help—make war on Iroquois. There are few Huron left."

The council moaned and wailed with grief as Atironto continued to describe the despicable acts of the Iroquois. They grieved for their Huron trading partners. When Atironto was finished speaking Young Gull's father rose to speak.

"Brothers and Sisters—Atironto: I am a Grand Chief of the Ojibwa. My heart is pained for you. We cry for your sorrows.

Huron Brothers—to make war on the Iroquois we would need approval of a Grand-War-Council. Much thought must be given to war. This council can only determine to call a war council—yes or no. This is how we must consider the request of Atironto."

Omuhwenahdaun or "He-Rushes-Upon-Him," a Chief of the Bear totem stood to his feet and spoke.

"Brothers and sisters—it is the purpose of the Bear totem of the Ojibwa to protect. War is well known to us. It deserves much consideration. As yet, we have not been called upon to protect our lands from the Iroquois. They have not attacked us. Nor have they threatened us.

Brothers and sisters—I think we move too quickly to call a war council. This is all I have to say."

Pugoosahbunga or "Looks-With-Hope" was an elder of the Crane totem. She was very old, about one hundred years. She spoke sitting down.

"Brothers and Sisters—my heart is heavy for our Huron friends. They have been good trading partners. Their corn has helped us through many winters and our meat and fish have been good for them. We must think of the future. Perhaps the Iroquois would trade with us also.

Brothers and Sisters—war is a terrible thing. I have always counseled against it. We have been fighting the Dakota in the west since before my time. Always we lose many good men. This breaks the hearts of their mothers. War is a terrible thing.

Brothers and Sisters—yet we must have compassion on our Huron friends. We must accept them in our lands and protect them here. This is my counsel."

One by one the chiefs and elders rose to give their opinions. Each one agreed with Looks-With-Hope's words. The council went on all day and into the evening. Finally Young Gull's father rose again.

"Brothers and sisters—this council has spoken. There will be no war council called. The Anishnaabek can only offer safe harbor to our friends.

Brothers and Sisters—it is decided then. As many of our Huron friends who wish refuge among us may have it. This Grand-Council approves it. I am in agreement with this council's decisions. This is all I have to say." All the chiefs and principal men at the Grand-Council voiced their approval with shouts and whoops ending the

Grand-Council on the Sorrows of the Huron. Atironto moved about two hundred Huron north to Ojibwa territory.

4

Young Gull was growing into a fine young man. As a hunter he excelled and his village never hungered. His father began to encourage him to seek his vision. His vision would show him the path he was to follow in life and introduce him to the spirit which would serve as his guide until death. So Young Gull began to seek his vision.

"Aanii!" he greeted Netahoosa, the band's holy man.

Netahoosa, which means, "He Walks Well" replied, "Boozhoo Young Gull!"

"I have come to ask you to purify me in preparation for my vision quest. I have been fasting for three days," said Young Gull.

"This is good. I will prepare the sweat lodge. Come back at noon," instructed He Walks Well.

He Walks Well went about building the purification lodge. This was a small lodge for one person, built without the benefit of shade. He heated four or five rocks in a fire all morning. When Young Gull arrived at noon he instructed him to remove his clothing and get into the lodge. After a while, when Young Gull was already soaked with sweat from the heat of the undersized lodge, Netahoosa placed the rocks in it. He also provided a birch-bark pail of water with the red-hot rocks as well as four sticks to turn them. He Walks Well then closed the flap of the lodge.

Young Gull began sweating profusely. He sprinkled water on the rocks as he turned them causing steam to rise. The temperature inside the lodge rose dramatically. Every evil thought and deed came out with the sweat, drop by drop. This is the purifying rite that prepares one to participate in other spiritual rites.

Meanwhile, He Walks Well offered a tobacco offering and chanted prayers to ensure a successful vision quest for the young brave. The whole village joined He Walks Well's ritual. They also wanted a successful quest because they had seen a great leader emerging in their chief's young son.

When the sweat was finished Young Gull put on his breach cloth and appeared from the lodge. He Walks Well presented him with a small medicine bag or bundle placing it around his neck and Young Gull left the village for a high place. He took nothing with him except his breach cloth, moccasins and his bundle.

5

The young teen climbed high upon a precipice, which overlooked the river below. There he settled in with a commanding view of the country all around. It was Ojibwa country as far as the eye could see. Young Gull fasted, offered his tobacco and prayed for his vision for three days.

All the while he thought, "The spirits are near. I can feel them. I can hear them in the wind. They will come."

The third day was very windy. Gusts of wind howled around the clefts below him. Young Gull was sure that day he heard his name spoken over and over again in the wind. Near the end of the day he felt a presence behind him. He had the same feeling in the pit of his stomach that he had when he first met Atironto. He was almost afraid to turn around.

"I have to face this spirit" he thought to himself.

Slowly he turned coming face to face with several of the spirit-creatures. They were smallish in appearance, about three feet tall. They had fine features with very long, slender fingers. They began to speak, all at once. Their voices were like the noise of the wind, but contained words that were incoherent. He could not understand them. Suddenly, there appeared in the midst of them another creature. This one was different. He was larger by a head and was covered in hair from head to toe. He had a strange, amber-colored aura around him. The others fell silent and the hairy one spoke.

"Aanii, Young Gull. The Great Spirit has sent me to you to interpret these spirit's words. They will tell you of the path in life you are to follow. They will be your helpers in life. You have been chosen to have not one spirit but many spirits. Your path will be one of greatness."

The strange looking spirit beings broke out in unison again, an eerie chorus of language mixed with wind.

"They say you are to follow the path of a warrior. You will become a prominent warrior of the Ojibwa and a renowned war chief."

Once more the spirit beings broke out in their ethereal language.

"They say this path of life will not lead you to an early death. You will live long and be great among your people."

Just then a tremendous gust of wind arose howling with the rage of a gale among the tops of the precipices. Young Gull covered his eyes with his forearm to protect them from the swirling dust. The wind died as quickly as it sprang to life and the young Ojibwa teen caught a fleeting glimpse of movement vanishing into the woods behind him. He strained to see a pack of white wolves fade into the underbrush as if into thin air. These would be his spirit guides for life and the wolf's characteristics would be their characteristics.

6

Several more years passed and Young Gull had grown into a mature, young man. His stature was large. He was tall and muscular. His body had been tattooed with various patterns, his nose had been pierced and his ears were fringed with beads. His hair was combed high with the top cropped and adorned with feathers. Young Gull had become a striking example of a fierce Ojibwa warrior.

Young Gull had an ever growing curiosity about the Black Robes Atironto had told him about. He had heard of two that had settled at Boweeting and he determined to visit there. He went to see his Huron friend to tell him of his plan and to seek his advice.

"Kaa!" said Atironto in Ojibwa when he heard of Young Gull's intentions. He was against any involvement with the French. "Do not go!"

"My nephew—Black Robes bring only death. Many Huron die from their sickness. Black Robes are sorcerers; practice evil magic. Black Robes curse Huron with sickness, but do not get sick themselves.

"My nephew—Black Robes divide Huron, one half against the other. Black Robes have no care for Huron; put French snow in water, make it sweet. Only want to throw water on people. Black Robes say this gives eternal life, but my nephew; the French snow is poison.

"My nephew—Black Robes call these people baptized. Black Robes treat baptized much better. Some Huron do not want sweet water. French treat these Huron much poorer. Huron are divided, even clans. Huron have become weak, no longer strong.

"My nephew—Avoid Black Robes! Avoid French!

"My nephew, this is all I have to say on this matter." This was Atironto's advice to the young friend he called, "my nephew".

"Miigwech," the young Ojibwa said thanking his Huron comrade. He thought well of Atironto and respected his opinions. He would have to think on this advice.

After about a week he was still determined to visit Boweeting. His curiosity would not subside even with the dire warnings of his Huron sage. He and seven other young Ojibwa warriors set out in two canoes along the shore of the lake called Gchigamii. As they approached the mouth of the river they beached their canoes and traveled downstream passed the rapids to the Jesuit mission.

"These are strange dwellings," thought Young Gull as he and his band approached the cedar log stockade. "This village is too heavy to carry. What do the Black Robes do when they have to move to hunt? They must live here always. How do they feed themselves?" As these thoughts filled the young warrior's mind a large man appeared at the entrance of the log palisade to greet his visitors.

The big man, whose face was covered with hair, greeted them enthusiastically in Ojibwa. "Aanii, welcome, welcome," the man in the long flowing black gown said motioning them to come into the mission. He wore a large brimmed black hat, black leather shoes and a shiny ornament around his neck.

"Such a strange looking symbol," thought Young Gull while staring at the crucifix intently. The proud looking warrior then quick glanced around the stockade, his keen eyes taking in all the strange sights; the log house, outer buildings and the large log chapel behind the house. Just then another, smaller man, but dressed the same strange way came out of the doorway of the log house. He stood beside the first Black Robe.

"Father Claude Dablon," the first Jesuit said pointing to his chest. "Father Jerome Lalement," he said as he put his arm around the second Black Robe. "The Saulteux are welcome," he repeated all the while smiling broadly. Saulteux was a French word meaning people of the falls or rapid tribe given to Young Gull's band because they lived in the district near the falls and great rapids of the St. Mary's river.

"These ones are too friendly," thought Young Gull. He told them his name and some of his exploits as a hunter and warrior.

When he had finished speaking the Black Robe called Dablon said, "We have heard of your great deeds, Young Gull. The Ojibwa who visit this mission tell of your victories against your enemies." After the compliments they exchanged gifts of tobacco and beads and the Black Robes offered them food. The Black Robes sat on wooden benches in front of the opening to the log house and the band of young warriors sat on the ground in front of them in a semi-circle. The one thing that Young Gull appreciated was that the Black Robes could speak some Ojibwa. When they had finished eating Dablon took his crucifix in his hand and began to speak.

"This is the symbol of our faith. God sent his son to die for all men's sins and this is how he died. He rose up from death and gives eternal life to all who believe this. You must believe this and be baptized and you will be given eternal life. There are many, many who have done so and all will live forever. Do you wish to be baptized?"

"I will think on this matter," Young Gull promised politely. He had already thought on it and had determined that Atironto had given good advice.

After the group of warriors left the mission the Black Robes called Saint Marie du Sault, they stopped to camp for the evening on the shores of Gchigamii.

"Have you thought on the Black Robes words?" asked a young warrior named Pemahshe, which means "He-Makes-A-Voyage".

"En" replied Young Gull meaning yes.

"I think Atironto is right. Why should I do the things the Black Robes ask? Do I not have eternal life already? Have I not seen the spirit beings; and spoken with them? Has not the Great Mystery, the Master of Life, given Young Gull powerful medicine?

"What is there new that the Black Robes offer? Nothing! These are my thoughts on the matter."

After the night's rest they continued up the shoreline until they reached their village.

Chapter 2

The Mohawk attack a village—The Mohawk attack a castle—The Mohawk attack the traders—Young Gull trades at Montreal—Young Gull meets Coureur de bois—Trading flotilla to Montreal—The Montreal Trade Fair

1

About this time Mohawk warriors from the Iroquois League began to attack Ojibwa villages on the north shore of Georgian Bay. They were a fierce enemy having a disposition for war, which made them proud and arrogant. After dispossessing the Huron, Neutral and Petun they were determined to subjugate the Ojibwa.

A runner carrying a message from an Ojibwa village in the south came to Young Gull's village. The chief of that village was Mechegegoona, which means Fish Hawk. A council of the village elders was quickly called to hear his words.

"Brothers and Sisters—hear the words of our chief, Fish Hawk. Mohawk warriors overrun our village. They came out of the French River at dawn one day ago. Most of our warriors are away hunting. They are killing many brothers, sisters, and children. They are about one hundred warriors. Many have guns. Fish Hawk sends me to seek the help of Young Gull. Thirty warriors from my village wait for me to return to Boweeting."

Young Gull rose to speak.

"Brothers and Sisters—we must turn back the Iroquois. They must be taught they cannot travel to our country and make war on our brothers and sisters; many of our warriors are also away hunting and fishing. My counsel is to strike quickly with the warriors at hand."

When Young Gull finished speaking Atironto spoke.

"My Ojibwa Brothers and Sisters—Young Gull is right. If Iroquois not answered quickly Iroquois become too bold. All Iroquois will attack Ojibwa country. All Iroquois should be crushed!"

Atironto had his own reasons for speaking this way and the council understood this, but this time he was also right in what he said. The council agreed with the two warriors. One by one they nodded their approval of the decision to repel the Iroquois.

A cedar post was put into the ground and the war council began. Every warrior attending the dance got up, one at a time and struck the war post telling of their previous deeds in battle. No one declined the call to war.

After this ceremony Young Gull and Atironto left with twenty warriors and Fish Hawk's messenger. They joined Fish Hawk's group waiting for them at Boweeting. They moved along the shoreline to about a mile from the captured village, which was near the mouth of the Garden River. There they made camp for the night. No fires were lit and there was no talking, not even a whisper.

As the birds began to announce the coming daybreak the brave warriors broke camp. They knew they were outnumbered and the Mohawk had the advantage of Dutch muskets. But they had a leader with powerful medicine in war. He was invincible. He was invulnerable to the enemy's shots. By joining him in battle his medicine would protect them also. In their minds, they could not fail so there was no fear in their hearts.

At dawn the band of fifty warriors surrounded the village. The Mohawk were still deep in slumber from the feasting and the celebrations of the night before. They could see, in the center of the village, the remains of their victims. They had been scalped, tortured and their lifeless bodies were impaled on long poles stuck in the ground. The sight of the warrior's loved ones desecrated in this manner drove the young warriors wild.

With loud war whoops they rushed the village. The sleeping enemy awoke in terror and confusion. The Ojibwa clubbed everything that stirred. Their tomahawks and war clubs were crimson with the blood of the despised Iroquois. Dead Mohawk warriors were heaped in a pile at the mouth of the River. Only one escaped to take the story back to his people.

The Ojibwa dead were buried with the dignity of the Ritual of the Dead. A mass grave was dug and after the victims were prepared for burial they were interned. Food was offered and the grave fire was lit. For four days the watch continued. There were long periods of silence interspersed with speeches about their loved ones. The men who knew them made the speeches and the women tended the grave fire.

After this the muskets, shot and powder that had been collected were divided between the two bands. This was the first time the Ojibwa possessed guns.

That day added to Young Gull's reputation as a warrior. He had recorded six slain enemy. Fish Hawk became a War Chief of much notoriety, but died about three years later.

2

The year of Fish Hawk's death his son decided to honor him by taking his name. He held a great feast on Manitoulin Island. Ojibwa came from far and wide. About sixteen hundred warriors attended.

At that same time a large Huron town, which they had built on the north shore of Georgian Bay, came under attack by their old enemy, the Mohawk. They built it after they had been forced out of their own country. It was built in the Huron way with a palisade surrounding it to protect the several hundred living there. The Ojibwa gave them permission to live there.

The Mohawk, who were seeking revenge for the defeat at Garden River, attacked the town from the southeast. They came down the French River from the Ottawa River district with about twelve hundred warriors. They put the Huron village under siege but the Huron sent runners to nearby surrounding Ojibwa villages. They learned of the celebrations being held on Manitoulin Island, so turned there for help.

The Ojibwa, which were led by Young Gull, arrived at the Huron town too late. The Mohawk had given up their quest of taking the fortress and had left. They had split into two groups, one returning by way of the Ottawa River and the other returned by way of Lake Simcoe and the Toronto portage. Young Gull and his warriors caught the second body of Mohawk at the mouth of the Severn River. A fierce battle was fought there on a large island and along the shorelines of the bay. Although the Mohawk had the advantage of firearms the Ojibwa and Huron had superiority in numbers. The Mohawk went down to total defeat so the Ojibwa gained more fire arms. The name of Young Gull became renowned throughout Ojibwa territory from Georgian Bay to Sioux country. In the land of the Iroquois it became feared and despised.

3

Young Gull's father died later that year and a council was called to name a new Head Chief. Although Young Gull had earned the position of War Chief his father had remained the Head Chief. Usually the two positions were kept separate to balance the leadership. However, Young Gull had shown leadership capabilities beyond the path of war. The choice was unanimous among the elders. Young Gull would also serve the community as Head Chief.

The council had also decided that the band needed more French goods. They made life much easier for the Ojibwa and many more muskets were required to defend themselves against the Iroquois.

"Aanii, Atironto," called Young Gull who was about to leave the village. "Tomorrow, I leave for Montreal with six canoes of pelts to trade with the French. Do you wish to join me?"

"En," replied the Huron chief. Atironto loved to travel along the edge of his old country. In this way he felt he baited his old enemies, the Iroquois. They had the habit of waylaying any traders they came across, killing them and stealing their goods. Atironto ached to fight the Iroquois.

The next day Young Gull rose before the sunrise. He started the breakfast fire and as the dawn broke he sat in the opening of his tepee facing east. The young warrior offered tobacco to the Great

Mystery and while the smoke of his offering disappeared into the air he raised his arms to the sun and prayed for a successful trading trip. The Master of Life had given the sun to his children the Ojibwa. Without it all living things would die.

After a breakfast of white fish and cedar tea, the small group of traders left the village. There were a total of six large canoes laden with furs, manned by ten Ojibwa and two Huron warriors. Young Gull and Atironto led the group. They moved steadily along the northern shore of Georgian Bay, up the French River, across Lake Nipissing to the place of portage. They made camp here to rest for the portage into Trout Lake and the Mattawa River.

Atironto was the first to speak.

"My Nephew—no Iroquois!" he exclaimed with disappointment.

"Not yet," replied Young Gull, "we have a long way to go."

Then Atironto began to relate past victories in his skirmishes with the hated Iroquois. His stories of valor were mixed with complaints of the peacefulness of the trip so far. Atironto was unaware what lay ahead.

Young Gull followed Atironto's stories of courage with his own. He had already won many eagle feathers for his bravery: several single awards for witnessing battles as a teen, ten double feathers for drawing blood, seven triple feathers for killing an enemy and two awards of five feathers each for capturing wounded enemies. His war bonnet was fast filling up with trophies and his reputation as a skilled and fearsome warrior was growing among the Iroquois.

The other young warriors sat around the evening campfire and listened in awe as the two leaders traded tales of bravery. After an enjoyable evening of stories they allowed the fire to die and they all retired to their temporary lean-tos.

At daybreak they began the long portage and all were glad when they dipped their canoes into Trout Lake.

As they traveled down the Mattawa a single Mohawk warrior who was scouting for a main party of fifty spotted them. He was perched high upon a cliff which gave him an unobstructed view of the river. His keen eyes informed him of the number in the trading party and of the booty. Then he quietly disappeared back into the forest to report his sighting. The main Mohawk party moved quickly downstream to wait in ambush.

They rounded a gentle bend in the river. Young Gull spotted a small island to the left. It was covered mainly by thick underbrush and long reeds hid the shoreline. Young Gull's keen sense of awareness of danger stirred within. He ordered the party to hug the opposite shoreline, which was lined with a high granite bank. Their canoes moved into the more dangerous rapids and they shot quickly past the island. The Mohawk did not expect them to take the more dangerous route and were surprised by the Ojibwa's action. The air rang out with Mohawk war whoops. The whizzing of arrows mixed with the odd musket shot filled the air.

Young Gull had maneuvered his party just out of range of the enemy's missiles, the arrows falling short and the lead missing its mark. As soon as they shot the rapids Young Gull beached his lead canoe. He knew with their heavily ladened canoes they had no chance of outrunning the Mohawk warriors. The others followed and they took the high banks to prepare a defense.

The enemy crossed the river at a ford just upstream. The hearts of the young Anishnaabek pounded in their chests. They knew they were outnumbered. They had heard of the fierceness of the Iroquois and now they would be tested. The young warriors drew courage from their two seasoned leaders. Now the Ojibwa lay in ambush. Young Gull had turned the tables to his advantage.

The enemy crept along the banks of the river. Soon they passed right by the Ojibwa who were spread out in a line hidden by the edge of the forest. Young Gull was on one end of the line and Atironto was on the other. Suddenly they unleashed a volley of arrows followed in quick succession by two more. Each found its mark. The remaining twenty-some fled for their lives being chased by the whooping Ojibwa. They caught several and killed them in close combat with their war clubs and tomahawks. They saved two of the wounded alive. Atironto was allowed to torture the two for a day to avenge the things the Iroquois did to the Huron. Then the two were released.

Young Gull spoke to the captives, "Tell your brothers you have suffered this humiliating defeat at the hands of the great warrior of the Ojibwa, Young Gull. The Ojibwa are strong and will not put up with the disreputable ways of the Iroquois. Tell your brothers that if they do not mend their ways the whole Ojibwa nation will make war on them. Repeat all the words of the great Young Gull to each of the Five Nations. Leave nothing out." The two were released with instructions to carry these words back to their people. The stature of Young Gull continued to grow. He became legendary as a warrior with great medicine, one who could not be killed, and one whose spirit guides also protected in battle.

4

After a couple of weeks of hard paddling they reached their trading destination. The small flotilla rounded the south end of the Island of Montreal where the Ottawa River empties into the St. Lawrence. They passed the mouth of the St. Pierre River and beached their canoes on the shores of the settlement. There was a large two-masted sailing vessel anchored in the harbor and Young Gull marveled at the size of it.

A host of greeters came out through the main gates of the stockade. There were two Black Robes, several soldiers and two officials with an Algonquin interpreter. They were prepared for the Ojibwa traders having heard of their approach by way of their own scouts. It was the Blue Coats that caught Young Gull's eye.

"These French warriors have strange customs," he thought as he admired the shinny brass buttons on their uniforms. "They all walk together and all stop at the same time!" He noticed the muskets they carried on their shoulders and thought, "We must trade for these thunder sticks that kill at a distance". The despised Iroquois had many and the Ojibwa had begun to appreciate the few they had captured in their skirmishes with them.

Suddenly, there appeared from behind the stockade three Mohawk braves. Young Gull's brave little band grew tense. Atironto's eyes flashed with hatred.

"What are these Mohawks doing with the French?" thought Young Gull as his hand grasped the handle of his war club. "Iroquois have been enemies of French," his mind racing with questions as it did when he first encountered Atironto.

The Ojibwa's countenance changed. The officials noticed it and recognized immediately that the sudden appearance of the Mohawk warriors was a problem.

"These Iroquois are renegades who are friends with the French. They live close to Montreal and scout for us," said one official through the interpreter. Young Gull relaxed his posture somewhat, but still remained wary.

"Welcome, welcome," the official said. You have come to trade? We are happy. This is Sieur de Maisonneuve, the governor," the one official said gesturing to the other official.

"The King of France welcomes the Cheveux Relevés," said the governor. The interpreter repeated, "Gzhegimaa welcomes High Hairs". This is what the French had called the Ojibwa because of the manner in which they combed their hair.

Young Gull introduced himself and Atironto as Ojibwa and Huron chiefs. Maisonneuve then invited the band to eat and rest before the trading would begin. That night they slept outside the stockade beside their canoes.

The next morning the town merchants brought their wares out and the bargaining began in earnest. Young Gull had determined to keep half the furs back to trade for guns. When they reached this point he asked the interpreter to fetch Maisonneuve.

"We are finished trading for goods," Young Gull said. "Now we trade for guns. Also is rum available?"

"It is a policy of the French not to trade for rum. We trade only for guns if the savages trading become Christian, and only one gun per trader," said Maisonneuve.

"What does this mean?" Young Gull asked.

"We will give one gun to each one who accepts the teachings of the Black Robes and are baptized."

"Others will trade for rum and guns," Young Gull replied. "English will trade for guns at Albany . . . also at Hudson Bay. Other

French traders with big canoes will trade at Odannong. Trade for guns and rum here or we will not return."

This put Maisonneuve in a predicament. It was his policy that no rum be traded to the Indians. The administrators of New France were more willing to bend his rules on guns and rum. The coureurs de bois Young Gull spoke of at de troit were trading illegally and the English had no such limitations. Maisonneuve desperately needed the Ojibwa to bring their furs to Montreal.

"Will your band become Christian?" he asked.

"No," replied Young Gull. "We will trade the rest of our furs for goods but we will not come back. We will trade with the English." Young Gull was firm and Maisonneuve gave in.

"If the Ojibwa return to trade we will trade for guns now," said Maisonneuve.

"And rum?" asked Young Gull.

"No rum," replied Maisonneuve. The morality that had led to his "no rum" policy would not allow him to acquiesce.

Young Gull had played all his cards and got what he wanted. When the trading was completed and the group left Montreal loaded down with blankets, iron pots, needles, thread, shirts, knives, hatchets, beads and most importantly, guns. They arrived home without incident some thirty days later and the whole village paddled out of the mouth of the Montreal River to meet them.

5

Fish Hawk, the son, came to visit Young Gull's village one day. He brought two strangers with him. They were Frenchmen.

Young Gull was visiting his mother's lodge and they came out of the entrance when they heard the commotion.

"Aanii Young Gull!" greeted Fish Hawk.

"Wemtigoozhii pegezemuhgud," Young Gull's mother said to him, meaning "He brings a Frenchman with him".

"This is the Grand Chief, Young Gull," Fish Hawk said to his French companions. "Young Gull has powerful medicine. Many spirits walk with him in life, protect him in battle. The Master of Life greatly favors Young Gull."

Fish Hawk had brought the Frenchmen to meet Young Gull. They wanted to meet with the most influential Ojibwa chief. They planned to organize a large trading trip to Montreal and they needed Young Gull's help. It was the autumn of the year and they had been traveling through the country for two years.

"These men call themselves coureurs de bois. This one is called Radisson," the chief from Garden River said. "This one is called Groseilliers," he said of the other Frenchman.

Young Gull called for a feast in honor of his guests and lodges were provided for them to rest in. They would talk later and a council was called for that evening. In the meantime the feast was prepared and served to the hungry travelers. First a dish of corn, squash, beans and cooked mushrooms followed by a bountiful offering of whitefish and berries. After an interval of about an hour a variety of fresh meats were offered. Two dogs were killed and served up along with roast bear, moose, and an assortment of fresh fruit and berries. After gorging themselves the tired band retired to their special lodges to rest for the evening's council.

While the Frenchmen were resting Young Gull and Fish Hawk, who were good friends, met to visit with each other.

"Where did these Frenchmen come from?" asked Young Gull.

"Potawatomi found them. Frenchmen return from Kewiinaw. Huron guides abandoned them. Potawatomi hunting party found Frenchmen very hungry. Potawatomi feed Frenchmen. Potawatomi bring Radisson and Groseilliers to Garden River." answered Fish Hawk.

"Are they good men?" inquired Young Gull.

"They are good men, only interested in trade. They carry words of French governor. French governor will give much for Ojibwa pelts, much more than English," responded Fish Hawk.

Young Gull countered, "This is good". He was about to find out that it was even better than he expected at the evening's council meeting.

The Frenchmen presented a plan to the council to trade furs at Montreal. For the distance traveled and if the Anishnaabek would bring all they could in one large flotilla the French would double the standard goods traded for furs. Gzhegimaa, the Ojibwa word for the French King, guaranteed the price.

The plan intrigued Young Gull because he saw in it a way not only to increase the wealth and prosperity of the Ojibwa but a large flotilla of canoes would discourage the raids of the Iroquois.

Radisson and Groseilliers had been away from Montreal for two years and spent another two years with Young Gull visiting other Ojibwa chiefs. They traveled from Georgian Bay to Lake of the Woods and on to Minnesota to arrange a large gathering of fur traders at Boweeting.

6

"My nephew—many canoes come!" exclaimed Atironto to Young Gull. For days they gathered at Boweeting, arriving from all directions. There were even Potawatomi, in about fifty canoes, who arrived from Mishigummee. Mishigummee means Big Lake. Today it is called Lake Michigan.

"Ojibwa arrive from every territory, bring many pelts. This will bring many French goods for our people, guns for our hunters. We will prosper by this trade. We will become even more powerful," said Young Gull.

"Powerful enough to make war on the Iroquois my nephew" said Atironto. Powerful enough to kill all Iroquois!" exclaimed Atironto. His heart seethed with hate for the Iroquois. He never gave up his dream of avenging their atrocities.

The drums echoed in the background as Young Gull and Atironto talked. Many danced to the drums the dances of happy festivals. Whoops of those warriors competing in a game of baggataway, or lacrosse, rose above the background sounds of the powwow. Great quantities of food were available all day long. The women of the Georgian Bay bands prepared whitefish, moose, porcupine and huge quantities of wild rice and corn.

"There are four hundred canoes, full of pelts. Still more arrive," said Sahgimah interrupting the conversation of Young Gull and Atironto. Sahgimah was an Ottawa grand chief who was as renowned a hunter and a warrior as Young Gull.

"Let us find Radisson and Groseilliers. We need to plan the trip to Montreal," said Young Gull.

"My cousins—we will find them near food tables," advised Atironto.

"No doubt," Sahgimah concurred.

The three leaders left the rapids area and returned to the powwow range to find the two Frenchmen. When they approached the food tables they found Groseilliers with food in mouth and hand. Radisson was watching the canoes arriving at the shoreline his eyes large as saucers. Neither Frenchmen could hide his excitement. No trading expedition anywhere near the size of this one had been seen before.

The five leaders of the expedition sat down that evening to formalize plans for the trip. Sahgimah suggested they not follow the route taken by much smaller expeditions. To avoid the harassing attacks of the Iroquois, and the rough waters and many portages of the lower Ottawa River they could take the Gatineau River and come down the St. Maurice to Three Rivers. This route had made Three Rivers an important trading center, but they finally decided that since their destination was Montreal they would take the shorter Ottawa route. Besides, the Iroquois were not likely to attack such a large and formidable force. Runners were sent on ahead so that Montreal could prepare for the large flotilla. The tobacco offering ceremony was completed at the end of the powwow to bless the excursion and the following morning five hundred canoes laded with pelts of all kinds began the arduous journey.

7

Young Gull was among the lead canoes along with the two Frenchmen as they landed at the shores of Montreal. The governor was there in the place called La Commune. It was an area between the river's shoreline and Montreal's stockade. There he sat in his armchair, wearing lace and a powdered white wig. He was prepared to greet the leaders of the flotilla, flanked by soldiers in fresh blue coats and a strangely dressed French holy man. Merchants had arrived from all over the territory and were anxious to begin the barter.

"Sieur Dupuis, we have accomplished our goals. We present you with the wealth of the western nations," Radisson said to the governor of Montreal. He was the first to reach the governor followed by Groseilliers, Young Gull, Sahgimah and Atironto. The governor rose to meet his guests.

"Young Gull, a great chief of much influence of the Ojibwa nation," said Radisson introducing him to Dupuis.

"These Frenchmen look very strange," thought Young Gull as Dupuis acknowledged him. "What kind of French chief can this Dupuis make? He is too fat and his condition is poor. He has no hair! He covers his head with fake white hair. He could not make a warrior. How can he protect his territory?" Many questions about these strange people swirled in Young Gull's mind.

As Dupuis spoke Radisson translated.

"Welcome to Montreal, great chief Young Gull. Allow me to introduce Bishop Laval, Bishop of Canada, who has come from Quebec to Montreal to meet and welcome you."

The bishop stepped forward. His dark eyes flashed and his enormous nose protruded far out from his pale face. His tight lips and unfriendly manner told of his strengths.

Young Gull thought, "This man must be chief of the Black Robes. He wears a chief's bonnet, white and gold in color, the height of a man's forearm. It has strange symbols. His coat too is white and gold and covered with the odd marks. In his right hand he carries a large staff with a curved top. He is flanked by two Black Robes".

Laval welcomed the leaders of the flotilla and expressed his wish they would come to know God.

"Why do these French holy men always think we do not know the Great Mystery?" thought Young Gull. The chief made note of the features and mannerisms of the bishop and concluded, "This one bears watching."

More niceties were exchanged. Then the pipe smoking ceremony commenced. Long oratories followed made by all who enjoyed talking. One chief after another rose and speeches continued far into the night.

The next morning the tables were set up in La Commune and they stretched around three sides of the stockade. There were magicians, jugglers, musicians and artists of all kinds performing both inside and outside the city. The carnival atmosphere only added to the din of the bartering.

Unfortunately, Dupuis' policy was not as moralistic as his predecessor, Maisonneuve. The sale of brandy was not curtailed and as the bartering began to wind down the Ojibwa warriors, painted and feathered, began to revel. The coureurs de bois who were in the city accompanied them in the drunken festivities. All stripped naked, whooped and hollered and fought amongst themselves. The citizens feared for their lives and locked their doors and shuttered their windows. Dupuis had the gates to the city shut and barred and posted guards inside the city. A good portion of the brandy the Ojibwa had traded for was consumed then and there and the party lasted several days.

Finally the huge trading party left Montreal. The huge quantity of goods acquired made their canoes run deep. The month long trip back to the homeland would be arduous but Young Gull was very pleased with the success of the expedition. The Montreal trade fairs continued for some time.

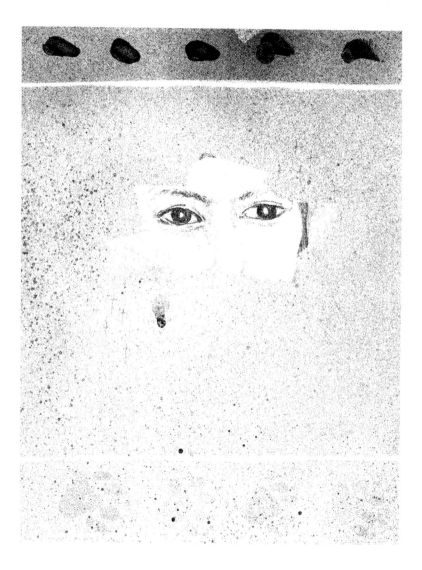

A Time of Turmoil

Chapter 3

Mr. Nanabush Vanishes—Young Gull Meets Chenoa—The Courtship—The Three Fires Council—Young Gull Hunts the Mahgwah—Young Gull's Marriage—Shahwanjegawin's Birth

1

Karen looked up from her desk to check the time. "Um, nearly four," she thought. "Mister Nanabush must be about done. I wonder how things went." Curiosity got the better of her and she closed the file she was working on. She got up out of the huge black leather chair and began to move toward the door. Remembering the open window she stopped abruptly and turned. She had meant to take out the stick that was holding the window up earlier and close it. Just as she did Brad White arrived at the door.

"Ahem," he cleared his throat to announce himself.

"Oh!" Karen exclaimed, dropping the stick out the window to the courtyard below.

"I'm sorry," apologized Brad. "I didn't mean to startle you. Please forgive me. "Of course—I'm just naturally—um—sort of jumpy. You know" said Karen trying to smooth over a rocky reaction to Brad's announcement.

"I'm going down to the cafeteria on a coffee break. Would you like to join me?

"I'd love to, but I was just about to go down to the lecture room to see how things went with Mr. Nanabush's storytelling," answered Karen. Her heart was beating faster than normal and she wondered whether it was because of her being startled or was it the invitation.

"That's OK. I'll go with you. We can retrieve your window prop from the courtyard after and then go for coffee."

"Sounds like a plan" answered Karen, the end of her statement raising an octave. She was trying her best to sound more composed than her emotions would really allow. Brad smiled.

The couple, looking very much a couple, left the antique office behind. They headed down the long, drab corridor that led to the third floor concourse and the elevator. When they reached the lecture hall on the first floor it was all but empty.

"Do you know where Mr. Nanabush is?" Karen asked a middle-aged woman who was standing just outside the room. The woman looked to the two teens standing with her for assistance.

"He left, just a few minutes ago. He went that way," answered the older of the two. He was pointing down the hallway that led to the esplanade, which backed onto the outside courtyard.

"Oh, he must be confused. He can't get out that way," Karen said to Brad. Just as the two started down the corridor they caught sight of Mr. Nanabush as he hobbled around the corner toward the esplanade.

"Mr. Nanabush! Yoo-hoo!" Karen called in a loud voice. Mr. Nanabush didn't hear her. He just kept shuffling along. The budding pair didn't go out of their way to hurry. They both thought they would meet Mr. Nanabush on his way back from the dead-end presented by the courtyard. As they reached the entrance to the esplanade they turned to go in.

The esplanade was a quiet retreat about thirty feet wide and a hundred feet long. The high, yellow brick walls were inlaid with reliefs of various exotic animals and beautiful, green ivy made its way up the brick to the ceiling. There was an indoor pool in the center of the esplanade and it had a statue of a girl holding a large Grecian urn, which had water continuously tumbling into the pool. On the right windows exposed the walkways, benches and vegetation of the outer courtyard. There were a few people enjoying the serenity of this aesthetic concourse, but no Mr. Nanabush.

Karen's eyes found the two double, glass doors leading to the courtyard before Brad's. There was no one at the closest set of doors, but she caught a glimpse of something moving through the far set. "There he goes!" she exclaimed with excitement. Brad and Karen moved more quickly through the closest set of doors. They entered the courtyard, but no one was there. Where had he gone? Brad and Karen looked at each other perplexed appearance etched on their faces. Suddenly there was the loud caw, caw of a very large, black crow as it lifted off from the center of the courtyard. The affectionate couple looked at each other in amazement, and then gazed upward to the bright blue sky. Their eyes followed the black winged creature intently, as it grew smaller, smaller, and then disappeared.

"That's strange!" exclaimed Karen.

Brad concurred, "It certainly is. Well, let's pick up the stick you dropped. We can talk to Mr. Nanabush next week." The two retrieved the stick and headed back to the coffee shop walking just a little more closely than before.

2

Mr. Nanabush arrived the following week right on time. When his audience had all taken their seats he began.

The Great Fall Powwow was taking place at Boweeting. All the Ojibwa totems: the leaders, the warrior, the teacher, the medicine and, the most important totem of all, the providers were there. They came from all around Lake Superior to celebrate a successful season.

This particular celebration was one of the largest ever seen as more and more Ojibwa from the western end of the great lake participated. The air was filled with excitement. The festive atmosphere had been in the air for days and the drums and singers could be heard for miles. A game of lacrosse had been going on for three days with several hundred participating while others were involved in games of chance, like the moccasin game.

"I will up the wager. Shirts for fifty Anishnaabek warriors!" exclaimed Young Gull.

"Agreed" Kechemahgwah, or Great Bear, retorted. He was a Grand Chief from the western tip of Lake Superior.

Young Gull took the long stick and pointed it to one of the two moccasins in front of Kechemahgwah and then he lifted it.

"Eeeeiiiii" Young Gull hollered! The marked bullet was under the moccasin so he moved another shot marker stick to his pile. The Ojibwa loved their games of chance and Young Gull was no exception.

"I cannot play well when I hunger. We should eat and then continue the game," said Great Bear half asserting, half asking.

"I hunger also. We will eat now and play the moccasin game later" agreed Young Gull.

They left the shelter of the trees by the rapids where they played their moccasin game and moved through the open field to the food tables. As they worked their way through the crowds Young Gull's old friend Atironto spotted him. He was with the celebrated war chief Sahgimah.

"My nephew! My nephew" Atironto called.

Young Gull waved his arm acknowledging his old friend. "Aanii Atironto, Aanii Sahgimah! This is Great Bear. He is a Grand Chief from the Minnesota district. We go to eat. Will you join us in the feast?"

"En, my nephew, corn soup best your uncle taste for many feasts," replied Atironto in his broken Ojibwa.

Several large iron kettles hung from wooden tripods over campfires releasing the appetizing aroma of corn soup. It hung in the air. The four leaders approached the soup area. Young Gull dropped behind the other three. He had caught a glimpse of an intriguing image. The confident young grand chief became uncharacteristically unsure of himself. This was a feeling he had not felt for a very long time. He felt like a wolf wary of the bait, overwhelmingly attracted but cautiously sensing danger.

"My nephew, did you come eat?" asked Atironto. As he prodded his friend he turned as saw the revelation that caused his companion so much concern. Atironto broke out in an ear-to-ear grin. "Young maiden attracts my nephew!" teased Atironto. The other two joined in with Atironto's guffaws.

"No! There is nothing here," exclaimed Young Gull as he tried, unsuccessfully, to hide his attraction to the young woman serving the soup. Then Great Bear greeted the beautiful young virgin. "Aanii Chenoa"

"Aanii Great Bear" said Chenoa returning the greeting. The four chiefs ate their fill and no more was said about the beautiful young woman. Then they returned to quiet solitude near the river for conversation, which was an activity also greatly enjoyed by the Ojibwa.

"Many more Ojibwa from Minnesota and Lake of the Woods attend the fall feast," said Sahgimah.

"We have signed a peace treaty with our old enemies, the Sioux. They have a great desire for French trade goods, which we have in abundance. They have become trading partners with us and have ceased their hostilities. This has brought much prosperity to both Ojibwa and Dakota" explained Great Bear.

"We have been trading in Montreal at the great trade fairs," said Young Gull, "but lately we have seen little of our western Ojibwa brothers."

"A Frenchman called Du Lhut opened a trading post at the mouth of the St. Louis River. He is a fair man in his dealings with us" answered Great Bear.

"My brother, have Black Robes been in your country?" queried Atironto.

"Yes, they have a mission they call Saint Esprit. A Black Robe by the name of Marquette is there."

"My brother, beware of Black Robes," warned Atironto. "Black Robes divide Minnesota Ojibwa. Minnesota Ojibwa become weak. Black Robes bring great sickness with them. Many die."

"Many have died, two winters ago. But the Great Mystery was greater than their God. Their plague could not prevail. No one listens to the Black Robe. No one accepts his Spirit" answered Great Bear.

"Their religion is strange. They are uncivilized. They worship a dead man who died an unworthy death. They are cannibals. They eat his flesh and drink his blood. They are uncivilized!" exclaimed Sahgimah. All agreed making coarse gestures. Then the conversation turned back to trade.

"Trade for French goods has brought peace to the west. Perhaps this strategy would work with the Iroquois" suggested Great Bear.

"My brothers, there can be no peace with Iroquois. My nephew, my brothers, Iroquois are belligerent people. Know only war, always war!" interrupted Atironto. The other three chiefs sensed Atironto's hostility and gave him a wide berth.

"Iroquois trade for English goods at Albany. Iroquois are hostile people. No interest in peace. Iroquois ambush Ojibwa trading party three summers ago. Kill twenty young men. Steal pelts. Iroquois make peace. Iroquois break peace this summer. Iroquois waylay hunting party. Iroquois are obstinate people who will be taught a lesson." Young Gull's prophecy was soon to be realized.

With this Atironto and Sahgimah decided to return to the game of lacrosse. Young Gull and Great Bear returned to their moccasin game but it soon became obvious that Young Gull was aloof. He had no concentration.

"There is something wrong?" asked Great Bear.

"You know the young woman, Chenoa," said Young Gull.

"Ah Ha!" remarked his new friend smiling broadly. "She is Pawnee. She was taken by a Sioux raiding party as a child and raised Dakota. She is part of the peace agreement. She replaces a daughter of one of our warriors called Red Stone. The Dakota killed his daughter four summers ago so he adopted her as his own. I will introduce you to Chenoa's father, Red Stone".

"That would be good," agreed Young Gull. His thoughts returned to the game and the two played long into the night.

The next day Great Bear introduced Young Gull to Red Stone. Red Stone knew of Young Gull because of his reputation as a Great War Chief and he was impressed that the great Young Gull should be interested in his new daughter. Normally a suitor would be required to prove his worth as a provider to the young girl's family. But in this case Young Gull had nothing to prove. His reputation went before him.

"Aanii Red Stone!" called out Great Bear to Chenoa's father. I have with me Young Gull, Grand Chief and Great War Chief of the Boweeting Ojibwa. He is interested in courting Chenoa." Great Bear gave Young Gull all the accolades the great chief deserved in his introduction to Red Stone.

"Aanii, Young Gull. I have heard of your many great deeds. We will smoke on this matter," said Red Stone. The three entered Red Stone's lodge where his wife, Tahkib was repairing a pair of leggings.

"Tahkib; Great Bear has brought Young Gull, chief of Boweeting. Young Gull seeks approval to court Chenoa. We will smoke on this matter," instructed Red Stone.

Tahkib, whose name means Spring Water, smiled a nervous smile. "Yes" she replied as she took Red Stone's pipe down from its place on the wall. They all sat on the bearskins on the floor of the lodge and Red Stone lit his pipe.

"Great Mystery, look upon our talk with favor. Bring success to all here. Bring the best for our new daughter Chenoa. She should prosper and be happy." Red Stone held the pipe high, offering the sacred tobacco smoke to the Master of Life. The smoke carried his chants to the invisible world. Spring Water began to shake the turtle rattle and Red Stone sang a prayerful chant. When he was finished Red Stone drew on the pipe and passed it to his chief, Great Bear. He did likewise and passed it to Young Gull. Young Gull followed suit then returned the pipe to Red Stone who placed it in the center of the lodge.

"Brothers", Red Stone began, "Chenoa is a new daughter. She replaces our daughter, Waubese, who was lost to the Dakota. Waubese was killed by a marauding war party that attacked our village. She was our only child."

Red Stone looked to Spring Water. She added, "Chenoa has filled a great void in my heart. When Swan was killed I thought I would die. Now my heart is happy. We are Chenoa's new parents. We have become a family. This is a new happiness. I cannot bear to have my heart empty again so soon." Spring Water paused, her voice breaking.

Red Stone broke in. "Chenoa will make a good wife someday. But I feel this is too soon, perhaps in a few years."

Young Gull said, "I will make a good husband for Chenoa. I am a good provider. I once killed three moose in one week. I have provided well for my parents as well as my whole village. The Great Mystery has given many spirit helpers and my medicine is great."

"Your reputation is great, Young Gull, and not in question. We would be proud to have you as a son-in-law, but this is too soon for us" Red Stone replied. Spring Water agreed as she dabbed a tear from her cheek.

Great Bear interjected, "Perhaps the courting could be extended. You could winter, as a family, at Young Gull's village. If the Great Mystery smiles on this relationship the marriage could take place next summer."

"Ah; I think this could work," said Red Stone, looking to Spring Water for her response.

"Yes" she said as she nodded her approval.

"Before we proceed we must tell Chenoa that Young Gull is interested in marriage. They must be formally introduced. We will talk to Chenoa tonight. Chenoa must consent. If she does Great Bear should bring Young Gull here tomorrow for introductions" instructed Red Stone. The talks finished with all in agreement.

The next morning the two chiefs approached Red Stone's lodge. Chenoa's parents greeted them at the entrance. Then they called Chenoa's name and she appeared in the doorway.

Chenoa was a vision of beauty. Young Gull slowly lifted his head and as he did he took in this vision from the ground up. Her legs were long and slender. The doeskin dress hugged her graceful figure. Her hands and fingers matched the shape of her body, long and slender. Her face was a vision of beauty. Chenoa's skin was bronze in color, which highlighted her ebony eyes. They caught the sunlight and seemed to twinkle and glisten just as her long black hair did. She smiled a smile that was white, straight and even.

"Aanii, Chenoa! This is Young Gull, Grand Chief of the Boweeting Ojibwa."

"Aanii Young Gull" greeted Chenoa. He felt a lump in his throat. He felt awkward, even nervous, not the feeling of confidence that was a normal part of his makeup.

"Ahneem, uh . . ." the great chief's voice broke with a high, mispronunciation of the greeting. Young Gull was overwhelmed. He felt foolish, even a sick feeling deep in the pit of his stomach. The Grand Chief of the Boweeting Ojibwa, War Chief and most notable hunter was smitten, left helpless. Chenoa's warm smile changed to a broad grin. She took Young Gull by the arm and the courting began!

3

The Freeze-up Moon arrived soon after the Great Fall Feast ended. It had been a good feast. Many bands had attended renewing family ties, friendships and military alliances, but now all had returned to their winter camps. The Great Spirit continued to smile on the Ojibwa.

"The hunters return! Here they come! Here they come!" the children of the village hollered. The commotion of the children mixed with the barking of the village dogs alerted the whole village.

Chenoa dropped the snowshoes she was repairing for Red Stone. She appeared outside her lodge to see which hunting party was returning. She could see four canoes, maybe five, coming down river toward the village. She hoped it was Young Gull. He and her father had been gone for days. Chenoa's heart began to beat faster and faster as the party got closer and closer. Yes it was them! She could now recognise the outline of Young Gull's powerful upper body as he urged the lead canoe on with the sure powerful strokes of his paddle. She began to move toward the shoreline of the river, slowly at first, then increasing her walk. The rest of the members of the village followed.

"Aanii how was the hunt?" hollered one excited, young boy as the canoes curled in toward the shore. The people could see the canoes were laden with big game as Young Gull answered, "The hunt prospered. Much game has given their lives for the good of the village".

After the canoes were beached the hunting party returned to their lodges and the young men carried the game to the center of the village for distribution. The entire village shared in the success of the hunt.

Chenoa and her mother, Spring Water, had been cooking a large pot of venison stew and corn bread. After Spring Water and Red Stone talked about the hunt he helped himself to a bowl of the stew. The succulent flavor of the meal lingered in his mouth. "Umm, this is good!" Red Stone exclaimed. Chenoa could contain herself no longer. She filled a pot, excused herself and headed toward Young Gull's lodge. It was him that concerned her. It was him that made her heart pound.

"Boozhoo Young Gull," she called from outside the entrance to his lodge.

"Come in," he said as he held the flap open for her. "It is good to see you."

"I have venison stew and fresh bread for you and your mother. Are you hungry?"

"Very," Young Gull replied enthusiastically. "It smells delicious."

Young Gull's mother interrupted, "It certainly does. You are too quick, Chenoa. I have just started to cook dinner for us."

"I'm sorry, I should have . . ." but Young Gull's elderly mother cut her off. "You have done right to be concerned for my son and we appreciate your sharing your dinner with us. I will take ours off the fire and finish cooking it later." Young Gull's mother was happy to see him in love and wholeheartedly approved of his choice of Chenoa as a companion to travel life's path with. She had watched Chenoa with the eyes of an apprehensive parent but had quickly put her concerns to rest. Chenoa had displayed all the qualities of a good companion. She was an excellent cook, could sew well, knew how to keep a garden and had a pleasing personality. She was very pleased with Chenoa.

After they ate Young Gull and Chenoa went for a walk. It was cold and there was some snow on the ground. The young couple made their way along the riverbank. It was twilight.

"When we are married I am going to keep a fine lodge for you," Chenoa said dreaming of the future. "We will have many fine children, sons and daughters, and I will make you so happy."

"And I will give you the whole territory, including all the lakes and rivers. I will always protect you and no harm shall ever come to you."

The two young lovers were making promises they only wished they could keep; the way young lovers have done since the beginning of time. The swift current of the ice cold river rushed passed and the cool air of the evening reminded them it was the Freeze-up Moon. Their thoughts turned to the cozy warmth of their lodges. The two held each other in a close embrace and Young Gull whispered tenderly, "Zaaghiin".

"I love you" Chenoa replied ever so softly into Young Gull's ear. Then they moved back toward the village. Although both were chilled from the late fall air their desire to be close to each other gave them no urge to hurry.

Three months had passed and Ojibwa territory was in the midst of winter's deep freeze. The previous year's harvest of fish, meat and corn had been good so that there was no need to use the village dogs to survive. The people of the village had gathered in the council lodge that evening to hear the legends told by Mundahminqua the band's storyteller. She was an elder about eighty years old and had been telling the stories for many years. She had been particularly good at keeping the village garden plot when younger and this is how she earned her name, Corn Woman.

Young Gull entered the council lodge, which was filled to capacity. The clamor diminished to an eerie silence.

"Aanii, Young Gull" greeted Corn Woman.

"Aanii," he replied as he made his way to the center of the lodge. He then began his welcoming speech.

"We are midway through the winter season. The Great Spirit has blessed us greatly. We have much to be thankful for.

Our winter stores are plentiful. The game has given itself freely so the hunting has been good. We have much to be thankful for.

The Winter Spirit's power is weak this season and his hardships are easy. We have much to be thankful for.

We should give thanks for Corn Woman who is the best storyteller in the district. Without elders like her to tell the stories our children's lives would die and our people would become lost. We have much to be thankful for."

As Young Gull continued speaking Chenoa watched the proceedings from the back of the lodge, near the entrance. She was so rapt with Young Gull that his voice trailed off and she slipped into a romantic fantasy. When Young Gull finished his speech Netahoosa began a prayer of thanksgiving.

"Gzhemnidoo, Great Mystery:

You are the Great Creator, Creator of the land,

Creator of the lakes and rivers,

Creator of the sky and all that are in them.

You have created the Ojibwa, your special people.

We are thankful for your provisions for the long winter.

We are thankful for the favorable nature you have given the game animals. Because of your edict they give themselves for our sustenance and well-being.

We are thankful for the spirit beings you have created for our guidance and protection.

You are Gzhemnidoo, the Great Spirit.

We offer sacred tobacco to carry this thanksgiving prayer to you in the spirit land."

When Netahoosa finished his prayer Young Gull began to drum the band's ceremonial drum. Netahoosa joined in with Young Gull's thank-chant. Kewadin, whose name meant North Wind, was Netahoosa's helper. Netahoosa chose him to teach the knowledge of medicine. It was Kewadin who offered the tobacco in the fire to the chants of the Grand Chief and the Medicine Man.

When the thanksgiving ceremony was over Corn Woman began to speak. She had a high penetrating voice that jolted Chenoa from her amorous daydream. Young Gull made his way to the rear of the lodge and took a place beside his darling Chenoa. He leaned over whispering in her ear, "Come outside. I have something to show you." The two slipped out the entrance into the night and the frigid arctic air.

A short walk from the village there was a small lake called Red Lake that emptied into the river. Young Gull took Chenoa by the hand and led her through the quiet village to the trail that led to Red Lake. When they approached the trail, which disappeared into the darkness Chenoa balked.

"We cannot go into the night!" she exclaimed. "The wiindgoo!" she gasped. "What about the wiindgoo? It is night and we will be devoured." Young Gull smiled a reassuring smile.

"The wiindgoo cannot harm us. I have very great medicine. Many spirit helpers accompany me through life. Don't worry. We will be protected". Reassuringly he took Chenoa by the hand and the two began down the long, dark trail.

As they walked the trail continued to peter off into the blackness of the night. They made their way slowly up to the small lake. Chenoa looked back and could see the trail fade into the darkness and the light of the village clearing had vanished. She clutched Young Gull tightly by the arm and he smiled confidently. This gave her a certain sense of security.

The forest was thick and the tall pines creaked with the light breeze. An unseen owl hooted an eerie call from just beyond the trail. Despite Chenoa's confidence in Young Gull the wiindgoo were never far from her mind. Suddenly a dim haze appeared ahead. It was the clearing of Red Lake. They had arrived and although she felt a sense of relief Chenoa realized there was still the long return journey to be made.

It was the time of the new moon and the night was clear and frigid. They reached the place where the trail spilled onto the small lake's beach. As the pair gazed up the night sky displayed a wondrous sight. It shimmered and fluctuated with brilliant colors, blues, greens and reds. The two lovers were awed at the glory of the Great Mystery's creation and their very souls rejoiced at the connectedness of his handiwork.

Chenoa shivered in the crisp night air so Young Gull drew her into his arms. Arms around each other they embraced and caressed each other tenderly. The sweethearts stared intently into each other's eyes and exchanged the vows again, Zaaghiin, I love you.

4

The Worm Moon came and went so the Ojibwa broke the small winter camps and had moved to the larger summer villages. Young Gull was away fishing at Boweeting when runners arrived from the Mississauga clan. They had traveled from the Nipissing district with a call for a Three Fires Grand-Council. They left the message with the elders and moved west.

The whitefish were moving in multitudes upstream from Lake Huron and Young Gull's nets were full. He and his band of fishers were processing the catch on the banks of the rapids when more canoes of fishers were seen arriving from the south. It was Fishhawk with his band.

"Aanii!" called Fishhawk from the water as his powerful strokes propelled his canoe toward Young Gull's processing camp.

"Aanii," said Young Gull as he helped Fishhawk beach his craft. His broad smile displayed the warm feelings he felt for his good friend. "It is good to see you. Was your winter easy?"

"Yes" replied Fishhawk. "The medicine was good. The supplies were plentiful. Our spirit helpers have smiled on our condition."

"The fishing is good. Many whitefish move upstream. We have caught our fill and leave for our village tomorrow."

The men that arrived with Fishhawk joined the processing of Young Gull's catch. The two chiefs walked downstream just enjoying each other's company. Conversation is something that the Ojibwa relished.

"How is Atironto? I notice he is not with you."

"Atironto is growing old. He is an elder on the council now. His son, Kondiaronk, has married a woman from The Bay. She is also Wyandotte. Many of them moved there a few summers ago. Kondiaronk is now a Grand Chief and wily like his father.

"Does Atironto still hate the Iroquois?" asked Fish Hawk, a sly grin appearing on his mouth.

"Atironto lives for the day old scores are settled with the Iroquois. But he is old now and will have to depend on Kondiaronk to exact vengeance."

"Maybe yes, maybe no, we will smoke on this matter at the Grand-Council at the new moon."

"Grand-Council?" asked Young Gull, unaware of the runners who had visited his village.

"You have not heard? Grand Chief Bald Eagle of the Mississauga has called for a Grand-Council. It is to be a Three Fires Council held at the next new moon. I do not know the details but it concerns the Iroquois."

The conversation with Fishhawk had Young Gull's curiosity up. He thought on this matter all the way back to his village. A Three Fires Council was an important event and not many were called. Many Elders and Chiefs would attend from the three nations of the confederacy; the Ojibwa, the Ottawa and the Potawatomi. Yes, Young Gull was curious indeed.

The new moon arrived and numerous bands of Elders, Chiefs and Holy Men had gathered at Boweeting, the traditional meeting place of the confederacy. The lodges of the conferees filled the woodlands that surrounded the field where the ceremonies would be held. There was a ridge that ran along three sides of the grassland and it afforded a natural listening place for the participants. This was a larger conference than Young Gull had ever witnessed and a somber mood hung over the whole place.

The first light of day, that light that turns the sky from black to blue announced the coming of the sunrise. The whole camp began to stir, moving to take their places in the field and on the ridge. The Fire keepers lit the ceremonial fire that would be kept going night and day until the Council had concluded. The Pipe Ceremony, a ceremony of reverence, greeted the sunrise. All who were there and a part of this religious experience knew that the Three Fires were a special people to the Great Mystery.

The Drum Ceremony, a ceremony of peace, followed. The Keeper of the Sacred Drum presented it to Young Gull, as he was a leading Grand Chief who also held the office of War Chief. He took the drum and tapped it slowly, lightly three times. On the fourth tap the other drummers began to drum with Young Gull. After a short space of time a lone singer began to chant with the drumming. Next other singers joined in building in tempo and excitement. The climax came with the dancers who made their way to the center of the grassland where the Keepers of the Sacred Fire tended the Sacred Fire. They danced the Peace Dance to show the desire of the people.

Orators were scheduled in the afternoon beginning with the caller of the Three Fires Council, Bald Eagle. He stepped up to the Sacred Fire and the Keeper of the Pipe offered it to him. He took it holding it high in each of the four directions then drew on the stem and blew the Sacred Smoke straight up in the air. He returned the pipe to the Keeper and then began.

"On this belt I speak to the people of the Ojibwa Nation.

On this beaver pelt I speak to the people of the Ottawa Nation.

On these beads I speak to the people of the Potawatomi Nation.

I bring a very grave matter before this council.

Brothers, Sisters; this matter makes my heart heavy.

Brothers, Sisters; this matter concerns the Iroquois.

They are an obstinate people. They have no honor. They are no more then murderers and thieves.

Brothers, Sisters; my own son was taken hostage along with a small trading party going to the French trading post. They were tortured and killed. Only one escaped to tell the story. They stole the furs to trade with the English at Albany.

Brothers, Sisters; three times this has happened since the end of the season of the snows. Seventy of our young men have been lost.

Brothers, Sisters; three times this has happened. The first time the Mohawk paid retribution. Three bales of furs for each man killed.

On the second occurrence, again, they paid the retribution. The third time they refused.

Brothers, Sisters; they laugh and make sport of the Mississauga Ojibwa.

Brothers, Sisters; these ingrates must be taught a lesson. We need to make them feel the power of the Three Fires.

Brothers, Sisters; if we do not act against this insolence they will only become bolder.

Brothers, Sisters; do not encourage them. If we do we will pay for our laxness.

Brothers, Sisters . . . Bald Eagle continued his passionate plea to the council. He talked until the sun rested on the treetops in the west. Then other orators took their turn. Finally the council broke for that first day and there were still speakers scheduled.

The next morning they continued. When the scheduled speakers were finished anyone else who wished to talk on the matter was given the opportunity. Many spoke for a punishing raid while others spoke passionately for peace. It was the speakers for peace, including Young Gull that felt the best course of action would be to send a warning from the Three Fires Council. When the Three Fires spoke the whole earth trembled in the eyes of their enemies. This would be the directive of the Three Fires Council. Celebration broke out. Peace would be the path and feasting and dancing went on for days.

Runners carried the warning to the Mohawk. They were to pay the regular compensation and cease their marauding raids on Ojibwa trading and hunting parties on penalty of annihilation of their village at The Narrows. The threat worked and wampum belts of peace were exchanged.

5

Spring had turned to summer and the band's hunters were busy throughout the territory. They had broken into the traditional small hunting parties moving from one temporary campsite to the next collecting pelts and curing meats. Each party made its way through the territory in a circular fashion arriving back at the main village a few days after starting out.

Young Gull was an excellent hunter. The Master of Life had endowed him with the skill needed to bring the blessings given the hunter to fruition. This is what makes a hunter successful and able to move on to greatness. All things flowed from the Great Mystery, the provision of game and the skill to bring it down.

Young Gull's hunting party, after offering tobacco, left their temporary camp at dawn. The eight hunters spread out, each traveling in a different direction. Young Gull headed due north and soon came upon the signs of a black bear. A small berry patch had been disturbed. Freshly broken branches and tufts of black fur caught on the prickly stems of the berry bushes told of the nearby presence of the quarry.

"Ah! My spirit guide has given Young Gull the black bear. It is the most prized of all game," the great hunter thought as he began to track the bear. Young Gull followed the trail through a small vale and up a modest incline to a ridge. The bear's trail moved along the ridge a short distance then broke off sharply down a steep embankment disappearing into the thick underbrush. Young Gull moved stealthily. Then he stood, perfectly motionless, listening intently, his keen eyes attempting to see through and beyond the dense brush. There was no sign of the bear. There was no movement. There was no sound.

Young Gull decided to move further along the ridge to a point where the thicket thinned out and the side of the embankment was populated with pine trees. He could see through the woods another, larger berry patch in the vale below. He stared intently. There was a slight movement at the far end of the patch.

"The bear is still feeding. I can use this time to overtake him" Young Gull thought. He moved stealthily along the ridge slowly circling around until he was in front of the bear's line of travel. Young Gull chose a place along the ridge where he was sure the bear would move back up the hill. The place he chose was upwind and also afforded him the protection of a high ledge that overlooked the lower ridge. Patiently he waited for the bear to have his fill of berries.

The sun moved from high in its arc to midway of setting. Suddenly the rustle of leaves, a snap of a twig could be heard moving along the ridge toward the place of ambush. Young Gull grew taut. Slowly, silently he drew his first arrow. The bear appeared sauntering through a small clearing directly below Young Gull. The bear was completely unaware of the danger. The missile whizzed through the air toward its mark, a mark that was lethal. The arrow struck the bear directly and death was instant.

Young Gull said a prayer for his brother, the bear. "My brother bear, I was in need and you provided. You will fill the needs of your brothers, the Ojibwa. May your spirit be happy in the Land of Souls. Thank you for your generosity."

Young Gull arrived back at the base camp. The tantalizing aroma of fish cooking on a campfire greeted him. He was hungry and weary from carrying the dressed bear and its pelt.

"Aanii Young Gull!" greeted Small Kettle one of the eight hunters. Small Kettle was born prematurely and cradled in a small kettle as an infant. This is how he got his name. Small Kettle's eyes grew wide and he broke into a broad grin upon seeing Young Gull struggling under such a heavy load. A second later he rushed forward to relieve the chief of his burden.

"Thank you" said Young Gull as he stretched and straightened his husky frame. The hunting had been good and the canoes were heavily laden with pelts and cured meat. The evening meal was gratifying and after a thanksgiving service offering tobacco to the bear's spirit the evening ended.

6

A few weeks later, Boweeting began filling up with participants of the upcoming celebration. Men, women and children were arriving from all over the territory. They were arriving for the marriage feast of Young Gull and Chenoa.

Back at the village the anticipation was also building, especially with the wedding couple. The marriage ceremony was simple but the celebration, which would be held at Boweeting, would go on for days.

"Two more days!" exclaimed Chenoa to Spring Water. "I am so filled with excitement that I cannot think of my duties to the village." They were to join an expedition of the members of the provider clans in the afternoon picking berries. As women they were members of one of these highest-ranking clans.

"Come and pick berries with us," answered her mother. "It will take your mind off things. It is better to be busy than idle. Time will go by much faster and the new moon will arrive much sooner".

"You are right, mother. Maybe we should pick berries all through the night too!" she exclaimed with laughter. The two women had lunch and then joined the group who were gathering at the council lodge. There were both men and women in the group and even the children were invited to come along and help. This was a privilege as well as a great adventure for the children and none refused the invitation.

Finally the big day arrived. Neither Chenoa nor Young Gull had slept the night before. Both were wide-awake and heard the birds announce the coming of daybreak. The whole village was stirring in anticipation. The ceremony itself would be private, taking place in the lodge of the groom. Only the marriage couple, their immediate family and the village holy man would be in attendance.

The whole village began to mill around the front of Young Gull's lodge and soon the participants had all arrived, all wearing their finest apparel and adorned with accessories of colored beads and brightly dyed feathers. They gathered inside the lodge and the ceremony began.

North Wind prepared the pipe of peace for smoking. He lit the pipe drawing on it with short bursts to get it burning well, then one long draw filling his mouth with the sacred smoke. Holding his head back he blew the smoke straight up in the air. North Wind then held the pipe high with both hands and pronounced a blessing on the proceedings. The pipe was then passed to each participant who shared in the sacred element with the honoured couple participating last. Young Gull returned the pipe to North Wind who set it in its holy place.

He then took the consecrated drum striking it once. Chanting several verses he punctuated each stanza with one beat on the drum. It was then time for Blue Bird's speech. As Young Gull's mother she represented the elder in the family. Usually this was the privilege of a grandparent but because Young Gull had reached the middle of his life his grandparents had gone on to the Land of Souls.

"My children," Blue Bird announced. "Your day has arrived. This day we have all waited for with great anticipation. I know that you have prepared yourselves well for marriage. As you know marriage is not to be taken frivolously.

I say to Chenoa; my child, you have shown great prudence in your choice of a husband. I do not say this because Young Gull is my son. I say this because he has no mean streak in him toward women. He has not engaged any sorcerer for love potions or to procure an evil hex. You have made a good choice.

I say to Young Gull; my son, you also have made a good choice. Chenoa has proven acceptable. She has shown the skills a wife needs to keep a lodge and the skills to be able to contribute to the village. You have shown wisdom and good judgment by looking beyond her beauty to the things that count the most.

I say to the both of you; my children, there is a great need for loyalty to each other. This will make your marriage strong. Remember to always help each other in life and you will arrive at the end of it together. Always stand beside one another. Always support one another.

Also remember to always be kind to one another. Also when your children arrive be kind to them. They will return this kindness to you in your old age. This is the way of the Ojibwa."

This ended the marriage ceremony proper and the newly weds emerged from the lodge to the cheers and celebrations of the village. The procession made its way down to the river, into the canoes and out into Lake Superior. The large flotilla made its way south along the shoreline headed for Boweeting and the expectant celebrants waiting to begin the great marriage festival.

The party arrived at Boweeting that evening to the whoops and shrieks of the waiting crowd. The drums began to beat immediately and the singing could be heard for miles around. Fancy dancers performed the various dances of celebration with the first being the wedding dance. The bride and groom led this. The dancing and feasting went on all night and drumming and singing greeted the rising sun.

Of course the wedding couple had left shortly after the wedding dance. Being full of romance and a great desire for one another they retreated several miles downriver to their marriage lodge. The couple of honor would rejoin the celebrations at Boweeting the following day.

Many had come for the celebrations from all over the territory. Potawatomi from Green Bay, Ottawa from Michilimackinac, Wyandotte from Lake Michigan, Mississauga from the Mattawa River and Ojibwa from Lake Superior were there to join Young Gull and Chenoa's band in celebrating the great marriage festival. That late week in August produced the largest gathering for a marriage festival in living memory.

7

Two more summers came and went. Once again the land was covered in deep snow and enough provisions had been laid in.

"Aanii Bluebird" Chenoa greeted the old woman as she entered her lodge.

"Aanii Chenoa" answered Blue Bird. "Where is Young Gull?" she asked.

"He is gone ice fishing on Red Lake. The lodge was closing in on him."

"Yes, I know how that feels. I even experience it on warm summer days!" the old woman laughingly exclaimed.

The two had become fast friends and had begun to share girlish secrets the way young adolescents do. Chenoa suddenly became strangely silent.

"What is the purpose of this visit?" Blue Bird began to wonder to herself. "Why does Chenoa struggle through the deep snow, since our last visit was just last night?" She was pondering these thoughts when Chenoa spoke.

"I have missed my last two moons," she blurted out.

"What of the other signs?" Blue Bird asked grinning broadly.

"They are there. Recently I have been sick each morning without fail."

"Have you mentioned this matter to Young Gull? Has he noticed anything?"

"I have not mentioned it to him yet and he has noticed nothing".

"He is just like his father" mused Blue Bird. She then began to reminisce her own long ago experiences as a young mother.

Young Gull arrived back at the village in the late afternoon. He had several large trout with him. They were frozen solid from lying for hours on Red Lake's ice. After sharing these with others of the village he drew back the flap of his lodge.

"Aanii Young Gull!" she greeted while stirring a pot of moose stew. She helped him off with his moccasins and put them near the fire to dry.

"I have news; good news," she said as she sat beside him. She was grinning like a young girl who had just received a valuable gift.

"Tell me," Young Gull said.

"It's a secret," teased Chenoa.

"Tell me," he repeated.

"After supper," she repeated.

"Have your way." Young Gull knew what her good news was. He had noticed the signs but had pretended not to. He continued to feign indifference in order to let Chenoa play her game and it was all he could do to hold his silence.

After the evening meal the young couple relaxed in each other's arms. Stroking one another lightly on the face and hair Young Gull whispered, "Tell me your secret."

"You are to be a father," Chenoa cooed.

At last Young Gull could release his excitement. It was an excitement he did not have to feign.

"I know," he laughed.

"You, how did you know?" she asked disappointed that he was not totally surprised.

"A small bird told me." Now it was Young Gull's turn to play the game.

"What small bird?" she asked sternly.

"The signs, I saw the signs," he said now being more serious. "I watched while you were not looking".

"No!" she exclaimed.

Young Gull turned the conversation from a game to a more serious note.

"This is wonderful news. You have made me so happy. I must call a council and announce this news to the whole village. I will do this in the morning," he advised his wife. "We must also choose an elder to conduct the naming ceremony." It will be their duty to consult the spirits in a vision or dream regarding the child's purpose in life and to give him a name reflecting this purpose.

"I thought He Walks Well should have this honor. He is the elder holy man and his visions and dreams are strong medicine," advised Chenoa.

"I agree. I shall talk to him in the morning before I call the council," said Young Gull.

Six more months passed, it was the Flower Moon. Chenoa was very near giving birth and Young Gull's mother was spending more time helping Chenoa with the daily chores. The two women were at the river's edge washing clothes, Blue Bird doing the lifting and carrying and Chenoa doing the beating and wringing. Chenoa had been feeling pangs all morning but they were irregular so she had said nothing to Blue Bird. Suddenly, Chenoa felt a release of fluid and she realized immediately the inside of her leggings were drenched.

"My water!" she exclaimed. Blue Bird realized at once what had happened.

"Here! Here!" Blue Bird cried for help from Small Kettle who was nearby patching his canoe. He responded immediately. Together they helped Chenoa to her lodge, which had been prepared with a clean flooring of cedar boughs, and a pallet covered with soft beaver pelts.

Small Kettle set out to find Young Gull while several of the women of the village joined Blue Bird to help with the birthing.

Young Gull and his friend arrived at the entrance of his lodge to the sounds of loud moaning. Young Gull's eyes were wide and his face was wrought with worry.

"Don't worry. The wailing is normal," said Small Kettle trying to reassure his friend.

"I know that!" snapped Young Gull. He immediately apologized to his companion. There was one last long groan followed by a few seconds of silence.

"Wahl" grunted Young Gull full of anticipation.

He had no sooner made the query under his breath than it came, a high-pitched squealing. That distinctive cry that told everyone who had gathered outside the lodge that all was well. Blue Bird appeared at the entrance.

"A boy!" she announced proudly. A loud cheer went up in thanksgiving and Young Gull entered his lodge to see his newborn son.

The next day old He Walks Well came to see the proud new parents. Chenoa was nursing the newborn when the old prophet entered their lodge.

"Hello, Young Gull, Hello Chenoa," greeted He Walks Well.

"Hello He Walks Well." Young Gull offered the old man a place by the smudge pot and then slipped outside to get him a cup of cedar tea, which had been brewing on the morning fire. When he returned the old man accepted the drink and began to speak.

"I have come about the child's name. I am ready."

"So soon?" questioned Chenoa. It was not normal to name a child so soon after birth. Often it could be a year or two and sometimes longer.

"The spirits have given me the name in a dream. The dream was very powerful, vast medicine. The naming ceremony will be in a week's time."

"In a week's time, fine," said Young Gull. Chenoa affirmed with a nod of her head. The baby had finished suckling and was being put down as the old man left the lodge.

A week later the couple assembled with the newborn in He Walks Well's lodge. It had been cleaned immaculately, inside and out and new cedar bough flooring had been installed. All this was done making the lodge ceremonially clean. Blue Bird joined them, being one of the grandparents. Chenoa's parents had returned to their home village, so were absent from the ceremony.

"We will smoke on this matter today. It is a very great day when one is given an identity. The spirits have been forthright in giving me a prophecy and a name for the infant." With this he lit the Pipe of Peace, drew a long breath on its stem and blew the mouthful of smoke straight up in the air. He then passed the instrument around and all took part in the smoking of the sacred tobacco. Then he began to speak.

"I have been given a very powerful prophecy regarding all of the Ojibwa. Your new son is to be used as an instrument of great blessing to all the people.

I dreamed I was standing on the banks of a wide, deep river. On the other side was the land of the spirits. One appeared on the other side and beckoned to me to cross over. There was no canoe, no raft, nor any way for me to cross over to the spirit being on the other side. I am an old man and it was too far for even a young man to swim.

"How can I cross?" I called out.

"Fly over the waters" answered the spirit.

I began to flap my arms like a bird flaps its wings and to my amazement I began to lift off the ground! I could feel the thickness of the air beneath invisible feathers that were attached to my arms. Higher and higher I rose as I pushed down on the heavy air with slow, powerful strokes. I crossed the river with ease and set down beside the spirit.

The spirit being was little, about three feet high and surrounded by a strange, amber glow. He was completely covered with orange tinged hair. Only his eyes, which were also orange, and his mouth showed. He said nothing but turned away from the river and moved his arm in an arc from left to right. As he did a vision appeared in the sky.

I saw, coming from the north, four spirits. As they got closer I saw that one was a bear, one was a wolf and the other two were eagles, a large one and a smaller one. The bear was on the left. It had fire with him and was fiercely bearing his teeth. The small eagle was on the right swooping down from high in the sky. The large eagle and the wolf moved in unison in the center of the vision.

They had all moved in on a common prey completely surrounding it. I did not recognise the prey. It was a fierce looking animal, something like a wolverine. It was flat with large pointed teeth and was a vicious beast. It had long, strong, tearing claws, three on one foot and two on the other. It was running from side to side, back and forth trying to protect itself from the others who were attacking it simultaneously and killing it. When it died it vanished and the four beasts doubled in size.

"What do these things mean?" I asked the spirit.

"I have been commissioned to show you this vision and also to explain it. It has to do with the new son of Young Gull. He will be The Great Mystery's instrument of blessing. Because of him the Ojibwa will benefit greatly.

The four spirits you saw in the sky represent the Three Fires Confederacy. The bear you saw attacking from the west represents the fire keepers, the Potawatomi. The small eagle that swooped down from the east portrays the Mississauga. The large eagle and the wolf that pressed from the north were the Ojibwa and Ottawa. The strange prey was the Iroquois."

The spirit then gave me the child's name and its interpretation.

Taking the infant in his arms He Walks Well held him high consecrating him to The Great Mystery. He then held the baby close to his chest, rocking him and chanting softly in the infant's ear. After this the old holy man began to speak again.

The spirit in the dream said to me, "The infant you are to name will be a boon to his people because of his considerable atonement for them. In light of this his name shall be called Shahwanjegawin, which by interpretation means One Who Provides Benefit. Now return to the land of the corporeal."

Once again I began to move my arms like a huge bird and to ascend high over the river. I felt a very strong updraft under the imaginary feathers of my arms and I soared higher and higher. The river and the two worlds on its sides disappeared far below and at this point I awoke.

He Walks Well returned One Who Provides Benefit to his mother and the party left the old man's lodge. The five participants joined the whole village. A great feast had been prepared in order to celebrate the giving of a name and everyone rejoiced late into the night.

Chapter 4

The Maemaegawaehnssiwuk protect Shahwanjegawin—
Shahwanjegawin's First Hunt—Shahwanjegawin's Blanket

1

Four more summers came and went and the fifth was upon the
chief's young son. Time was moving like a fleeting doe distracting
a hunter from the hiding place of her fawn. Shahwanjegawin was a
now a little boy and he was already exhibiting the prominent side of
his nature, a side that hinted at the part he might play as the great
benefactor to his people.

"Shahwanjegawin is a fine son" Young Gull said to North Wind.
"He loves his mother very much and shows this by preferring her
company rather than playing with the other children of the village.
He shows no interest in the hunting games of the other children. He
is very sensitive to the well-being of the creatures of the forest."

"He is still young," answered North Wind. "Children go through
stages and changes. He has plenty of time to choose the path he will
take in life."

North Wind perceived that Young Gull was concerned and was
only trying to alleviate those concerns. He did not realize that it was
not concern that motivated Young Gull but a desire to prepare the
medicine man for a future apprentice.

"I do not mean that I wish Shahwanjegawin to remain in the
wolf totem and be a provider like his parents and grandparents. It
would please me just as well if he was to join the medicine lodge"

"Ah, I see," the holy man said. "His vision quest is still far in the future and it will be up to his spirit guide to show him his path. Only time will tell."

Suddenly their conversation was interrupted with the desperate calling of Chenoa.

"Young Gull! Young Gull! She repeated the calling as she made her way through the village. Young Gull appeared immediately at the entrance of North Wind's lodge.

"Here!" called out Young Gull as he motioned his arm to Chenoa. "Over here!" he repeated.

Chenoa rushed over to Young Gull. "Shahwanjegawin is missing. I can't find him!" she cried, tears streaming down her face.

"Slow down." Young Gull took her by the hands and tried to calm the frantic mother down. "Now tell me, what is this all about?"

"We were picking berries by the river. I turned to check on Shahwanjegawin and he wasn't there. I looked all over. I could not find him. Oh, the river," she moaned.

"Don't worry, he'll be all right. We'll find him," Young Gull reassured her as he moved quickly to the center of the village to organize a search party.

Meanwhile, the small toddler moved deeper into the forest. He had begun following a butterfly but when he realized Chenoa was nowhere to be seen he began looking for his mother. "Wagemind . . . Wagemind." the young boy called. Over and over again he called, "Mother . . . mother." It was getting dark and he began to cry.

"Don't cry." The voice came from behind Shahwanjegawin startling him. He began to wail and shake. "Don't cry. It will be all right. We will take care of you."

The little boy turned to see who was speaking to him. To his surprise it was a very little person, half the size of the five-year old, yet he looked like man.

"I want my mother," Shahwanjegawin said.

"Don't worry. We have been sent to take care of you." As he was saying this two other small people appeared from beneath the tall ferns. One was another man, the other person was a woman, but they were so small. The little boy's crying turned to sob's and sniffling.

"I can't find my mother," he explained.

"Don't fret. We will help you get home to your mother, but we can't do that until the morning. You see, we must return to where we live by nightfall, but we will show you a safe place to spend the night. You sleep there and we will take you home tomorrow."

"I will," was Shahwanjegawin's childlike response. The little people then led him to a large, hollow log. It was so huge that the boy's head barely touched the top of the inside as they led him in. There were cedar boughs for bedding already inside the log. Dusk was upon the little band when they arrived safely inside the hollow log. The light was very dim and Chenoa's pride could hardly see his tiny protectors.

"You sleep here where it is safe. You can't come where we live, but we will return in the morning to take you home."

"I will," replied Shahwanjegawin and as he lay down on the bed he could see the little people disappear right through the wall of the log! The log felt cozy and safe and the little tyke was so tired that he shut his eyes and immediately fell into a deep sleep.

Unfortunately, Chenoa and Young Gull did not have so restful a night. Search parties had been organized and with the daylight left they scoured the woods in the area of the berry patches. Others had searched down river on both banks in case the small child had fallen in and drowned. Chenoa whimpered most of the night in Young Gull's arms and he tried to comfort her.

"It is good that the search parties have found nothing. It means he is all right," Young Gull whispered trying to convince himself as well as alleviate Chenoa's burden. "We will look again in the morning. We will find him."

The birds began to sing announcing daybreak and the whole village began to stir. After a quick breakfast search parties were organized and the quest for their chief's son resumed. Only a few elders and some of the young mothers stayed in the village to mind the very young. Suddenly voices could be heard at the edge of the forest. The voices were strange sounding, very high pitched. Then, to the amazement of the villagers the young boy appeared from behind a thicket.

"Shahwanjegawin, it's Shahwanjegawin!" cried Shahwanjegawin's grandmother. Blue Bird rushed toward the little boy and scooped him into her arms. She was so happy that tears of joy streamed down her face. Others searched around the area for the source of the high-pitched voices but found nothing. A young mother was sent to advise the search parties of the happening at the village.

"Where have you been?" the grandmother quizzed young Shahwanjegawin. He explained what happened to him and described the little people all to the amazement of those who heard.

"Tauhau!" exclaimed Blue Bird expressing her astonishment. "Maemaegawaehnssiwuk have protected my grandson. The Great Mystery has spared his life by sending the little spirit beings, the special guardian of children, to protect him and guide him home. After making this pronouncement she rocked the child in her arms repeating over and over again, "Miigwech, thank you."

Young Gull and Chenoa were among the first to arrive back at the village and they rushed toward the small crowd that had gathered around Blue Bird and her treasured grandson. Chenoa needed to see for herself in order to believe the news fully. As the crowd parted and she saw her precious little boy she broke into sighs of relief mixed with joyous laughter. Blue Bird released the child to his mother, stepped toward her son and said in a low voice, "Maemaegawaehnssiwuk." Young Gull understood.

2

Seven more summers passed and Shahwanjegawin's time had come for his First Hunt. Unlike the other boys of the village this was something he did not look forward to. The other boys anticipated the day they would make their first kill. They all relished the thoughts of the praise the whole village would heap upon them when they would bring in their first game. It was a rite of passage.

Shahwanjegawin had spent enough time in the forests and meadows of their hunting territory. He also carried a bow and arrows with him, but somehow had always felt deep within himself that he should only use them for protection. He had a love in his heart for the creatures of the forest and a feeling of kinship that prevented him from harming them. Also, the animals seemed to sense this. They showed less fear and were less wary when it was Shahwanjegawin roaming the territory.

"Must I do this?" he asked his father.

"Yes. You must try. It is important that each person contributes to the village and this is the primary way of contribution. So, you must try. Do you understand son?" answered Young Gull.

"Yes father." Shahwanjegawin replied dejectedly.

Young Gull understood that his son may have a different path in life to follow but he also understood the principal ways must be tested first. He said nothing of this to Shahwanjegawin because it was important that the boy not think there was a way out of his dilemma.

Early the next morning the young adolescent prepared his morning offering. He went through the ritual of offering the sacred tobacco in the fire and praying for a successful First Hunt, but his heart was not in the prayer. In fact, he felt a sickness in his heart and it was heavy due to the deed that he must now accomplish. After his morning devotional he finished his breakfast of whitefish and cedar tea. Then he struck out for the hunting grounds.

Shahwanjegawin had no trouble locating or even making contact with game. They seemed to trust him more than others and now he felt that somehow he was betraying that trust. He reached the hunting grounds with a sense of guilt that was almost overwhelming.

"I know. I'll not seek the game out," he thought to himself. "If I should happen across a brother, then I will do what I have to do." With this thought in mind he built a small campfire by a little stream and sat down to rest. A fire was not in the hunter's repertoire for attracting game.

As he sat beside the fire he began to daydream. He thought of his mother, Chenoa, whom he adored. He thought, "If only I had been born a girl. I would not have to be doing this. I could be like my mother and contribute to the village by tending the garden plots. Or

I could make clothing, or cook, or something, anything but hunt." But thoughts of being a girl turned his thoughts to Dehmin.

"I wish I was back at the village playing the hiding game my friends, especially with Dehmin. Dehmin was a young girl the same age a Shahwanjegawin. Her name meant Strawberry and she was named this because of the color of her skin when she was born. She had a pretty face with large ebony eyes, long, straight, silky, black hair, dark skin and her lips matched her name. She had always been a playmate but since the melting of the snows he had felt a strange attraction to her. His desire to be in her company was beginning to override all his other activities. Thoughts of her quelled anymore desire to have been born a girl. Life now had Shahwanjegawin quite confused.

Suddenly he heard a rustle in the underbrush across the stream. He peered intently through the thicket trying to determine what was there. Crack . . . the sound of a sizeable stick snapping under the weight of something very heavy resounded through the forest. Shahwanjegawin silently picked up his bow and deliberately loaded an arrow. "Perhaps it is a bear, I hope he doesn't charge. I hope he sees me and turns tail," he thought. He didn't have to think much longer.

Out of the brush and into a small clearing moved one of the largest bucks he had ever seen. The deer's stature was magnificent. It stopped dead in the clearing and stared directly at Shahwanjegawin. He deliberately lifted his bow, took direct aim, and slowly drew the arrow back all the while thinking, "Run! Hurry! Run! Can't you see I mean to kill you?" But the big buck did not run. He just stood there staring dolefully into Shahwanjegawin's eyes. "Isn't he going to flee? Why doesn't he take off?"

Eventually the large whitetail buck turned and slowly moved off into the brush. Shahwanjegawin lowered his bow along with his head and cried. He felt a failure, a disappointment to his mother and he cried for the shame he thought he would bring on his father, even upon his own name. He stayed at that place in the woods until the sun was low in the sky and he had no alternative but to head for home.

When he arrived home empty-handed it was no surprise to his parents, but they could see that he was distraught and the black smudges on his cheeks evidenced the fact that he had been doing some serious crying. This concerned them and they asked the boy how the day went.

"I had no luck," said the young teen dejectedly.

"You will do better tomorrow." said Chenoa.

"Maybe"

"You've been crying." declared Young Gull.

"I'll do better tomorrow." promised Shahwanjegawin not wanting to talk about his experience.

"Let me." Chenoa whispered to her husband. Young Gull left the lodge and Chenoa gently drew out her son's feelings.

Shahwanjegawin broke down and confided the whole story to his mother. She consoled him by reassuring him that he was not a failure.

"You have not disappointed me. In fact I am more proud of you than ever." she proclaimed. Shahwanjegawin was relieved but also puzzled. At this point Young Gull returned to the lodge and Chenoa related their son's story to him.

"There is no shame in being close kin to the animals of the forest," declared his father. "They are our brothers and often give themselves up for our maintenance. But one who can communicate with them has a special gift and a different path in life than one of a hunter."

"A different path?" asked Shahwanjegawin.

"You must seek guidance from the spirit beings in a vision quest. They will give you direction. I will speak to North Wind in the morning. He will prepare you for the quest."

The fire inside the lodge was dying and with the light growing dimmer the small family retired. Shahwanjegawin turned his back to his parents, his feelings of depression turning to relief and then to excitement. "My vision quest, usually a vision quest is for young men. I am still a boy and I am to go on my vision quest!" he thought. Shahwanjegawin had trouble sleeping that night, not due to despondency but due to the stimulating of his mind brought on by the excitement of a vision quest.

3

Two more summers passed. Shahwanjegawin had his vision. His spirit guide repeated old He Walks Well's prophecy also revealing that his path in life would be like a shooting star. This was a very good omen for the Ojibwa and North Wind interpreted the vision to mean that Shahwanjegawin's path in life would be in the Medicine Lodge.

The Medicine Lodge was made up of Anishnaabek holy men and all priests trained in this Society. The training began early in life under the supervision of the village holy man and took years to move through the various levels of discipline. Shahwanjegawin would begin his training in medicine under the tutelage of North Wind this summer.

Chenoa was filled with pride for her son and showed it by talking about him at every chance. He had been chosen to become a member of the Medicine Society, a very high honor, and this was the source of her happiness. She was so happy for him that she decided that it was time to present him with his own blanket.

"You know this means he will no longer be a child," advised Young Gull.

"I know."

"He will no longer be under our authority; no longer subject to your influence."

"I know."

"He may move into his own lodge."

"I know." Chenoa repeated adamantly.

"If this is what you want to do I am in agreement," Young Gull capitulated.

"He is becoming a man. He will start his training with Kewadin this summer. He is mature beyond his years and it is time." explained Chenoa.

"I said you were right. I agree."

"It is good. I will do the presentation tomorrow."

The fire in their lodge dimmed and the night became quite quiet as Young Gull and his small family drifted off to sleep. Young Gull began to dream.

He was like a hawk soaring high above a land that was unfamiliar to him. There was a large, sparkling blue lake. It seemed similar to the Great Lake of the Huron. Far below him there were rapids, like the rapids where the river at Boweeting empties into the lake. The river in his dream was wide and its color deep blue, but here the lake emptied into the river.

Young Gull followed the course of the dark blue river a short distance where he could see below him a smaller black river coursing its way toward the greater river. The waters teemed with all kinds of fish. He swooped down to have a closer look at the lay of the land.

The rivers were bordered with an infinite number of apple trees, an abundance of plum trees and also chestnut, walnut and cranberry trees. He saw a large quantity of vines loaded with fairly large and good grapes.

At intervals he came upon very large meadows full of tall grass and wild rice. They were only broken by fruit trees or tall hardwoods of various kinds, such as butternut, walnut, maple, white and red oak, poplar, elm, ash, basswood and cottonwood. This variety continued as far as Young Gull could see even from the great height at which he soared.

He saw inhabiting this great variety of foliage a great quantity of game. Sharing the forest were wood buffalo, white tail deer, bears and turkeys. The woodland and wetlands provided a habitat for a profusion of pheasants, quail, partridges, and a variety of ducks, cranes, swans, geese, and pigeons. They abounded with a great diversity of beaver, otter, muskrats and foxes. Young Gull knew this was a realm that could only have been created by the Great Mystery but its purpose was not given. The dream faded.

Young Gull rose early the next morning and described his wonderful dream to Chenoa. Together they wondered what it meant. He then left for the hunting grounds. He left in order to leave his son alone with his mother.

The blanket presentation was a personal rite of passage that occurred between a young man and his mother; it was a private thing.

"Where is father? Shahwanjegawin asked his mother. "He has gone hunting. Do you want me to cook breakfast now?"

"Ah, yes. I am hungry," the young teen answered.

After morning devotions to the Master of Life they shared breakfast. Chenoa then spent most of the rest of the morning talking with her son, no, more listening to her son talk about his upcoming instruction with North Wind. He was full of dreams and aspirations about the Society of Medicine.

When they were finished talking Shahwanjegawin arose and said, "I am going to Red Lake this afternoon with North Wind. He said he has much to discuss with me. I will be back in time for supper."

"I have something for you before you go."

"What is it?" Shahwanjegawin asked with a smile of anticipation on his face.

"Just this." said Chenoa as she took out a new blanket. It was a beautiful blanket with traditional quill designs and in the center was the family totem representing the oak tree.

"Ah! Thank you mother, it is a beautiful blanket" Shahwanjegawin said as he received the present from Chenoa. He knew what this simple ceremony meant and felt good about the measure of responsibility that she was releasing to him with the blanket. He also couldn't wait to show it to Strawberry. The young girl had turned into a young woman herself, and the two young people had become very close.

Chenoa knew the blanket would serve him well as he matured and traveled further and further from the village that was his home. She also had a tear in her eye put there by the mixed emotions of pride and happiness tinged with a sense of sadness that she was giving up the boy she loved so deeply.

Chapter 5

Seneca Defeat at Irondequoit—Chenoa Saves the Village—Mohawk Treaty at Sahgeeng—War Council at Boweeting

1

The Flower Moon had just ended and the warm summer sun shone daily over the band's territory. In the distance several canoes could be seen making their way up the river from Lake Superior. As they drew closer the lead canoe, manned by Pemahshe and Small Kettle, escorted the others. Young Gull, shading and straining his eyes, recognized the occupants of the other ensuing canoes. It was Fish Hawk and several of his young Ojibwa warriors. The small band also included four Frenchmen, one a Black Robe.

"Aanii Fish Hawk, welcome!" exclaimed Young Gull as they beached their canoes at the village.

"Aanii, good friend" replied Fish Hawk.

"You bring strangers with you and your young men are painted for war. Does Fish Hawk carry bad tidings to his friend?

"Fish Hawk, War Chief of the Ojibwa, desires a council with the Boweeting band" answered Fish Hawk in a serious, official sounding tone. "Fish Hawk would talk to his friend in private first" he added.

"Good! Talk is always good," Young Gull said as he and his good friend walked the familiar trail that led to Red Lake. The others were led off to the main lodge where they could rest while a feast was prepared for them.

"The strangers are from the trading post at Michilimackinac. The French Governor at Montreal wants to make war on the Seneca in Seneca country. He has ordered these coureurs de bois to trade at half price with any Ojibwa who join in the battle. The special payment is to last until the first snow. We will also receive all of the spoils and they will pay for Seneca scalps in French coins. They can be traded for goods at any of the French posts"

"Who is the Black Robe?"

"He is the Frenchmen's shaman. He is called Marest. He blesses their actions asking their god for success. He also wishes to gain Ojibwa followers to his religion."

"The Black Robe wastes his time. The Great Spirit will bless any council in Boweeting. I met an Ojibwa hunter from Minnesota once who had embraced the overseas people's god. He was sorry he had done so. He told me one he was once a great hunter but the dreams no longer worked for him. He told me that the Black Robe's prayer had ruined his life."

"This I understand, but the traders believe in him. They are called Du Lhut, La Durantaye and Tonty. They wish to strengthen the French force with the power of Ojibwa warriors. The Potawatomi War Chief, Ouenemek, The Pike, War Chief of the Ottawa and the Wyandotte War Chief, Kondiaronk are joining Chichikateco, War Chief of the Miami at Round Lake. I will also join them at this lake the French call St. Claire.

"Three summers ago the French Governor, La Barre, said the same words. We journeyed with the Frenchman, Perrot, to meet them at Niagara. When we arrived at the water falls La Barre sent us his words on the Frenchman's paper telling us to go home, they had made peace!"

"The French have a new Governor now. He is called Denonville. He is different, a grand leader with great inner strength. He will not change his direction. He has a force of two thousand. We have two hundred warriors with us and I know if my good friend, Young Gull, Grand Chief and Great War Chief of the Boweeting Ojibwa, should choose to join us we could more than double our strength."

"If the council agrees, I will join my good friend, Fish Hawk, in battle."

Several days later, when the elders of the surrounding villages had been gathered, the council sat. It quickly reached a consensus that the venture would bring both honor and profit to Boweeting. This council was followed by a week's spiritual preparation for war. During the war dances many young warriors chose to follow Young Gull into battle.

On a warm, late-summer morning Young Gull left his village with Fish Hawk, the strangers from Michilimackinac, and a war party of two hundred and fifty. The party made their way along the shores of Lake Superior to Boweeting. Fish Hawk's fifty warriors joined them but the Jesuit, Marest, left to return to Michilimackinac.

The awesome party of three hundred, feathered Ojibwa warriors, faces painted vermilion and black, made their way down the western shores of Lake Huron into the St. Clair River where they silently past the newly constructed French post Fort St. Joseph. They made camp south of the post. To Young Gull's amazement he recognized the territory. It was from his dream. Everything was the same, the great rapids, the dark blue river, the black river that flowed into it as well as the abundance of fruit trees, hardwoods, marshes and game. Again he wondered what his dream was telling him.

The next morning strong Ojibwa arms propelled their light canoes down the river past the delta at its foot. One hundred and fifty Miami, Wyandotte and Potawatomi warriors were camped on the western shore of Lake St. Claire waiting for their Ojibwa allies.

A council was held on the shores of the round lake. The small party of war chiefs chose Young Gull to fill the temporary position of Grand Chief of this party. Under his direction they made their way past Detroit into the White Water Lake or Lake Erie. After passing along the northern shore line they made the portage at the waterfalls and into the Beautiful Lake or Lake Ontario. They met Denonville and his force of two thousand at Irondequoit Bay at the mouth of the Genesee River.

When the French governor appeared the three coureurs de bois stepped forward. The one called Du Lhut spoke to Governor

Denonville and La Durantaye acted as interpreter for Young Gull and the other war chiefs.

"We have commanded these four hundred and fifty warriors from the western tribes to serve the French King in His Majesty's extermination of the Seneca," Du Lhut said to Denonville. "They follow us because we are looked upon as the greatest of warriors and the elders of the land. I now place them under your command."

La Durantaye interpreted the French words. "These are Ojibwa warriors. Their power makes the earth tremble and they are here to teach the insolent Seneca a lesson." He continued, "This great force allied against the Seneca will follow Young Gull's warriors because they are the greatest in all the earth".

"Put our savages in the front and let them take the brunt of any resistance by the Seneca" ordered Denonville.

"Because the Ojibwa are the greatest warriors they will be given the honor to lead in the battle. The French will follow up with reinforcements" La Durantaye translated.

Young Gull spoke. "The French Governor is wise to acknowledge the power of the Ojibwa. It is good that the French submit the honor of the battle to us."

La Durantaye translated Young Gull's words for Denonville. "The chief of the savages submits his authority and agrees to follow the order by your Excellency to lead in the battle." Denonville smiled at the words of La Durantaye.

The following day Young Gull led the Western Nations, including the three coureurs de bois, up the Genesee. The French army followed.

The Seneca were alarmed by the news of the advancing force and of its size. The fact that the Ojibwa was leading it was even more alarming. They prepared a hasty plan of defense. They would ambush their enemy on a bend of the river several miles from their main village.

The village had a population of more than two thousand including a fighting force of six hundred. It was fortified with a palisade protecting the long houses and surrounded by acres of tall corn interwoven with the vines of huge, ripening pumpkin and squash. This bountiful harvest meant that most of the six hundred Seneca warriors were available for the trap at the river's bend.

Young Gull was in the lead canoe, followed by ninety canoes manned by the best of the Western Nations. Four hundred canoes manned by Denonville's French army followed them. The hidden Seneca let the Ojibwa contingent pass and waited patiently for the French who were less adept at forest warfare. The French regulars and conscripts passed in front of the strung out Seneca and they opened fire with Dutch muskets. Confusion reigned. The French abandoned their canoes and rushed up the hill and into the surrounding forest. The French soldiers panicked and in the confusion began firing upon each other.

The warriors of the Western Nations heard the din behind them and returned to the battle as quickly as they could. Four hundred and fifty warriors charged wildly up the banks shrieking fearsome war whoops. Some were firing French muskets while others waved their war clubs. The Seneca broke ranks and turned in full retreat toward their village. They passed the abandoned and burning village in full flight deep into Seneca country.

Denonville was so disheartened by the panic of his troops that he ordered his men to only clear and burn the cornfields. They found and burned a few smaller villages in the surrounding countryside but did not pursue the fleeing Seneca. Ten days later the governor ordered his troops to withdraw.

The failure not to capitalize on the rout of the Seneca and complete the extermination of their old enemy was not appreciated by Young Gull and the other war chiefs. It deprived them of valuable scalps and the spoils of a larger conflict.

"This will teach the scoundrels a lesson they will never forget. They will surely come groveling for peace now!" exclaimed Denonville. La Durantaye interpreted for the war chiefs.

"Denonville is a fool! The French make poor warriors. They vow to annihilate our common enemy, the Seneca but only make war on their cornfields. They have only succeeded in creating a swarm of angry hornets by knocking the nest down. We will never again give such an effort for so little return!" exclaimed Young Gull. La Durantaye did not translate nor did Denonville ask him to.

The disgruntled war chiefs left in a huff and immediately returned to their own country to tell of the French treachery. Denonville withdrew to Niagara where he ordered his men to begin the construction of a large fort. But the most ominous consequence of the French's scorched earth policy was the longhouse council being held at Onondaga. All five nations of the Iroquois were enraged at the arrogance of the French and their allies and the infuriated chiefs were planning their revenge.

2

The Blackberry Moon had arrived and the time had come once again to collect berries for the winter's provisions. Berry picking season was always a joyous occasion for the Ojibwa. The whole community participated, all members of each family even down to the little ones. There were great numbers of berry bushes along the shores of Lake Superior immediately north of Boweeting. On a particularly warm summer morning the whole village set their canoes in the water and struck out for the berry grounds. The trip was uneventful and they arrived around midday.

It was hot that sunny afternoon, too hot to start picking berries. So, the whole band moved into the shade of the pines, which grew, to the north of the large peninsula that contained the berry grounds. They spent the afternoon setting up camp in the pines overlooking a large, sheltered bay. Most of them gathered around a grand-fire after supper to listen to Corn Woman tell stories. Because of the heat wave they would only collect berries in the morning and late afternoon. They would spend the heat of the day at their campsite enjoying the shade and the cool breeze that blew off the large bay and up the incline to the pines.

The camp rose early the next morning as the birds were announcing the dawn. After offerings and a light breakfast they set out for the grounds. They made their way around the neck of the peninsula to the berry patches.

"Ah, the bushes are loaded! How good the Master of Life is. He has provided bountifully the whole summer," Young Gull said to Chenoa as they beached their Canoe.

"Yes, the winter will be easy this year," Chenoa answered as a second canoe was beached beside them.

"Aanii! Look at the harvest!" exclaimed Shahwanjegawin as he and Strawberry removed their birch bark baskets. The young couple had traveled with Shahwanjegawin's parents but paddled their own canoe. They had become as close as bark to a tree and suffered the pangs of new love. They were to be married in a year.

The foursome worked fast and before long they were encroaching on the family next to them. This slowed them down so they decided since midday was approaching they would return to the camp with most of their baskets full.

Back at the camp Young Gull declared, "At mid-afternoon we shall go to the south end of the grounds, at the tip of the peninsula, and work our way up."

"Yes, this is a good plan. That way there will be no-one to slow us down," his son said in agreement. They put their produce into the large, temporary, storage bin that had been built to keep the animals out and moved up to the camp to relax. When the sun had reached midway between high and setting they struck out again, this time for the southern tip of the peninsula.

This time Young Gull and Shahwanjegawin paddled together in one canoe and the two women traveling in the other. When they reached their destination the two women started at the southern most point and the two men moved up the shore a distance out of sight. They did this because although Strawberry desired to be with Shahwanjegawin she also enjoyed being with Chenoa who was like a second mother to her. They relished their time together.

After spending some time in the berry patches Chenoa exclaimed to Strawberry, "Look at the sun! Let's break for a rest and enjoy the view." The sun had turned from dazzling white and impossible to look at into a large red ball that hung over a small island offshore. It seemed suspended precariously over that small isle while it decided whether or not to engulf it. Suddenly Chenoa noticed something in that idyllic scene that was ominously out of place.

"Do you see that?" she asked Strawberry.

"No. What?"

"There, I see it again!" Chenoa whispered.

"Where" Strawberry inquired? "Ah! I saw it" exclaimed Strawberry! They both observed a wisp of smoke as it rose above the island. It was the smoke of a campfire. They quickly loaded their baskets into the canoe and paddled hard up the shore to find the men.

When the sun had set and all had returned to the base camp Young Gull called a council. It was decided by the elder council members of the band that Young Gull should take three scouts with him and reconnoiter the cause of the smoke seen on the island. Four men set out in two canoes hidden by the dark of night. They paddled hard across the wide straight between the peninsula and the island.

Soon they beached their craft on the west shore of the isle. They could hear the din of a Mohawk war dance; drums beating and whoops and howls from the warriors as they petitioned their spiritual helpers in preparation for war.

"What are the Mohawk doing this far into Ojibwa territory? We must know how many warriors they have here," thought Young Gull. He motioned to Small Kettle and his comrade to swing wide around to the south of the noise. He and partner would approach from the east. Slowly, cautiously they crept through the pines to the edge of the Mohawk camp. The enemy was making so much noise and so engrossed in their dancing that even if their dogs did bark they would not have heard the warnings.

Both parties successfully scouted out the enemy and returned covertly to their base camp.

The news had spread through the camp like wildfire. The whole encampment was buzzing with whispers of shock and astonishment. The Mohawk had never before dared to penetrate so deeply into their territory. Young Gull thought of his old friend Atironto, who had died the last winter. He would be livid, ranting and raving against his hated adversaries. A council was called.

"These Mohawk get more insolent with each passing season. They must be taught a lesson. This is Ojibwa territory. They have no right to be here. Even now they make preparations for war; war against our village" declared Young Gull.

"There are about one hundred Mohawk warriors. All have guns. We have fifty warriors and about twenty guns with us. Yet, the odds favor us. Our medicine is stronger" proclaimed Small Kettle.

"Small Kettle speaks the truth. Our medicine is stronger than the Mohawk's. Chenoa's spirit guide has shown her this thing. It is for our benefit. Our spirit helpers have delivered them into our hands" declared Kewadin.

"We must act. We can take them completely by surprise. They don't know we are here," advised old Corn Woman. The entire council shook their heads and grunted sounds of agreement.

Solemn offerings of tobacco were given and each warrior prayed for the help of their personal spirit guides instead of dancing. The drum was also dispensed with keeping noise to a minimum. Sometime after midnight they slipped twelve canoes into the bay; four warriors in each craft. They made their way down the coast of the long berry peninsula and across the straight with strong, silent strokes of their paddles.

When they reached the island Small Kettle broke off with six canoes. Swinging around the south end of the island they landed their craft on the west beach. Young Gull beached their canoes on the east shore. When the two groups reached the Mohawk camp all was quiet. The enemy had exhausted themselves with hours of dancing in preparation for war. The Ojibwa warriors surrounded the outpost.

Suddenly there was a stirring in the camp accompanied by low growling sounds. Small pieces of fresh meat were tossed from the behind the pines. The dogs were won over and the Ojibwa waited patiently for the first light of day. With the bird's greeting of daybreak the attack was on.

The Mohawk were taken completely by surprise. Young Gull's warriors were vicious in their assault upon the sleeping enemy clubbing many before they could gain their senses. Many were slain before the sleep could be rubbed from their eyes. It was all over in a matter of minutes, not one opponent was left alive, and not one shot was fired. The dead Mohawk warriors were beheaded and the bodies piled in mounds and the heads were piled in one large mound on the east beach as a warning to others. Bones and skulls would be found there for a very long time.

Young Gull, Small Kettle and the rest of the Ojibwa assailants gathered up all of the Mohawk's guns and provisions and headed back to the base camp for the victory celebration. Unknown to them their village had been visited by an advance Mohawk scouting party. The Mohawk scouts were puzzled by the apparently abandoned Anishnaabek village and horrified when they returned to their outpost on the island. There was nothing left for the two confused scouts to do but to return to their own country and report the dismal failure of their incursion into Ojibwa country.

3

The Mohawk's foray so deep into Ojibwa territory was an affront to their sovereignty. Young Gull called for a Grand-Council to determine an effective response and their course of action. It convened during the Corn Moon. After the invocations Young Gull rose to speak.

"Brothers, Sisters, the Iroquois have once again heaped scorn on the power of the Ojibwa. It is the Ojibwa that have supremacy in all the earth. No one can refute our strength. Not the Dakota, nor the French, nor the English, and not the Iroquois. The whole of the earth trembles when the Three Fires Council speaks.

Brothers, Sisters, the Iroquois covet our trapping grounds. Our grounds are rich in fur and theirs are drying up. We have improved our lives by trading with the French for overseas goods. They would push us out if possible, stealing our territory. They need to expand in order to keep up their level of trade with the English at Albany.

These Iroquois become more and more belligerent. This cannot be allowed to continue. We must teach these Snakes a lesson.

Brothers, Sisters, the Iroquois also seek revenge on our people and on Young Gull for leading so grand a force against them at Irondequoit. On the Genesee River they were vanquished completely. They dropped their weapons and ran at the sight of our warriors. They have seen that it is the Ojibwa that they should fear. They war with the French, who only make war on the cornfields, but cannot win against them. How can they win against our warriors?

Brothers, Sisters, I propose a show of force to encourage them toward peace. We should call for peace wampum to be exchanged at Sahgeeng. I, myself, offer to lead an armed force to the peace powwow. It should be a large force, no smaller than four hundred warriors.

Brothers, Sisters, this is what I have to say on the matter."

The elders and chiefs considered Young Gull's words by talking in council for three days. The Grand-Council came to a consensus that Young Gull's words were wise and runners should be sent to the Mohawk village at the mouth of the Sahgeeng to elicit their response to peace. The runners were sent and returned with an invitation to Sahgeeng.

Young Gull led the armada with two hundred Ojibwa warriors. They were followed by Fish Hawk with seventy-five brave fighters, The Pike with seventy-five Ottawa and Kondiaronk with one hundred Wyandotte. The impressive flotilla was joined by Potawatomi war chief Ouenemek and fifty of his best men.

Unknown to the peace seekers a small Mohawk raiding party was waiting just south of Boweeting for them to leave Michilimackinac. At the first indication that Young Gull's warriors were moving south the Mohawk raiding party headed straight for Young Gull's lightly protected village.

"Shahwanjegawin" Chenoa called. The tall, good-looking teen turned when he heard his mother's voice. She beckoned him to come to her with a wave of her arm. "I know you are going spear fishing at the rapids upstream but first I need you to take this tobacco to old He Walks Well. Tell him I want him to offer it as a sacrifice for peace and as an appeasement offering to the Master of Life for the success of your father's endeavor."

"Yes, I will take it right now" he said as he clutched the deerskin medicine bag. He knew that He Walks Well was fasting at the mouth of the river where the presence of the spirits was very strong. He slipped his canoe into the river and headed downstream to meet his destiny.

The old holy man was sitting cross-legged in front of his lodge where the swirling river spills into the frigid waters of Lake Superior. He had ceremonially sacrificed a dog and its head was held high on a peace pole behind him while in front of him the flames from his ritual fire licked the air high above their coals. He sat, trance-like, deep in meditation when Shahwanjegawin beached his canoe. The two never had time to greet each other.

Shrill Mohawk war whoops broke the serenity of the scene. The raiding party had rounded the south point of the river's mouth and they headed straight for the lone campsite. The stealthy warriors could hardly believe their good fortune. They knew their quarry by sight and they took him without a struggle. He Walks Well was felled with one swift swing of a Mohawk war club. Two powerful, young warriors bound and gagged Shahwanjegawin and placed him in the bottom of one of their canoes.

They left the site and headed south as quickly as their long, powerful strokes would carry their canoes. The Three Fires Confederacy was making its way slowly along the west shore of Manitoulin Island when the raiders passed them on east side of the island. Quickly they moved down the east side of the Bruce Peninsula to the portage at Owen Sound. They arrived at Sahgeeng via the back way a full day ahead of the peace party led by Young Gull.

The Mohawk welcomed the conferees with shouts of ho, ho as they raised their arms in honor. The Three Fire's show of power was impressive, more than twice the warriors of the Sahgeeng, but the Mohawk were undaunted. The main force camped all around outside the palisade. The chiefs and a small guard of feathered warriors entered the village. The Mohawk welcomed their visitors like relatives but their kindness seemed insincere to Young Gull.

"I don't trust these people," he whispered to Fish Hawk when the smiling host beckoned the chiefs and their small guard into one of the long houses for a parlay. The Mohawk chiefs capitulated on every point. Wampum belts were exchanged signing the peace into reality. Gifts of pelts, English goods and produce were heaped upon their visitors.

"We must feast to celebrate this great day!" exclaimed the Mohawk Grand Chief.

"Ho! Ho! Ho!" the other hosts shouted.

"We must parlay first," announced Young Gull and the Ojibwa emissaries withdrew to their camp outside the village.

"I feel very uncomfortable with our hosts," Young Gull said to his chiefs and principal men.

"My brothers, these Mohawk cannot be trusted!" exclaimed Kondiaronk.

"I agree. They are up to something. They are too willing in negotiations," added The Pike.

Fish Hawk spoke up. "What could it mean? We have them outnumbered and surrounded. They can't be waiting for reinforcements since they knew for weeks we were coming. Besides they seem to want to settle and get rid of us quickly."

"Perhaps they have ambush in mind. They could have an armed force waiting up the peninsula. Their Sahgeeng warriors would be at our flank," interjected Ouenemek. He was well seasoned in the art of warfare.

The council was bewildered so they decided to accept the peace and the gifts but not let their guard down. They would keep a watchful eye on their return home by sending scouts continually ahead of the main party.

The feast was on and such a feast between these two perpetual enemies had not been seen before or since. The food was served in abundance, corn, bread, squash, pumpkin, whitefish, lake trout, berries and fruits. Various kinds of meats, moose, deer, bear, porcupine and dog.

The Mohawk Grand Chief honoured Young Gull by serving him the first plate loaded with samples of all the abundance spread before them. Young Gull was hungry and devoured the heaping plateful in what seem like seconds, hardly enough time to taste the food, but not quite. He was impressed with the meat. It had a strange, sweet kind of taste. A taste he could not place but he enjoyed it thoroughly. He passed the strange taste off as perhaps some unknown herb or spice used by the Mohawk.

The celebrations continued for several days, as there was also an ample supply of English rum to wash down the bountiful tables of food. Gorging was intermixed with drumming and dancing, but little sleep. Finally the visitors left on the best of terms.

They followed through on their decision to send scouts ahead but the precaution was unwarranted. There was no sign of trouble until they reached Manitoulin. There they were met by a party of young teens from Young Gull's village. They carried an ominous message. A blow to the head had killed old He Walks Well and Shahwanjegawin was missing.

"This is the work of the Mohawk" he thought. When he arrived home he was heartsick and Chenoa was frantic with worry but there was little they could do. The whole village was in mourning when the worst of all news arrived by an Ottawa runner.

A council was called to hear his words. It was solemn. No sound could be heard in the council lodge when the young messenger began to speak.

"Brothers and Sisters of the Three Fires, the Mohawk have done a grievous thing. They are laughing and bragging how they put the Ojibwa to shame. How they outwitted us at the peace council at Sahgeeng.

Brothers and Sisters, their vengeance is despicable. For their humiliating rout at Irondequoit and their utter defeat on Berry Island they have wanted revenge. But their revenge is not an honorable one.

Brothers and Sisters, they are telling their Iroquois brothers of the capturing of the son of the Great Chief Young Gull. They tortured and killed the young boy, cooking his flesh and feeding it to his own father . . ."

The courier's words were interrupted with loud wails of grief. Chenoa fell on her face as if dead. Young Gull staggered out of the lodge, his stomach heaving, but he could regurgitate nothing. Later he began to shake with the shock of the news and he could not stop. The village had never known such mourning and the wailing went on for days.

4

Chenoa and Young Gull were devastated. The story of the Mohawk's abominable act spread quickly through the land of the Ojibwa and beyond. All the bands clamored for war. A Three Fires council was called. It was to be held at Boweeting before the first snowfall.

Chiefs, elders and principal men and women gathered for the council. They represented most bands of the three nations of the Confederacy and the Ouendat, or Wyandotte as they were now called two thousand leaders in all. Young Gull attended but did not speak, although leader after leader spoke for war. All conferees concurred. The entire Three Fires would take the path of war beginning following spring. The council dissolved with the Grand Chiefs and the War Chiefs staying on to plan strategy.

"War canoes must be built. This can be done over the winter," suggested Sahgimah. "Each band must build enough to carry the young men they will send into battle. Each War Chief will be responsible for overseeing the construction of the canoes."

Young Gull finally spoke. "We must drive these craven Snakes back to their homeland. They have inflicted their depravity on the land that once gave life to our friends the Wyandotte. We must send them to their own home south of Lake Ontario." Now the great chief understood the lasting bitterness of his old friend, Atironto.

He continued, "It is best to surround Southern Ontario. Our forces should be split into four divisions. The first should leave Boweeting twenty days ahead of the other divisions. That detachment should be made up of part of the Ojibwa force and should include the Wyandotte from Green Bay and the Potawatomi.

Surprise is our greatest ally. It should move down the eastern shore of Lake Michigan to avoid detection. It can pick up Potawatomi warriors along the way gathering finally at Round Lake. From here they can invade Southern Ontario from the west.

As they gather at Round Lake Bald Eagle should take his Mississauga warriors east to the Ottawa District and attack from there.

Sahgimah should drive south, with his Ottawa braves, on an easterly course to Blue Mountain. There he can wait in ambush for the Iroquois forces that are sure to come by way of Lake Simcoe. They use the old Wyandotte portage from their villages on Lake Ontario to get to the Great Sea of the Ottawa.

At the same time the other Ojibwa division should also move in southerly direction on a westerly course and attack the large Mohawk village at Owen Sound."

"My brothers, this is a good plan!" exclaimed Kondiaronk. Sahgimah, Bald Eagle and the other chiefs concurred. Young Gull's stratagem was adopted and he was chosen to lead the St. Clair division, named after the lake that would be the springboard for their western offensive. An Amikwa Ojibwa Grand Chief from the north shore of Georgian Bay named White Cloud would lead the north division of Ojibwa south from Boweeting. Like Young Gull, White Cloud had built a reputation as a fierce warrior in battle and a clever strategist in his many skirmishes with the Iroquois.

On one of the cool, late afternoons Young Gull walked the familiar path along the Boweeting rapids with his good friend Fish Hawk. Fish Hawk exemplified the Ojibwa meaning of the word friend, "one who cries for my sorrows." The mood was solemn. War was a serious thing and the prospects of it cast a pall over the whole area. The gray skies paired the milieu with Young Gull's depressed state. Fish Hawk was the first to speak.

"The war will have a negative affect on our trade with the French. Also our food supplies will not allow a sustained campaign."

"You are right. Perhaps the French will help with supplies once the war begins."

"Do you think they will be sympathetic to our cause?" Fish Hawk asked the Grand Chief.

"They are still enemies with the Iroquois. Kondiaronk has seen to that."

"Kondiaronk?" quizzed Fish Hawk.

"He is a good chief and just as crafty as his father, Atironto. After the rout at Irondequoit the Iroquois feigned peace overtures to Denonville. When Kondiaronk heard that peace emissaries were on their way to Frontenac he intercepted them. He killed one Iroquois chief and took the others prisoner"

"Ah!" Fish Hawk exclaimed.

"The prisoners cried out that they were on their way to make peace with Denonville. 'Denonville' Kondiaronk exclaimed! 'Denonville sent Kondiaronk to destroy advancing Iroquois. Denonville claimed Iroquois party was war party! Go, tell your people of the French treachery' he said. Kondiaronk then released all the prisoners but two which he kept as hostages."

"That was crafty indeed," laughed Young Gull's good friend.

"That's not all," explained the Grand Chief. "When he returned to Michilimackinac he handed one of the Iroquois over to the French chief commanding the fort there. Upon Kondiaronk's advice the French leader had the prisoner shot dead in front of all. After this, Kondiaronk released the other prisoner with enough provisions to get him home. This is how Kondiaronk killed the peace" Young Gull said as a slight smile crossed his face. It was the first time Young Gull smiled since the Sahgeeng peace powwow.

The War Council broke as the first of the winter snows began to fly and the Grand Chiefs and War Chiefs returned to their home territories to prepare for war.

The Iroquois War

Chapter 6

Mr. Nanabush and the Subway Station—St. Clair Campaign—
Battle of Skull Mound—Siege at Owen Sound—Support Offered
at Boweeting—Battles of Blue Mountain and Skull Island

1

The coffee was good but the conversation much better. Both
ended too quickly. An hour had passed and the two had just begun
to explore each other's being.

"Look at the time!" exclaimed Karen. We've been talking for an
hour. I need to get home and walk my little dog. He's been in the
apartment all day."

Brad agreed but the time together had been far too short for his
liking. As the two descended the front steps that formed part of the
entrance to the ROM Brad spoke.

"Would you like to meet again for coffee—perhaps some
evening?" he asked rather hesitantly.

"Oh yes!" Karen blurted out. "Darn! Why can't I be more
composed? Why do I always have to speak without thinking?" she
thought.

The two stopped on the sidewalk agreed to meet the following
evening then went their separate ways.

Brad waited anxiously at the small coffee shop around the corner
from Karen's apartment. It was seven o'clock. Brad thought "she
should be here anytime." Sure enough no sooner had that thought
crossed his mind when he saw her approaching through the glass
doors.

The two settled into the booth Brad was holding and ordered their coffee. Their conversation picked up where it left off the day before as if there was no interval. It was captivating and led to a movie date the following Friday. The romance had begun!

The new week dragged on for both Karen and Brad. All week long they looked forward to their movie date with great anticipation. Yet neither spoke of it to the other. Finally Friday arrived but their eight hour work day seemed to be taking forever.

Brad was in Karen's office looking over the project for his department that Karen had prepared. The drawings were laid out on a large early twentieth century work table. In front of the table Mr. Blackman had the matching wall mirror installed.

Suddenly a slight movement in the mirror caught both their eyes. For less than a second they saw the image of a young Ojibwa warrior. His was tall. His lean, muscular body tattooed in the old fashion. The rims of his ears were studded with small ornaments and two large earrings hung from the lobes to his shoulders. The warrior's sleek, long black hair was adorned with three hawk feathers.

But the image was subliminal. It changed so quickly that both Brad and Karen weren't sure they saw it at all. They quickly turned and there in the doorway stood the old man confirming the image they were sure they saw.

"Come in" Karen instructed Mr. Nanabush. Mr. Nanabush came into the office and sat in one of the black leather guest chairs.

"We can finish going over the project drawings next week" Brad said to Karen. "It's near quitting time now" he said leaving the office.

"How are things going with the lectures?" Karen inquired.

"The people are enjoying my story. Many more came this week"

"I wanted to ask you how you left the museum at the end of last week."

"By the front entrance—that is the only way out that I know of" replied the old man.

"You didn't go down the esplanade?"

"I don't know of an esplanade. What is it?"

"It's the long walkway that leads to the outer courtyard—toward the rear of the museum" Karen replied rather perplexed.

"No" repeated Mr. Nanabush.

"I'm sorry. We thought we caught sight of you going into the courtyard. We must have been mistaken" she apologized although she knew she wasn't mistaken.

"That's all. I was just wondering how your storytelling was going. I'm glad the people are enjoying them." The old man struggled out of the soft leather chair and shuffled out.

Karen neatly piled the drawings in the center of the table and secured them with Mr. Blackman's heavy paperweight. She quickly grabbed her clutch and hurried out the door. The only thing on her mind was her date that evening with Brad.

As Karen left the entrance to the museum she caught sight Mr. Nanabush. His familiar figure circumvented a barricade and disappeared down the entrance steps to the subway station. She hurried to catch him. The sign hanging on the barricade read "Subway Closed". The ROM station had been closed for several days for repairs.

Karen followed the old storyteller down the steps. Again she caught sight of him as he vanished around the step's entrance to the platform. When she reached the bottom of the entrance steps she could see the turnstiles had been removed. The workers had left for the day and the station was completely empty. Again—no Mr. Nanabush! "How can he vanish into thin air like this?" thought Karen. As she stood there dumbfounded her keen eyes detected a slight movement at the end of the platform. A rat scurried along the edge of the wall and disappeared along the tracks and into the darkness.

Karen left the station and continued home. Now she was not only filled with anticipation for her big date but she was anxious to tell Brad about the mystery of the ROM subway station.

2

Week three arrived and Mr. Nanabush appeared early this time. He was anxious to continue his story; after all it had reached his favorite part. His audience began arriving shortly after him. Many of them were early as well. The old man was a gifted storyteller well able to captivate an audience. The seats were all taken and some were even standing at the back of the small lecture hall. The storyteller began.

Patches of snow were still on the ground and the moon was waxing half full when the first division had gathered at Boweeting. It was month of the Lost Moon, this extra moon being added at the end of every thirty-moon cycle. The campaign was planned to begin on the first day of the Sucker Moon so Young Gull's division of warriors needed to be at St. Clair during the Naked Days, which were the three and one half days between the end of the illumination of the Lost Moon and the beginning of the Sucker Moon.

Kondiaronk arrived with six hundred Wyandotte warriors. The Ojibwa had gathered from the west including Minnesota, Wisconsin and even as far away as southern Manitoba and the Thunder Bay District. Their war chiefs brought two hundred and seventy five war canoes in all, eight warriors to a canoe. Young Gull would pick up another one hundred and twenty five Potawatomi war canoes as they skirted along the eastern shores of Lake Michigan. By the time they made the Kalamazoo portage and spilled out into White Water Lake, or Lake Erie, they were thirty-two hundred strong. The new moon was still a few days away so they camped along the banks of the Raisin River.

"My brother, Young Gull!" Kondiaronk called as he moved through the camp of the Ojibwa toward Young Gull's lodge. Young Gull had summoned both him and Ouenemek to a parlay to refine strategy.

"Aanii!" replied Young Gull. "Come in." Both chiefs has spent years skirmishing with the Iroquois and had much experience. Both were tall, powerfully built men but had reached the end of middle age and this would be their last campaign.

Ouenemek joined them. He was younger than the other two by two decades. He was also shorter than them but stocky with a powerful upper body. His head was shaved on the sides. The hair on the top of his head stood straight up like six inch bristles. His ears were pierced and he wore long shell earrings. His face was painted vermilion on the right side and indigo on the left.

"When we attack the Seneca town on the Horn River they will send reinforcements from their home land. Their town is a large one protected by two palisades; there will be a siege so we need to protect our flank. The Seneca cross Lake Erie at Long Point where it is the narrowest. Take your warriors there and wait for them in ambush."

"We will leave at day break, my brother," said Kondiaronk. Ouenemek nodded in agreement and the two returned to their respective camps.

The next morning at day break two hundred Wyandotte and Potawatomi war canoes slipped out into Lake Erie and along its northern shoreline to Long Point. Here they would make camp and wait in ambush for the Seneca reinforcements.

North Wind was traveling with the First Division as the armed force's spiritual leader. As the large war canoes of Kondiaronk and Ouenemek glided along the shoreline to Long Point Kewadin performed his ceremonies in order to seek a vision of how the battle would go.

First he prepared a sweat lodge to purify himself. After fasting for three days he offered tobacco and performed the drum ceremony. He chanted to the resonance of the drum for hours but no vision came. The various camps of warriors waited patiently showing no concern because they knew North Wind's medicine was strong. On the fourth day a council of the War Chiefs was called. Speeches of encouragement by the Grand Chiefs opened the council then North Wind rose to speak.

"Brothers, Chiefs, I have received a vision of the coming battle. It is good. It came in a dream as I slept last night.

I was exhausted from fasting, drumming and chanting and knew I needed to rest in order to renew myself. As I lay on my mat last night I fell into a deep sleep. The dream sent to me by my spirit guide entered my head and I began to see.

I could see a river valley with deep forests on both sides. The river was deep and moved slowly toward me. In my dream I heard a commotion behind me. I turned to see what the commotion was and saw an ominous storm approaching from the west. The sky was black and there was continuous lighting and thunder. The wind began to pick up as the storm approached. Suddenly, the storm was all around me. I could hear the wind, howling with rage. I could hear the crack of thunderbolts as if right on top of me. Hail fell pelting the ground as if shot from a thousand slings, but I could feel none of it. Not the hail, nor the wind, nor the resonance of the thunder.

The storm ceased as suddenly as it had begun and the sky opened up to a brilliant blue. Out of the clear sky it began to rain, but not water; weapons! Muskets, hatchets, knives and war clubs fell around me. Not only weapons fell but the bodies of dead warriors, all of them Seneca!"

"Eeeeiiiii!" the War Chiefs sounded as they exhaled with relief.

"Go, tell your warriors to sleep well. Tomorrow the victory is ours!" exclaimed North Wind.

The next day the party moved out into Lake Erie and into the channel that leads to Round Lake. The village was about twelve miles up the river the Ojibwa called Horn. The large war party did not enter the mouth of that river until just before dawn. When they did they advanced single file, a column of two hundred war canoes strung out over three miles of river.

The sky was beginning to lighten from black to dark blue when they were spotted by a small band of Seneca fishermen who were heading down a trail on the north bank to check their nets. They rushed back to warn their kinsmen, most of who were still sleeping. This gave the enemy time to close the gates and begin to mount a defense.

Young Gull led the charge across the fields that had been cleared for maize and pumpkin. The air was filled with the sounds of war whoops and the din rose to a fever pitch. The stockade held and arrows and musket balls whizzed through the air around the attacking warriors. The Seneca were able to place two hundred marksmen on platforms located between the double palisade and this forced the attackers to withdraw to the edge of the forest. Young

Gull's stratagem was foiled by the fishermen so new tactics would have to be devised.

The Seneca were outnumbered four to one but their stockade proved a formidable defense. All day long Young Gull's warriors rushed the walled town only to be beaten back. They were suffering losses of two or three warriors to every one of the enemy's. As evening drew they retreated to the protection of the forest and to devise a new plan.

"We can leave them under siege until they starve. That would cut our losses to next to nothing," advised Small Kettle.

"We don't know how much provision they have, so we don't know how long that would take," replied Fish Hawk.

"It can't be much. They have just gone through winter so their supply must be low."

"This is true," said Young Gull, "but time is precious to the overall plan. We are to unite with White Cloud on the next new moon. We will wait them out for a while and try to pick off their warriors one at a time from the edge of the forest.

Meanwhile, under the cover of darkness the Seneca discharged several couriers who were to try to slip through Young Gull's lines and make their way to their homeland. Several didn't make it and were taken prisoner, tortured and killed.

However, two did make it through the lines. They moved as quickly as possible up the river to a short portage to Kettle Creek and into Lake Erie. They paddled their dugout canoes as quickly as possible straight across the lake and on to their kinsmen on the Genesee. A large Seneca war party was raised and one thousand painted warriors put their canoes into the lake and headed for the portage on the neck of Long Point.

"Seneca!" exclaimed a Wyandotte lookout as he peered out into the lake. His companion strained his eyes and could see them also, many dugouts appearing out of the haze on the horizon. They moved through the trees to their canoes on the west side of the point and hurried down to the base camp to alert the force waiting there. Kondiaronk moved his warriors up the west side of peninsula to the tip of the point. Ouenemek moved his Potawatomi to just above the neck. They waited for the Seneca to come within range.

The first of dugouts were about a quarter of a mile from the portage when the Potawatomi, led by their great chief, Ouenemek, came rushing and shouting out of the trees and onto the beach. Into the water they slid their light birch bark canoes and paddled out to meet their hated enemy. They were able to circle around the heavier dugout canoes used by the Seneca and this gave them great advantage

In the heat of the battle Kondiaronk unleashed his Wyandotte warriors from the tip of the point and they swooped down on top of the Seneca armada attacking its flank. The battle was over in a matter of minutes. The whole Seneca contingent was completely annihilated. Kondiaronk and Ouenemek then gathered their forces and retraced the courier's trail to join Young Gull.

Young Gull had decided to try to burn the adversary out and so rained flaming arrows down on the Seneca town. Many long houses caught fire and burned destroying both homes and provisions.

At night his warriors made lightning forays to the wall putting them to the torch. The Seneca countered with water but that was not always successful. A large piece of outer stockade had burned through on the north side of the town and they were working on the inner palisade when the Wyandotte and Potawatomi forces arrived.

The sight of the extra warriors arriving instead of Seneca reinforcements took the heart out of the staunch defenders. It was just a matter of time until they breached the north wall and poured into the town. The din of the battle was deafening with the firing of hundreds of muskets and war whoops. They completely overran the town and the Seneca capitulated. During the battle old people, women and children were killed. The women were killed because they are the life givers and produce warriors. The children were killed because they grow up to be, or produce, warriors and the elders were killed because they give the enemy's community wisdom. But after the surrender those left alive were taken prisoner. When the battle was over there was only a smoldering ruin where the town had once stood. A few of the Seneca warriors had escaped to the forest but they were quickly hunted down and taken prisoner.

"Decapitate all of the Seneca's dead," ordered Young Gull.

"All?" asked one of the minor War Chiefs.

"All: warriors, elders, women, children. All! Leave the bodies but pile the skulls in a pyramid above the ground." This served notice that the Three Fires Confederacy had gone to war and they were a force that was invincible. The enemies' headless bodies were left lying on the ground exactly where they fell so the sun would bleach their bones. The mutilated bodies rendered them desecrated and so they could not enter the Land of Souls. Without a proper burial with the provisions needed to make that long journey their spirits would be lost.

The Three Fires' dead were buried in mounds with provisions for their next journey and the benefits of the Ritual of the Dead ceremony which was performed by North Wind.

3

At the same time Young Gull's forces attacked the Seneca from the west the other divisions left Boweeting for their theatres of war. Bald Eagle took fifteen hundred Mississauga warriors up the French River, across Nipissing to the portage to the Mattawa River where he sent part of his fighters along the old trade route to the north. The rest continued along the River.

Sahgimah took two thousand Ottawa and Ojibwa warriors along the eastern shores of Georgian Bay to a place called "Sahgimah's Livery," at Blue Mountain on the Penetanguishene Peninsula. They made camp here and waited for the appearance of the Iroquois whom they expected to come down the Severn and Nottawasaga rivers. Meanwhile, White Cloud led twenty-one hundred Ojibwa fighters across the Main Channel of Georgian Bay to the tip of the Bruce Peninsula.

Young Gull left the Horn River via Round Lake and turned north. As the first of the flotilla's canoes past old Fort St. Joseph the last were just leaving the lake. They had left behind only smoldering ruins, several large burying mounds and a huge pile of human skulls, some two thousand in all.

Again Young Gull passed the through the territory of his dream. Again he wondered what it meant. His dream had recurred to him several times and he had asked North Wind for the interpretation but there was none. The dream was so vivid and intense that it had weighed heavily on his mind, so much so that everyone in his village had heard about it at least once.

Their powerful strokes carried them up the eastern shore of Lake Huron. They were making haste to meet White Cloud's forces in the area of the Bruce Peninsula. Young Gull particularly wanted to be the first to arrive at Sahgeeng.

On the sixth day of hard paddling they beached their canoes at Sahgeeng Beach. They were about six miles south of the large Mohawk town at the mouth of the Sahgeeng River. After moving inland to make a hidden camp Young Gull called his war chiefs to plan the next campaign.

"Sahgeeng is very close by. The Mohawk will know by now that the Three Fires make war on them. Their town will be on high alert so we have lost the ally of surprise. Our numbers will still prevail. We should use the same tactics as we did at Horn River; lightning raids from the forest, attacking their palisades with fire and wearing them down. These are my thoughts" Young Gull said while surveying his war chiefs.

Kondiaronk spoke next. "My brothers, we may still be able to use our old ally, surprise. The Mohawk have not yet discovered our presence. They do not know they are in imminent danger.

My brothers, if we move into position under the cover of night we can catch the stockade guards unaware. If we can take out the sentries at the gates our warriors can throw them open. Sahgeeng will then be ours to take while they sleep.

My brothers, this is my counsel."

"It is not good to move through the forest at night. It is not good to fight at night. Evil Spirits roam the forests at night. We would be prey to the Wiindgoo," complained Little Iron Man, a young chief from Lake of the Woods.

"Little Iron Man speaks with wisdom. To attack at night would arouse the Evil Spirit and leave our warriors open to his evil ones. This is what I have to add," He Makes a Voyage, one of Young Gull's old friends, said.

"Our Spirit helpers are strong; stronger than the evil ones. Kondiaronk is the one who speaks wise words. If we can take the town at night, it will be ours in a few hours instead of days. It will also preserve many of our warrior's lives. I am in favor of Kondiaronk's strategy. This is what I have to say," said Fish Hawk forcefully.

"We have not heard from North Wind. Although I also am in favor of Kondiaronk's plan our decision should rest with the holy man. It is a spiritual matter," said Young Gull nodding to North Wind.

"We have a strong force and many spirits in our camp. However, the Evil One is also very powerful. I shall have to seek wisdom from my spirit guide. I shall prepare myself for the shaking tent". North Wind stood after speaking these words and the council broke up. Only the holy man would reconvene it.

North Wind set about constructing a small sweat lodge, which he would use to purify himself in preparation to converse with the spirits. The rest of the warriors settled down in their separate camps which were spread throughout the forest surrounding Sahgeeng Beach.

Young Bear, North Wind's young apprentice was also traveling with the war party and he set about following North Wind's instructions. He chose a small glade which was perpetually shaded by the forest where he drove the six poles of the shaking tent deep into the soft, black earth of the forest floor. Then he banded the poles with two strips of bark, one band half way up the poles, the other at the top. Young Bear then covered the sides of the tent with bark leaving only the top open and one small opening on one side so the holy man could enter. His task complete he left the shaking tent alone among the abundant ferns and trilliums that blanketed the forest floor throughout the glade.

North Wind fasted for three days and on the fourth morning entered the sweat lodge. After purifying himself he went to the glade accompanied by Young Bear and another young warrior. Young Bear bound North Wind hand and foot and the two placed the holy man in the tent. They then covered the entrance with a bark door and retreated to the edge of the glade. They could hear North Wind in the shaking tent singing and chanting. This went on for about an hour.

The wind picked up filling the glade with the sounds of sighing and creaking limbs as it moved through the treetops. Suddenly the tent began to shake violently. Strange talking could be heard coming from the tent while it shook. There were many different voices all speaking in a strange dialect, which they couldn't understand.

After this all went quiet and a few minutes later North Wind emerged from the shaking tent unbound. The three returned silently to camp and Kewadin called a council.

"The spirits have spoken to me in the shaking tent. I asked them if it was wise to attack Sahgeeng at night. I said we were afraid of the evil one. Here is what they answered.

"The whole earth trembles when the Three Fires travel through the land in concert. The spirits who are not Three Fires spirits also tremble in fear. The Iroquois spirits tremble before you. The evil spirits have all fled. Take Sahgeeng at night. It is yours and all who live there are yours'".

North Wind said no more. The War Chiefs all nodded their heads in agreement and Kondiaronk's plan was adopted. They would take advantage of the cloud cover that had moved in and attack that night.

At midnight the various camps began to stir. The warriors filled the bay with their war canoes and headed north to the mouth of the Sahgeeng. Young Gull led the large party and he felt good. This would be his personal retribution for the false peace and utter humiliation he was made to suffer at this very town.

The drizzle turned to rain as they beached their canoes and surrounded the town. Several warriors, who had been selected based on their personal spirit helpers, were sent into action to take out the stockade guards. One warrior named Silent Being quietly made his way between the two palisades and appeared behind a lone sentinel at the main gates to the town. The sleepy lookout never took another breath. Two others swung down inside the compound and opened the gates so the flood of death could rush in.

And rush in it did. Wave after wave of feathered warriors, faces painted black, indigo and vermilion. Thousands of voices screaming in unison the war cry of the Three Fires. In the confusion of screams, smoke, musket fire and the smell of burning flesh some of the Mohawk warriors escaped out a door at the rear of the town. Others escaped out the sides. Many were cut down as they poured out the ends of the burning long houses. The ones who did not escape the flaming longhouses were burned alive. By daybreak the entire town was burned to the ground. Scouts reported two groups of escaping Mohawk warriors, one moving up the shoreline of Lake Huron and the other moving up the Sahgeeng.

Young Gull dispatched Ouenemek to overtake the fleeing enemy up Lake Huron and disposed of them. Kondiaronk took his Wyandotte fighters and made haste up the Sahgeeng to finish off the other group.

Ouenemek overtook the band of fleeing men at the fishing islands. The Potawatomi warriors were relentless. Only a few Mohawk were left standing. They surrendered and were taken prisoner. Bodies were felled over a wide area and left for the sun to bleach the bones of the enemy. Chief Ouenemek named the small bay Red Bay because the water ran red with blood of the slain foe.

The trail Kondiaronk was following split at a fork in the river. One group fled up the main branch of the Sahgeeng while another escaped up a branch called the Teeswater River. Kondiaronk split his forces sending two hundred up the Teeswater while he led the other three hundred in pursuit up the Sahgeeng.

The brave Mohawk warriors, about fifty in number, made a stand on Indian Hill near the Teeswater River. They were on the ridge of the hill, a good vantage point, as they watched their old enemy charge up the hill. They recognized their ancient adversary by their stature, which was tall and muscular, and their hair, high in the center and shaved clean on the sides. This made them all the more determined not to capitulate until the last man so they fought valiantly. However, they were badly outnumbered and the Wyandotte who were exacting vengeance for long ago deeds wiped them out.

The other group of escaping warriors made their final stand on the clay banks at Walkerton. They also fought with the ferocity of badgers but quickly succumbed to the overpowering numbers. Kondiaronk may have won the day but he paid a high price. The fleeing Mohawk, who numbered one hundred in all, killed one hundred and fifty Wyandotte.

Back at the town of Sahgeeng the Ojibwa were gathering their few dead and burying them in mounds. Ouenemek and Kondiaronk returned with their dead while North Wind prepared for the Ritual of the Dead. Then the skulls of the enemy, just as at the Horn, were piled in a high mound near where the entrance of the town used to be. After this the taking of Sahgeeng became know as the Battle of Skull Mound. Young Gull then prepared his forces for the portage to Owen Sound where White Cloud had another large Mohawk town under siege.

4

When Young Gull arrived at Owen Sound White Cloud was using the same tactics that Young Gull used at the Horn. He had the town surrounded and the stockade was on fire at several places. As Mohawk warriors threw water on the various blazes White Cloud's Ojibwa marksmen would take pot shots with their guns driving them back. Occasionally they would hit one or two of the defenders despite the inaccuracy of the French muskets.

Just as at the Horn the heart went out of the Mohawk defense when they saw the arrival of thousands of Three Fires reinforcements instead of the Iroquois reserves they had sent for.

It was only a matter of time and the stockade was breached. The warriors led by Young Gull and White Cloud poured into the town. As it was at the Horn and Sahgeeng every living resident gave up their lives to the fierce onslaught. Panic griped Mohawk families at the sight of hordes of painted, feathered warriors pouring into the town all whooping war cries and brandishing war clubs and hatchets above their heads. The Mohawk warriors were resolved to protect their families and fought courageously. They fought so fiercely that they killed an equal number of their enemy before they succumbed to overpowering numbers.

Young Gull and White Cloud warriors massacred everything that moved amid the din of hollering, gunfire and the smoke of burning longhouses. Only a few prisoners were taken. After it was over the bodies of most of the dead warriors, women, children, old people, even the Mohawk's pet dogs lay strewn over the burning site.

The two major War Chiefs' dead were being prepared for burial but the Mohawk dead suffered the same fate as at the Horn and Sahgeeng. Young Gull was surveying the battle site when White Cloud approached from the center of the aftermath.

Young Gull greeted White Cloud as he approached.

"Aanii!" replied White Cloud.

Young Gull and White Cloud retreated to meet in council with their war chiefs on a small ridge overlooking the cornfields that surrounded the once prosperous town.

"How does your campaign go?" asked White Cloud.

"It goes well. We have destroyed two Iroquois towns the size of this one. Because of the power of the Three Fires many Iroquois have forfeited their lives. Large towns on the Horn and at Sahgeeng have given up perhaps one thousand warriors. We also took a large force by surprise at Long Point killing another one thousand of their warriors." The conversation switched to more immediate concerns.

"There were many Mohawk here also but few warriors. Perhaps we should send out scouts to find the few hundred warriors that are missing" queried Young Gull.

"It is true. The main force from this village was not here, but scouts won't be necessary. They are all dead. When we reached the tip of the peninsula we met their main force at Cabot Head. They were about four hundred strong. They fought bravely but could not resist. After we slew a quarter of their braves the rest fled down the coast. We caught them on the Islands at Colpoys Bay. The main force made a last stand on the inner island where we slew three hundred. My warriors are calling this island White Cloud after the victory."

"White Cloud is the bearer of good news. It is possible now to hasten to Blue Mountain. Sahgimah is waiting there to ambush the Iroquois reinforcements. Runners have brought word that there are one thousand warriors making their way down the Nottawasaga River. He can use the support of our combined forces."

All agreed and prepared to leave at daybreak.

Young Gull sent word to Boweeting asking for harvesters. The fields surrounding Sahgeeng as well as here were loaded with produce and it would help support their people through the winter.

5

At the same time the Anishnaabek runners reached Boweeting with their good tidings another party of couriers arrived. They also carried good news.

A leading elder of the council by the name of Gabanquè spoke for the Ojibwa at the gathering place beside the rapids. A large voyageur canoe flying a large blue and white banner in the rear could be seen making its way up the river. Six Menominee and two coureurs de bois manned it. The old chief could tell that it was from Michilimackinac by the two passengers it carried. One was the Black Robe, Marest. The other was a French officer. The paddlers beached the big canoe at the south end of the portage and Gabanquè prepared to receive his visitors.

"We bring greetings and warm wishes of prosperity from Comte Louis de Buade Frontenac, Governor of all the French territories," greeted Marest.

"Gabanquè, Ojibwa Elder and Chief," said a stocky, powerfully built young brave introducing the old chief. He would act as interpreter.

"This is Antoine de Lamothe Cadillac, Commandant of Fort Michilimackinac. He brings you words of great benefit for your people from the Governor in Montreal."

"We will smoke together first. Then we will discuss the French Governor's words," said Gabanquè through his youthful translator.

The group moved into Gabanquè's lodge where all participated in the Pipe of Peace ceremony. After this Cadillac spoke.

"We are here under the orders of the great French King across the salt water sea. He commands us to distribute liberally these many presents because of the thirty Iroquois scalps delivered by your brave warriors to our Fort Michilimackinac a season ago.

The Great King and his Governor wish his good friends and allies, the Ojibwa, to take up arms against our enemies, the Iroquois. The Great King would support such an endeavor with the necessary provisions to carry out a sustained conflict. The Great King would also deliver to Boweeting, for the benefit of your people who would remain at your villages, goods in enough supply to sustain them. These presents would be delivered in the spring and fall of each year for the duration of the encounter."

The young Ojibwa translated the Commandant's words. The old chief sat expressionless for a very long time while he contemplated the timely offer made by the Frenchman from Michilimackinac. Then he smiled complacently.

"We are greatly overjoyed at the words of the French King who lives across the salt water sea. All of our young warriors have taken the path of war and will be greatly pleased to hear of the means to continue."

The French negotiators left for the fort the following morning overjoyed at the speed at which their plan to set their powerful allies against their troublesome adversaries to the south succeeded. When Frontenac received the word of the agreement from Cadillac he thought he was directing the Ojibwa. He had no notion of the real reason for the war.

Ojibwa runners also left that day for Blue Mountain happy to be carrying the news that French support of arms and provisions was in place for a sustained campaign. They saw the French only as a supporter of their war effort.

6

The wild strawberries were already ripe and Sahgimah was fervent for the thrill of battle. He had waited patiently; his warriors camped throughout the Penetanguishene Peninsula, for the expected flood of Iroquois from their towns in the south. Now word had arrived that he would soon get all the battle he could handle.

The Iroquois responded to the destruction of the towns in southwestern Ontario by bolstering their numbers of warriors. They were supplying divisions from the homeland to their towns in the Rice Lake district and on the north shores of Lake Ontario. They were using these towns as staging areas for a two-pronged offence.

One thousand warriors were moving down the Nottawasaga River from their towns along the northern shoreline of Lake Ontario. This was known as the Toronto route. Another one thousand were moving along the Lake Simcoe route from Rice Lake. Sahgimah split his forces keeping one thousand Ottawa hidden in the Penetanguishene interior and sending eleven hundred Ojibwa down the eastern coast to meet the advancing Nottawasaga division.

Meanwhile, Young Gull and White Cloud were advancing east along the shoreline of Nottawasaga Bay to lend support to Sahgimah. Although their combined forces had been reduced to forty-three hundred there was still more than ample firepower to repel the advancing enemy divisions. The Iroquois were unaware of the size of their adversary and that they were outnumbered three to one.

Sahgimah allowed the Lake Simcoe division to make its way through Severn Sound without confrontation. They set up a large camp at the top of the peninsula on the site of the old Huron town of Ihonitiria. Sahgimah waited patiently while his enemy danced their war dance most of the night. At last, exhausted by the long trip and the preparations for battle, they fell fast asleep. Sahgimah moved his Ottawa warriors into place surrounding the Iroquois camp.

As the sun first gleamed over the Blue Mountains the Ottawa struck. War whoops echoed across the still, silent waters of Georgian Bay. The dazed Iroquois warriors struggled to gain their wits and make some kind of stand, but it was to no avail. Sahgimah had gained the upper hand using their old ally, surprise, to his complete advantage.

A small contingent of about two hundred escaped out into the bay. They moved out of sight behind a large island then turned sharply inward, landing on the north shore, and hid among the pines. What they didn't realize was that Bald Eagle, who was returning from ridding the northland of Iroquois marauders, was converging on the scene of the battle from the north. His advance scouts had spotted the Iroquois fugitives hiding their canoes on the island. Sahgimah, meanwhile, was finishing off the enemy warriors trapped in their camp.

"We will not kill all these craven Iroquois!" he screamed. He repeated his command. "We will not kill all these craven Iroquois!" There were a few of the enemy still alive and standing when the slaughter stopped. They dropped their weapons thinking they would be taken prisoner. Sahgimah chose two out of the prisoners. "These two shall be released to return to their kinsmen. They shall carry the story of what it is like to meet the Three Fires in battle. They shall tell them how utterly hopeless it is to confront the Confederacy of the Three Fires. They shall tell them of the ferocity of our Ottawa warriors.

But first let us array our battle site. Cut off the heads of all the dead Iroquois. Raise them high on poles facing our great lake, the Lake of the Ottawa. This will serve notice to all who pass by what it means to make war with the Ottawa." The two enemy fighters were forced to watch the degradation of their comrades. They were then released with enough provisions to get them back to their towns, where they fled straightway with all haste.

Bald Eagle's Mississauga hordes washed over the island killing most of those in hiding. Although they knew their escape was in vain, the Iroquois fought hard, like trapped wolverines. In the end the island was left strewn with headless bodies. Their heads were piled high in a mound at its south beach. Afterward this island became known as Skull Island.

An Ottawa War Chief named The Pike was leading Sahgimah's Ojibwa. They met the advancing Nottawasaga division near the old Huron town of Ossossane on the beaches of Nottawasaga Bay. When they came in sight of each other both divisions beached their canoes and advanced toward each other on foot. They met in deadly hand-to-hand combat on the beaches and in the pines. They were evenly matched and both sides were suffering heavy losses when they broke off to regroup and take up positions in the pines. The gunfire was continuous as small bands used the hit and run tactics of forest warfare on each other.

The advance scouts of Young Gull returned with news of the battle and how it was going. The powerful paddlers picked up the pace of their war canoes and rushed to the support of The Pike. The combined forces of Young Gull and White Cloud beached their canoes to the flank of the enemy's position and moved through the forest toward the sound of the battle.

White Cloud moved his division farther inland and strung his forces out in lines to the east of the battlefield. Young Gull positioned his warriors in the same formation on the south side of the site. They attacked simultaneously taking the foe by surprise. They cleaned out the surrounding forest of Iroquois killing most. Only a few were taken captive and ferried north. The Three Fires' fallen were buried properly in mounds but the Iroquois were left on the ground wherever they fell.

All four divisions of the Three Fires Confederacy gathered at Penetanguishene. They then moved up the Severn River burning several small abandoned Iroquois hunting villages along the way. The leaves were beginning to change color when they arrived at the Narrows, so they set up many camps on both shores of Couchiching Lake and called a council to plan strategy for next spring's campaign.

Chapter 7

1

"Aanii!" greeted Young Gull as he entered the council circle. They
were meeting in the open on the west side of Lake Couchiching.

"Aanii Young Gull, Bald Eagle was just telling of his exploits in
the north" said White Cloud. "Bald Eagle has cleared the northern
districts of all Iroquois!"

"That is good" replied Young Gull. He smiled to acknowledge
the chiefs sitting in the circle. There were six War Chiefs in all:
Young Gull, Bald Eagle, White Cloud, Sahgimah, Ouenemek and
Kondiaronk.

"The Iroquois dogs are also no longer to be found in the western
or northern parts of Ontario. We have expelled them totally. The
whole earth shakes at the voice of the Three Fires. No nation can
stand when we flex our power!" Sahgimah exclaimed. Sahgimah was
always windy in council.

"We must make plans to support our warriors over the long
winter" interjected White Cloud.

"The French have offered to assist us with provisions for our
war with their old adversaries. They have sent food, kettles, knives,
axes, fishhooks, cloth and blankets to Boweeting to supplement the
supplies for our home villages. They have also provided vermilion,

knives, hatchets, flints, powder, shot and ball, and guns to replace the ones buried with our warriors in the mounds.

There are many fields of corn, squash, pumpkin, beans and sunflowers at Owen Sound and Sahgeeng. This land is also rich with game and there is no better fishing then here at the Narrows," advised Young Gull.

Ouenemek and Kondiaronk offered to reap the Mohawk harvest that was left standing at the two destroyed towns. They would use their war canoes in a continuous supply route until the harvest was complete. The others would split their forces into hunting and fishing parties and spread themselves throughout the newly conquered territory. The plan was set and the council broke.

"Tell me about your expedition in the north," Young Gull said to Bald Eagle as they walked along the trail. This was the first chance he had to spend time with the Mississauga Grand Chief.

"There were many Mohawk raiding parties along the Mattawa. We chased them down the river killing many. We caught the last of them at Sand Point, on the Ottawa River, taking thirty warriors captive.

One of my War Chiefs, Strong Wind, took a party up the north trade route and wiped out raiding parties at Whitefish Lake and Lake Minisinakwa. There are no longer any Iroquois to harass our traders along the great trade route."

Support for the war effort was coordinated from Boweeting by Gabanquè. Runners carried messages back and forth between the front at the Narrows and Boweeting. Runners were also dispatched regularly from the different districts to retrieve news from the front.

Back at Young Gull's village the whole community eagerly awaited the arrival of the runners coming from Boweeting. Young Dog, a young teen came running into the village.

"They are coming!" he gasped. "I saw the signal . . ." he stopped to gasp for air, "from the mouth of the river." Young Dog was completely out of breath but his heart was filled with pride that he was the one to bring news of the arrival of the couriers.

The whole village rushed to the river's edge, young wives, young sons and daughters, elders and the few young men who did not have war in their blood. Some were so intent they waded into the water to greet the canoes. Chenoa was one of these, up to her knees in water, desperate for news of her beloved Young Gull.

"Ho! Ho!" the people shouted when the first canoe rounded the bend. Both adolescent boys and young women manned them. They were also riding low in the water, loaded down with French goods. When the first canoe pulled up to the people they helped the paddlers out and beached their craft for them.

"What about Little Bear?" asked one?

"Is Flying Cloud among those on the list?" asked another. All began to ask questions at once. The air became a sea of voices all with questions about their loved ones. So loud was the din that their words became indistinguishable.

"Ho! Ho!" exclaimed one of the elders named Long Pipe. The clamor began to subside. "Ho! Ho!" he repeated. The crowd grew quiet to listen to the old man.

"First we will assemble in the council lodge to receive news of the war. After this we will unload the canoes." Many, mostly young wives anxious for news of their husbands, immediately made their way to the center of the village. Others remained to help beach the heavy-laden canoes. Finally, all arrived at the council lodge, but they had to meet outside the lodge because it was too small to hold all of the attendees.

First a general account was given of how the war was going. This was good news and most greeted the descriptions of Horn River, Sahgeeng, Owen Sound and Penetanguishene with gasps of awe. Others were only interested in hearing the names on the list, the names of the killed or missing.

After the glowing descriptions of the different battles the whole village grew silent. The atmosphere was thick with tension. It was time to announce the names of the dead. Chenoa grew taut. Her heart began to pound. She knew if the name of Young Gull was to be heard it would be the first one uttered. After all he was the Grand Chief and the names were called out in order of importance.

The first name was called out. A loud wail arose from the back of the crowd. Children began to cry. Chenoa exhaled a long held breath. Other names quickly followed and more wailing joined that first young mother. Old mothers lost sons, children lost fathers and there was no opportunity to release the grief, nobody to say goodbye to. For the loved ones left at home there was only the emotional rise of anticipation followed by the let down of relief or the collapse into devastating grief. For the loved ones left at home there was no glory in war.

Young Gull made his way to North Wind's lodge. The winter had not been a particularly hard one. The snows that normally come off the great Ottawa Lake on a daily basis did not materialize. This meant more winter game than usual was available. The whole Ojibwa nation attributed this to the powerful medicine of North Wind and his apprentice Young Bear. A council had been called and the two leaders arrived together at the large gathering of warriors. Spring had arrived and once again they had called on their great holy man to prophesy the coming invasion of the south.

"The spirits have spoken to me in a vision. We will completely surround the enemy and annihilate them. When the cold rain turns once again to snow there will be no Iroquois left in Ontario." Then the prophet painted a pictograph on a large rock overhanging Lake Couchiching to commemorate the prophecy. He used paints of indigo, vermilion, black and yellow provided by the French to symbolize their support. He then painted a warrior falling to represent the defeated Iroquois. In front and behind the collapsing brave he painted two warriors of the Three Fires, the one behind striking the defeated warrior with a war club. The other warrior facing their adversary looked on while holding a musket. The drawing represented the upcoming pincher movement foreseen by Kewadin in his vision.

The pictograph painted by the old holy man was a great inspiration to all that saw it. Many war dances were held in all the camps in the days before the assault began. In Young Gull's camp the dance began with him.

The drum throbbed with a pounding cadence. The war pole was in place and well lit by the grand fire whose flames danced high into the crisp spring air. Young Gull began dancing around the war pole. He carried a war club in his right hand and in his left his spirit stick. His stick that had wolf's paw for a handle and the head of the stick was decorated with a wolf's head. It was also painted with the war colors of red and black. It was used to enlist the aid of personal spirit helpers, who for Young Gull were symbolized by wolves.

"Eeeeiiiii! Ho! Ho! Who will follow me into battle? I have killed many of our enemies," he hollered as he moved rhythmically up the pole. Crack! He hit the pole a great whack with his war club. He held his spirit stick high in the air as an invitation to his spirit helpers to join him. Around the fire and back to the pole he danced. Crack! He dealt the war pole another death dealing blow.

"Eeeeiiiii! Ho! Ho! I killed fifty warriors on the Mattawa in my youth. Who joins me in the war dance?

Young Gull danced and extolled his many deeds both to his warriors and his spirit helpers for several hours. When he was done each of the War Chiefs took their turn followed by the principal warriors. The young warriors were the last to dance the war dance. The day after the last dance was finished the great camp broke and moved south.

2

At the Talbot River, on the east shore of Lake Simcoe, Bald Eagle took his Mississauga warriors east into the Kawartha Lakes. The others continued south to the end of the lake and up the Holland River where they crossed the portage to the Humber. This was known as the Toronto route.

Meanwhile, the Iroquois were building their forces in Ontario from their reserves homeland south of Lake Ontario. Their towns were overflowing with warriors anxious for the thrill of battle. They did not know that they were about to be inundated by a flood of superior numbers.

At the mouth of the Humber River stood the town of Teyaiagon. It was another large town, which, like most Iroquois towns, was fortified by a palisade. Their scouts had warned them of the large Three Fires force that was approaching down the Humber and so preparations for defense were in full swing. The women, children and elders had fled to the neighboring towns of Ganestiquiagon to the east and Quinaouatoua to the west.

The Three Fires warriors arrived at Teyaiagon at mid morning. More of their war canoes passed by the town than the town had warriors. A cloud of Potawatomi surrounded the town so they dug in prepared to fight to the last man. Ouenemek laid siege to Teyaiagon while White Cloud and Sahgimah moved their forces out into the lake and headed eastward. Young Gull and Kondiaronk moved west toward Burlington Bay.

Ouenemek used the same siege tactics used at Owen Sound unwilling to lose one more man then necessary. Patient for the breach they only made lightning runs to the stockade at night setting and re-setting it on fire. The days were spent taking pot shots from the edge of the surrounding forest at any movement discerned on the stockade platforms.

Finally the walls were breached. A surge of Ouenemek's warriors flooded through the large gaping hole in the stockade. Howling war whoops, brandishing axes and war clubs, the feathered, painted assailants poured into the town.

The Iroquois responded by meeting the surge of frenzied combatants with a wall of determined warriors of their own. All of them had either Dutch or British muskets. They fired a volley into the tide of Potawatomi. Many fell. The warriors who had French muskets returned the fire indiscriminately and the flood of brutal warriors kept coming. The Iroquois were forced into hand-to-hand combat. They fought ferociously killing many but the numbers were just too great to overcome. The battle was over as quickly as it had begun. The Iroquois had accomplished what they had determined to do; they fought bravely to the last man.

At the same time that Ouenemek had Teyaiagon under siege, White Cloud did the same to the town of Ganestiquiagon. Ganestiquiagon, being at the mouth of the Rouge River, was blockaded the same afternoon as Teyaiagon. Sahgimah continued on to blockade the town of Ganaraske at the mouth of the Ganaraske River the following day.

In the mean time, Young Gull and Kondiaronk approached a long beach where one smaller village was located at the east end. The beach stretched westward to the outlet of Burlington Bay where there was another village. Palisades did not protect these villages because it was not expected that enemy raiders could get past the heavily secured towns surrounding them. Besides, who would dare to strike at the heart of the recently acquired Iroquois territory?

The Iroquois were prepared. The non-combatants were sent on with the other Teyaiagonian refugees to Quinaouatoua on the portage to the Grand River. Large holes, about one hundred feet in diameter, had been dug in the sands of the beach. They were spaced only a short distance from each other and reinforced with a breastwork. This line of defense was manned by several hundred determined Iroquois warriors bolstered by the power of their confederacy and the advantage their muskets had given them over others. They did not understand the force that was about to come upon them. They did not grasp the fact that although they were equal in firepower they were badly outnumbered.

Kondiaronk continued west with his Wyandotte warriors and five hundred Ojibwa. They were to take the town on the portage. Young Gull knew that it housed many women, children and old people and he wanted the son of Atironto to savor the sweet taste of retribution for what the Iroquois did to his people fifty years earlier.

Young Gull could see the folly of trying to take the beach by storming it head on. He sent Fish Hawk west with fifty canoes. Keeping just out of range of the enemy muskets he made his way to the outlet of Burlington Bay. Meanwhile, Young Gull beached the rest of his division east of the main beach. Unfortunately, this part of the shoreline had only a narrow, short beach, which ended abruptly at the face of a high bluff whose top ridged around behind the villages. They landed their canoes on the inadequate beach piling them one on top of the other. Then the resolute Ojibwa scaled the bluff and made their way through the thick underbrush spreading out behind the villages below.

At the same time Fish Hawk attacked the line of defense from the west Young Gull led his forces down the side of the ridge, through the villages and attacked from behind. They set fire to the abandoned longhouses and totally annihilated the village. Their line of reinforced holes in the sand did not repel their foes but instead had turned into a deadly trap from which there was no escape. The frenzied warriors killed every living soul mutilating the bodies by decapitating them and leaving them to rot in the sun. Not only did this show their hatred for the depravity of the Iroquois but these dead would not enter the land of souls.

Moving along the portage to the Grand River Young Gull's forces approached the town of Quinaouatoua. They could hear the din of battle long before they could see it. The distant sound of warrior's war whoops and the sound of gunfire mixed with the cries of terrified women and children stirred the blood of his warriors. They picked up the pace. When they reached the Iroquois town the battle was all but over. Young Gull held his warriors in check so as to allow Kondiaronk to exact his retribution. Although many died many more were taken prisoner.

With the north-west end of Lake Ontario expunged of any Iroquois presence Young Gull moved his forces eastward along the north shore of the lake past the smoldering ruins of Teyaiagon and Ganestiquiagon. With powerful strokes of their paddles the Three Fires warriors moved their canoes along the shoreline.

Ahead they could see large plumes of black smoke billowing into the air. It was the town of Ganaraske and as they approached there was no doubt they were following the trail of Sahgimah. Along the shore of the lake on both sides of the mouth of the Ganaraske River were, set in the ground, poles about twice the height of a man. These poles stretched for a distance of about eight hundred feet. They were spaced apart about the length of a canoe all adorned with the heads of the town's former occupants all facing the Iroquois homeland.

Young Gull and Kondiaronk, whose name means The Rat, moved past the town of Quinte, where they witnessed the same trademark of the great Ottawa War Chief. Finally, they assembled themselves at the portage to the Bay of Quinte called Onigaming or the Carrying Place. Sahgimah, White Cloud and Bald Eagle had been waiting there with their forces camped throughout the neck of the peninsula.

3

In the beginning of Bald Eagle's Kawartha Lakes campaign he lead his Mississauga warriors into Balsam Lake where they encountered a large enemy war party. The fighting was furious but not long-lived. Many warriors on both sides gave up their lives. Although the Mississauga numbers were too great for their enemies a few escaped through the system of lakes to Lakefield. They prepared a defense here with reinforcements from their town at Peterborough.

Bald Eagle sent an advance party to pursue the fleeing Iroquois while he took proper care of his fallen warriors by providing them the proper burial. The advance party had several running skirmishes with the escaping enemy until finally they received refuge at their town at Lakefield. Bald Eagle's warriors pulled up short of the town and waited along the shores of Clear Lake for the arrival of their main force.

When they did arrive they moved on the town with full force attacking it by both land and water. After burning through the palisade they found, to their dismay, that it was only defended by a small force that were acting as a rear guard for a general retreat. After killing all the Iroquois rear guard and burning the town they quickly set off in hot pursuit. They bypassed the deserted town at Peterborough leaving only a small party to destroy it also by fire.

They moved quickly down the Ontonabee River; as quickly as their powerful strokes would carry their canoes. They caught the exodus at the bend in the river at Campbelltown where the Iroquois, after having sent their non-combatants on to the safety of their large town at Roch's Point, made a staunch defense.

Bald Eagle led his warriors in battle with a long, loud war whoop followed by several short cries. The Mississauga charged whooping and firing their muskets randomly. After the first volleys of musket fire from the defendants, who were dug in, the fighting quickly turned to hand-to-hand combat. Once again the fighting was fierce but the Iroquois were hopelessly outnumbered. The bones of a thousand warriors were left to bleach in the sun at this site.

Some of the Iroquois, when they saw the battle was lost, fled down the river into Rice Lake and to the safety of the large town at Roch's Point. It was also a town with a double palisade and protected about two thousand souls. Bald Eagle gathered his forces on the south side of the lake opposite the town and prepared a two-pronged attack to the east and west of the fortress. Bald Eagle led the western prong of the attack and Strong Wind led the eastern one. Having surrounded the town he put it under siege.

It wasn't long until the outside stockade was burnt through at several places. The Mississauga braves flooded into the town. Again, the scene was the same. The air was thick with smoke from the burning stockade and longhouses. This smoke was mingled with the smell of gunpowder and the air was filled with the sounds of battle; war whoops, gunfire, women and children wailing.

At one point Strong Wind approached the entrance to a storage shed that was used to store corn. Suddenly, a tall, powerful looking, Iroquois warrior appeared out of nowhere. He confronted Strong Wind. The brave was half a head taller, more muscular and a decade younger. His eyes were wild with rage; his head shaved on the sides and his hair was spiked four inches high. His face was painted vermilion and black matching the many tattoos that marked his upper body. He swung wildly first with his axe followed quickly with his war club. Strong Wind ducked, leaned, swerved and backed away skillfully avoiding the life ending swings of the younger warrior's weapons.

Strong Wind ducked low swinging his own tomahawk in a wide, forward arc. It found its mark taking the youthful adversary's legs out from under him. Strong Wind was on him in an instant with his reliable old flint knife artfully opening the jugular vein.

Strong Wind wondered why the young brave fought so desperately. What was in the storage shed that he was so frantic to protect? He slowly swung the door open and moved inside. Standing there in front of him was a young woman with two small children clinging to her legs. Strong Wind could see the terrified look in their eyes and they could see the wild, frenzied look in his. Their last vision was one of a Mississauga warrior. His face was painted yellow on one side, indigo on the other. He had feathers woven into his long back hair and was bedecked in painted shell earrings and pendants. His war club was raised high above his head. The last thing they heard was the traditional Mississauga victory whoops.

When the battle was over prisoners were shuttled north. Bald Eagle had the fallen Mississauga warriors buried with their weapons and provisions in front of an ancient, large serpent-shaped mound in front of the smoldering Iroquois town at Roch's Point. The remnant that had fled the battle at Roch's Point were caught at Cameron's Point and after a sharp skirmish succumbed to the same fate as their comrades. Bald Eagle held council on the north shore of Rice Lake at the site of the previous battle.

"Our scouts report a small village on Chuncall Lake. It is called Ganydoes in the Iroquois tongue," said Bald eagle. "It has few longhouses and no stockade."

"I would take a small force and annihilate the last of these craven dogs," replied Strong Wind.

"It is good. Take a force of five hundred with you and turn your vision into truth," the wily old Grand Chief of the Mississauga commanded. "We will move on to the appointed meeting place at the Carrying Place. Join us there when it is finished."

Strong Wind annihilated the small village of Ganydoes where the lake called Chuncall empties into the Moira River. They then moved down that river to be the last to join the gathered forces of the Three Fires at the Carrying Place on the Quinte peninsula.

The rising sun of the morning no longer filled the dales with the mists of the sultry heat of summer. The mornings were cooler now, almost crisp. Young Gull met in council with the other chiefs. Bald Eagle and Sahgimah would take out the last two Iroquois towns left in Ontario while White Cloud and The Rat would take their warriors back to the decimated towns and harvest the Iroquois crops for winter supplies. Young Gull sent runners back to winter at

Boweeting and arrange for French supplies to continue the effort in the spring. The Three Fires had decided to strike at the very heart of the Iroquois by invading their homeland south of Lake Ontario.

Bald Eagle and Sahgimah surrounded the town of Ganneious. It was located at the mouth of a small river that flowed into Napanee Bay. The fighting was intense but short in duration. Some Iroquois escaped to an island near the Bay of Quinte where they were caught and massacred. They then moved on to the last town of Toniata at the mouth of the Gananoque River. The Iroquois here met the same fate as their brothers and sisters, except the few that had fled into their own country to seek refuge at their town of Onontague across the great Lake Ontario.

4

The whole Anishnaabek horde wintered at Onigaming. The short winter days were spent hunting in the rich forests of Southern Ontario and ice fishing on the Bay of Quinte. This added to their supply of corn harvested from the destroyed Iroquois towns. The long winter nights were spent visiting one another and exchanging stories of deeds of war or playing games, such as the moccasin game, the game of straws and the dish game.

The promised French war provisions arrived with the spring rains that wash away the snows of winter. These included shot and ball along with more guns. These along with the Dutch and English muskets taken from the Iroquois meant that more and more Anishnaabek warriors were armed with firearms.

Once again the traditional preparations for war were performed. This time, however, the dances, religious feasts, and ceremonies were delayed. They were done during the Flower moon because of the lateness of the arrival of the French provisions. When the preparations were complete they set their canoes into the waters of the Bay of Quinte and made for Iroquois country.

The entire force kept together, seven hundred war canoes, each being propelled along swiftly by sixteen powerful arms. They crossed the entrance of the St. Lawrence River then moved along the south shore of the lake and approached the town of Onontague. Outside the walled town several women were planting beans around the small shoots of corn in the cleared fields. Some were on the ridge of a hill in the front of the town between the main gates and the bay. Out of the early morning mist they saw movement. They strained their eyes to see what was out on the lake. The mist began to lift. To their utter astonishment the whole lake seemed filled with enemy war canoes!

They ran to the gates of the town hollering all the way. Several warriors ran to the ridge to confirm with their own eyes what the women had told them. It was true!

The Iroquois were taken by surprise. No town in the heart of their country had been attacked before. The leaders of Onontague ordered the town's people to flee up the Onondaga River and seek refuge at their main town of Gannentua. As the people fled up river a few warriors stayed behind and set fire to the whole town.

"Wagwahge! Look! See!" an Ojibwa warrior called from one of the lead canoes. Large billows of thick, black smoke could be seen rising just inland from the mouth of the river. The warrior's blood began to race and they picked up the tempo of their paddles.

When they passed by Onontague it was but a smoldering ruin. They continued up the river until they came to a main fork where the Seneca River joins the Onondaga. At this point the Three Fires divided their forces. Young Gull and White Cloud moved up the river and into Lake Oneida while Bald Eagle and Ouenemek entered the Seneca. Shortly after this they came upon the large town of Gannentua and put it under attack. Meanwhile, White Cloud put the main town of Oneida, at the east end of the lake under siege while Young Gull and Kondiaronk crossed the portage to the Mohawk River and entered the Mohawk Valley. No enemy force had ever been this deep in the Iroquois heartland. A delegation of chiefs hurried off to Albany to appeal to the British for support.

"My Brother! We have come here with a lamentable complaint. The Dowaganhaes have once again attacked and killed many of our people. Woh! Woh! The ones who established the hunting grounds are all in their graves! The hunting grounds are now again lost and all who lived there are dead.

My Brother! Even now they attack us and kill us in our own country. The Governor of Canada, at Montreal, refuses to take the war club from the hands of the Far Nations unless we submit to him! Woh! Woh!

My Brother! As our allies and trading partners we ask for help. A covenant chain binds us. Allow your soldiers to return with us to the Valley of the Mohawk that we may save our towns and live.

The Governor of New York, the Earl of Bellomont advised, "The Iroquois speak the truth, that they have been good allies and trading partners, but the Governor of New York has no troops to spare. I advise the good chiefs to co-operate with the Governor of Canada. Submit to him and sue for peace with him and his Indian allies, or else their continual warring on you will, in a few years, destroy you."

This left the Iroquois in a quandary and they angrily left Albany with nothing more that the sage advice of Governor Bellomont. The crafty old Governor had the foresight to understand that if the Iroquois blockade to trade with the Dowaganhaes were breached this would open up the rich hunting and trapping grounds of the Far Indians to British trade.

Back at the main town of Gannentua the defense was short lived. Most of the inhabitants had fled to the capital town of Onontague and beyond. Only a small contingent of about one hundred warriors was left to defend the town. Sahgimah and Bald Eagle had one thousand Ottawa and Mississauga warriors under their command so the town was quickly overrun. After killing the Iroquois warriors and desecrating their bodies they burned the town and moved on to attack the capital.

When they reached Onontague it was deserted. Everyone there had fled into the hills and thick forests for refuge. Some of the stronger ones escaped into the western end of Iroquois country via the many trails that wound their way through the forests. The capital town of Onontague was burned and this Anishnaabek division turned back to unite with the main force.

The Ottawa and Mississauga division passed the smoldering ruins of Oneida and crossed over into the Mohawk Valley. They arrived at a place where the Iroquois had three villages built on a hill. Young Gull was just finishing the job of setting them ablaze. The three Grand Chiefs held council.

"The Iroquois have all fled before us. They do not have the strength to resist the power of the Three Fires," said Young Gull.

"We also found this to be true. The hills and mountains are covered with thick forest and they all flee to hide themselves from our presence. We have found two towns all but deserted and so we have put them to the fire," reported Bald Eagle.

"We make war on empty towns and deserted rivers. There is little honor in our victories here," added Ouenemek. At this point runners arrived from the advance division led by White Cloud and Kondiaronk.

"White Cloud and Kondiaronk have left the capital town of Tionontoguen in ruins. They caught a small force of Iroquois down river near the village of Holendowe. They have wiped them out and have moved on. Scouts have reported that a large party of warriors is gathering at a large lake north of the British town of Albany," reported the courier. The three Grand Chiefs decided to follow and the council broke.

Meanwhile, the Governor of Canada prepared to receive visitors at the French fort at Montreal. Four Iroquois Grand Chiefs, Tonatakout, Aouenano, Aradgi, Ohansiowan and two minor chiefs had arrived accompanied by twenty warriors. They had come to confer with Governor Callières regarding the invasion of their country by the Far Nations. Tonatakout spoke for all.

"Onontio, my brother. We are here to talk of peace between our peoples. As you know the Dowaganhaes are attacking us in our own land. They burn our towns and kill those of us they can. They cut our bodies into little pieces and remove our heads and scalps so we cannot release their spirits to enter the Land of the Souls to join our brothers and sisters who have gone before us.

Onontio, we are a small people and cannot stand this continual warring. We will be destroyed. We ask you to take the hatchet from the hands of the Far Nations. We ask you to compel them to cease their attacks and return to their homes. They are your allies and we know that you support them in their ventures. We ask you to withdraw this support, to council with them to stop this warring and make peace.

Onontio, we offer in exchange our friendship. We will cease all hostilities toward you. We offer you a peace that will last and our trade that we now do at Albany. We offer the support of our warriors against any of your enemies.

Onontio, I now tell you a truth. There is no falsehood in the words I am about to speak. These Dowaganhaes are your allies now, but you cannot trust them to always be so. They seek a covenant chain with the British and wish to trade at Albany. I am telling you something you have not known before. Several years ago a party of Dowaganhaes chiefs and sachems arrived at Albany to arrange relations. They remained among their English hosts several months but all got sick and died there.

Onontio, you need our strength to keep the Far Nations from Albany and the British. We ask you to take from them the provisions of war that give them the means to destroy us. In this way Onontio will get all the trade and the British will be cut off."

Callières listened to the Iroquois orator intently. When Tonatakout finished his speech the governor looked to his left at his captain and then spoke.

"I think it wise to break this council for the remainder of the day. We shall reconvene tomorrow at which time I shall give Tonatakout and the Great Chiefs of the Iroquois that accompany him my response to his words." Callières wished the time to confer with his advisors.

The following morning they reassembled to hear the governor's reply.

"I have considered the words of Tonatakout and weighed them carefully. I have decided that the Great Chief's words carry much wisdom.

We also desire nothing more than peace with all the Indian nations and profitable trade for both them and us. Therefore, as Governor of Canada, I accept your overtures of peace and trade and I am prepared to provide you with a small force of one hundred troops to accompany you to your homeland. My captain will take my commands to the chiefs and sachems of the Far Nations who attack you to make peace."

The Three Fires were reported to be in the eastern extremity of Mohawk territory so the company left Montreal and traveled up the Richelieu River and into Lake Champlain. They came upon the Three Fires who were camped along the west shore of Lake George where they had caught the large party of Iroquois and destroyed them.

Upon hearing Governor Callières' words Young Gull called a council. The French along with the six Iroquois chiefs and their small party waited apprehensively. Neither had ever seen so many warriors in one party. Their lodges dotted the shoreline as far as the eye could see. Young Gull spoke for the Three Fires Confederacy.

"We have followed the path of war for three seasons now. We have considered the French Governor's words of peace and have agreed that our vengeance upon the Iroquois has been spent. We know also that our loved ones in our own country wait anxiously for our return. They wait daily for news of us and are given to worry, always. Our young warriors' hearts are also heavy with desire to return to their country and their families. The Three Fires do not wish to exterminate our enemies. We now even only desire peaceful trade.

We will retire to our own country to decide the terms of peace after which we will send word to our good friend the Governor of Canada."

The relieved Iroquois chiefs left with their small party returning to their country via the Hudson and Mohawk rivers. The French returned to Montreal escorted by the whole Three Fires Confederacy who continued on to Boweeting.

5

The Corn moon was nearly over when the Anishnaabek arrived back in their country. There was great celebration all over the land. Mothers greeted sons with tears of joy. Wives greeted husbands with hearts ready to explode with rapture. Children danced and sang songs to their fathers, songs of delight at their return. The feasting and ceremonies continued until the first snows of winter.

The following year a Three Fires Council was called at Boweeting. The Grand Chiefs, sachems, and elders of the nations met to discuss the terms of peace to be demanded of the Iroquois. Young Gull rose to speak to the council.

"Brothers! Sisters! We have won a great victory over our enemies, the Iroquois. They have been expelled from Ontario. This is a large country full of game. Its rivers teem with fish of all kinds. The winters are not long nor are they harsh. It also contains huge quantities of beaver whose pelts both the French at Montreal and the English at Albany crave.

Brothers! Sisters! The Iroquois now deal for peace. They have lost many in the war and are in a weakened condition. The Ojibwa also lost many fine, young warriors but we are still strong. We are powerful enough to continue the war until the Iroquois are no more. We are in a strong position.

Brothers! Sisters! First the Iroquois must agree that Southern Ontario is now part of Ojibwa territory. It is ours!

Brothers! Sisters! It is necessary that we trade for English goods at Albany. Since the French have left Michilimackinac and we must still trade, Albany is no further than Montreal. The English wares are of a better quality and the English give more in trade than the French. If the French learn that we trade at Albany they will give more for each pelt.

Brothers! Sisters! The route to Albany still runs through Iroquois country. It is ours to take by war or peace. For myself, I would choose the path of peace. The British to the south, the Ojibwa and French to the north, now hem the Iroquois in. They have enemies to the east and to the west. Their homeland has become depleted of beaver, which they need for trade. They are in no position to dictate terms.

Brothers! Sisters! I, Young Gull, War Chief of the Ojibwa, Grand Chief of the Three Fires Confederacy, advocate these terms of peace. All prisoners the Iroquois may have taken are to be released to their own country.

Brothers! Sisters! The Iroquois have made their marks upon the British governor's paper ceding Southern Ontario and putting it under his protection. This paper means nothing. Southern Ontario is now Ojibwa territory and we will, in return for a clear and peaceful trade route to Albany, grant the Iroquois hunting and trapping privileges in our territory of Southern Ontario. I declare that there should be peace and by these terms we will prosper and they will live.

Brothers! Sisters! This is all I have to say on the matter."

The council endorsed Young Gull's words and runners were sent to the Iroquois capital of Onontague to arrange peace talks.

Meanwhile, Governor Callières was trying to negotiate peace with the Iroquois to entice them to both trade at Montreal and to keep Iroquois country a barrier between the English and the Far Nations. Callières had also sent ambassadors to the Nations in the west to invite them to come to Montreal for a vast peace parlay. This project was immense considering many of the Nations were traditional enemies.

Governor Bellomont, of New York, had a great desire to trade with the Ojibwa. He had, however, no bargaining position to act as a peace broker since his only influence lay with the Iroquois. He had plans to establish forts in Iroquois country and even on the southern shore of Lake Ontario in order to open up trade with the Far Nations. However, the British government did not back his Indian policy so his strategy was thwarted.

Before the peace negotiations could be arranged at Onontague, a French delegation arrived at Michilimackinac. Runners were sent throughout the territory and a council was called. It was to be held there in order to hear the words they brought from their brother the governor. The two French ambassadors, a black robe by the name of Father Jean Enjalran and a military man called Augustin Le Gardeur de Courtemanche, were loaded down with wampum belts with which to seal agreements with as many of the Far Nations as they could. Courtemanche rose to speak to the Three Fires first.

"My friends, I bring words of praise from your brother, the Governor of Canada, Louis-Hector de Callières. Your father, the

King, has heard that you are pursuing peace with the Iroquois at Onontague. Your father the King desires that you cease, for now, this line of action.

Instead, your father would rather you join all the nations, including the five nations of the Iroquois, at Montreal to sign a peace treaty with all the Indian Nations."

Father Enjalran rose and stood beside Courtemanche.

"My Children," he began. "It is true that you have been staunch allies of your brother the governor and that you have not wavered in your devotion to him and to Canada. I have no fear that you would not adhere to the words of your father the king.

To seal this agreement, that you should cease your advances to make peace with the Iroquois alone and instead, come to Montreal to be part of a larger design for peace among all the nations, we have brought many presents from your brother, the governor. Also we leave with you this wampum belt to signify your adherence to your father the king's words."

Each Grand Chief rose in turn to give a response to the words that the two had brought from Montreal. Young Gull, Sahgimah, Bald Eagle, Ouenemek, Onanguisse, Hassaki and many other chiefs spoke at the council. All spoke in favor of adherence, even though it was too late to stop the negotiations at Onontague, since the peace delegation had left Boweeting three weeks earlier. Despite the agreement reached not to pursue peace on their own the peace party had already secured an arrangement allowing safe passage for trade negotiators to travel to Albany to talk with the Governor of New York. However, there was, as yet, no formal agreement to allow access to actual trade.

After the council at Michilimackinac the French ambassadors split their party with Courtemanche heading west to travel among as many nations as he could reach. When ice began to form on the rivers he abandoned his canoes and carried on by snowshoe.

The following summer chiefs and principal men from different nations and bands from all over the western frontier descended on Montreal. They were joined by representatives from four of the Five Nations of the Iroquois Confederacy. Representatives from the

Onondaga, Cayuga, Oneida and Seneca were present with only the obstinate Mohawk missing.

A total of thirteen hundred representing over thirty different nations or distinct bands attended. Dakota chiefs were there bedecked with buffalo robes and full eagle feather headdresses. Among them mixed feathered, tattooed Ojibwa, Potawatomi and Mississauga. Sauk, Fox and Ho-Chunk mingled between former enemies Menominee, Ottawa and spike-haired Ouendat along with Illinois, Miami and Kickapoo all clad in buckskin and their finest shell jewelry.

The Potawatomi chief Onanguisse attended sure to wear his buffalo robe complete with horns and the Fox head chief Miskousouath delighted the delegates with his French powdered wig. The huge camp was spread out around the post of Montreal and the peace conference was to be held outside the city walls.

The night before the conference was to begin Young Gull began to dream his dream again. But this time the dream was different. As he wheeled high above the lush land below he noticed many wigwams stretching a great distance along the river that was black. Whose villages are these he thought. He swooped down for a closer look and to his amazement he recognized the people. Chenoa was washing clothes at the river's edge. Small Kettle, Silent Being and Kewadin along with his young charge Young Bear were all there. The familiar dream once again faded.

When Young Gull awoke he felt such a sense of relief that he whooped a large cry. Several nearby came running to see what was the matter. Kewadin was among them and Young Gull said to him, "My dream! My spirit guide has given me the interpretation!" Young Gull told Kewadin the new elements of the dream and both agreed it meant the People of the Falls would be moving.

A large platform was built complete with thatched roof where Callières sat in a satin upholstered chair along with other official French dignitaries and the clergy.

The honor of opening the ceremony was given to Hassaki, a Grand Chief of the Ottawa. He was a tall, handsome man with high spiked hair, shaved on the sides and adorned with hawk feathers.

Around his neck he wore a necklace of bear claws and in one hand he held the pipe of peace and in the other he held high the wampum belt he had received as the seal of peace. He was a fine orator and delivered a resounding speech. This was followed by a few words from Callières.

"My brothers, listen to my words. As the Governor of Canada, and the representative of your father, the King across the Great Salt Water Sea, I hold the power of war and the power of peace.

It is the wishes of your father, the King of France that you cease your warring among yourselves and live in peace and harmony. Also, your father understands that some of his children are short of goods. To this end he has determined to open, once again, the trading post at Michilimackinac.

My brothers, your part is to remain at peace with one another and trade with Canada. To this end, I, Louis-Hector de Callières, Governor of Canada, will act, with all the power vested in me, as mediator in any disputes that arise among you. If one side in a dispute refuses to receive the fair compensation determined, then, the power of Canada will side with the other, ending the dispute by force. The Governor of Canada will even invite the Governor of New York to join him if necessary. However, your father, the King of France, and his representative, the Governor of Canada knows this drastic action will not be necessary.

Accompanying the peace will be the exchange of prisoners of war. Also property taken during acts of hostility will also be returned.

These are the goals of this great peace parlay and we will remain here, resolute in our efforts to secure a lasting peace, so that we may obey our father, the King of France. That is, to live in peace and harmony to the prosperity of all."

After these opening speeches the negotiations began in earnest. Much of the time was spent on haggling over the exchange of prisoners, much to the chagrin of Callières, who wanted to spend more time on locking in trade agreements. His main goal in this area was not only to prevent the English from trading with the Far Nations but to also woo away their covenant chain trading partners the Iroquois. However, this was not to be. Not only was too much time spent on prisoner exchange but also there was another event that derailed the talks.

The wily, old Wyandotte chief, Kondiaronk, died. All dialogue ceased and the body was prepared for return to his country. Kondiaronk was dressed in his finest robes. His face was painted with bright vermilion and his hair combed and decorated with feathers. His finest jewelry was put on him and a new porcelain choker put around his neck. He was laid on a mat in a fetal position and the necessities of life laid beside him, that is a tobacco pouch, a bowl of fish stew, a jar of water, his musket, shot and ball, tomahawk and knife.

He lay in state for three days. Streams of people passed through his lodge leaving the most lavish of gifts. Only a few of these gifts would be interned with Kondiaronk's body. The rest would be shared among his family and kinsmen.

Offerings of tobacco were given followed by the chanting of prayers. Drumming could be heard continuously. Throughout all of this eulogies were interspersed.

On the third day the mat Kondiaronk laid on was lifted up about eight feet and placed on top of six poles and then the whole fixture was set on fire. The whole congregation cried the Wyandotte cry of souls, haéé, and haé. Once the flames had licked the bones clean of flesh they were retrieved from the fire, cleaned and polished in preparation for burial in his country. Then a great feast was given which was not concluded for several more days. All of this aggravated Callières to no end.

After this elaborate, pompous funeral, Young Gull along with several other Ojibwa chiefs met with the Iroquois head chiefs Tonatakout, Teganissorens, Aouenano, Aradgi and Ohansiowan at Onontague the Iroquois capital to complete the negotiations for a safe trade route to Albany. While these negotiations were going on a separate negotiating party was simultaneously striking trade prices with the new Governor at Albany, Robert Nanfan.

The Ojibwa had prospered greatly by the securing of new territory and by being able to place themselves in the enviable position of playing the French against the English in trade. As the negotiators remarked to Governor Nanfan, "We will bend our course to where we find goods the cheapest."

The Treaty of Montreal, which was signed by only some of the Nations, was ratified by all through the exchange of wampum belts the following summer. Now, Young Gull began to realize the significance of old Netahoosa's vision and the meaning of his beloved son's name, Shahwanjegawin, or One Who Provides Benefit.

A New Home

Chapter 8

Mr. Nanabush and the Wolf—Move to Aamjiwnaang—A night with the DBaajimod—Chenoa Dies of Shaking Fever—Lord Cornbury—The Fall Feast

1

The movie date was all the enamored young couple had expected. The movie was good but the two were more interested in each other that the film.

They also had friended each other on facebook and had begun messaging each other as well.

"I'm more used to texting than messaging" Karen told Brad. "I'm normally not on facebook too much."

Brad didn't have a problem with that although he hadn't really texted much. He thought he'd send her a text. Fumbling and learning as he went he entered "Hi! How are", oops—he somehow hit the wrong key. "Saving to draft" his cell phone replied.

"What?" Brad exclaimed. He found the half sentence in the drafts folder, retrieved it and continued. "you? I'm trying out", oops—wrong key again! "Message Sent."

"Darn!" he thought and started a new message. "this texting thing. I'll get the hang of it" Brad continued. That message was sent ok.

"One message in two" Karen thought as she smiled to herself. Brad did get better at texting and they found themselves communicating that way every night. There seemed to be a recurring theme with each session—Mr. Nanabush and the strange occurrences that seemed to accompany him.

During work hours the two kept very professional although they did take their lunch and breaks together most often. On one of their breaks, midweek, Brad asked Karen if they could have coffee at the usual shop near her place. It was becoming a regular spot for them to meet after work. They would meet that evening at their regular time, seven o'clock.

The evening went just as all the others. The coffee was good, the conversation great and the time too short. Ten o'clock arrived and Karen indicated it was time to go. Brad concurred and the two left the coffee shop.

Karen lived in an older part of the city. The frame houses were built during the depression on small lots. The lots were divided by a narrow alleyway which single-car, wooden garages faced. The two, holding hands, turned down the alleyway which leads to Karen's back door.

Suddenly they found themselves confronted by three unsavory looking young men. Their appearance was menacing. The glint of a steel blade caught Brad's attention. The one in the center, the one that seemed to be the leader was holding a knife.

"Aw no, this is not good" Brad thought. The young couple stood frozen, Brad trying to formulate a plan to protect Karen and Karen's panic stopping her from thinking at all.

As suddenly as the three young hoodlums appeared they all heard the deep, vicious growl of something very large coming from the side of one of the garages.

To everyone's surprise it leaped to the middle of the laneway facing the three young thugs. Brad and Karen could not believe their eyes. It was a wolf—a full grown timber wolf! Bearing its large, canine teeth it growled and snarled its warnings to the three. They backed up. The leader turned and ran with the other two in full pursuit. Just as quickly as it appeared it disappeared in a single bound over the fence of one of the backyards and out of sight.

"Do you believe that!" exclaimed Brad. "What is a wolf doing in downtown Toronto?"

Karen said nothing. She could only tremble. Brad put his arms around her and drew her close to comfort her.

"It's ok. It's ok now." The two embraced for a long time before continuing home. Just as they reached Karen's backyard gate they caught sight of that familiar figure disappearing down the next street.

"Mister Nanabush?" they both said quizzically at the same time.

"He doesn't live near here" Karen said half stating a fact and half questioning it. Now this latest episode was the most enigmatic yet!

2

The following afternoon was Friday. Mr. Nanabush arrived as usual eager to continue explaining Ojibwa culture by storytelling. The lecture hall quickly filled up and he continued the story of Young Gull.

The crisp fall air the Harvest moon brings greeted Young Gull and his party each morning of their long arduous journey home. Young Gull thought how good it felt to rise each day and not be concerned that an Iroquois raiding party might be concealed around the next bend waiting to pounce. Yet in the back of his mind he wondered if the Great Peace signed at Montreal could be trusted.

At last he rounded the final bend in the Montreal River and his village came into view. Young Gull's heart began to pulsate matching the increased tempo of their paddles. He could see the young braves launching their canoes into the cool deep water and their first strokes propelling their vessels toward the arriving party. The shore was lined with the elders and women and children. The women were waving and the children were jumping in circles. The whole village abounded with excitement.

Wives and families rushed toward the peace delegation as they beached their canoes on the shore. The greeters included Chenoa and after a long embrace the two retreated to their lodge. Chenoa made her dear Young Gull a cedar tea.

"How did the conference at Montreal go?"

"There were many there. All the nations of the lakes including our enemies were there. A great peace treaty was signed. All exchanged wampum belts and exchanged prisoners to seal the agreement. Only the Iroquois brought no prisoners. The Mohawk did not even attend. Otherwise it was a great success. The French Governor Callière is more interested in trade and worked very hard to bring all together."

"That is good" interjected Chenoa.

"I have some sad news from the conference though. Our old friend Kondiaronk died while there."

"Kaa" Chenoa murmured with a concerned look.

"He was given a funeral deserving of a Wyandotte Sastaretsi. His bones were blanched and they are being returned to Michilimackinac."

"The trading post at Fort Michilimackinac has closed."

"I know. Callière said there is to be a new post opened at de troit."

"The commandant of the old post, Cadillac, arrived at Michilimackinac last month with many presents and brandy for the Wyandotte and Ottawa villages there. He was encouraging them to move their villages to de troit with him."

"I knew this. Cadillac left Montreal before the Great Peace Conference. A council of the elders is to be called to discuss the closing of Fort Michilimackinac.

I have more good news. Before the conference began my dream came to me again." Young Gull then explained the new elements of his dream and what the interpretation was.

"I will speak at the grand council and inform them of this. We will be moving to Aamjiwnaang territory.

"Oh" replied Chenoa and the conversation ended. The two settled into an embrace and more intimate companionship.

The smoke of the council fire rose slowly toward the outlet of the great hall erected for the Grand Council of the Three Fires. Machonce, Wapisiwisibi, Seginsiwin and Tonquish all elders from Boweeting represented the Saulteux Ojibwa on the council. Each Grand Chief rose in turn to give his thoughts on the closing of

Michilimackinac and the opening up of Saganan to the council of elders.

The Wyandotte and Ottawa decided to stay at Michilimackinac because of the warnings of the Black Robe de Carheil. He warned them that if they moved to Detroit they would be dead men and so beleaguered them to move near the Miami for the winter but to return to him at Michilimackinac the following year.

Ouenemek spoke for the Potawatomi expressing their desire to move from the Bay back to their old territory near the St. Joseph River. White Cloud spoke for the territory along the southern shores of Georgian Bay while Bald Eagle wanted to move his Mississauga into the eastern part of Southern Ontario. Young Gull rose to speak for the Boweeting Ojibwa.

"Brothers and Sisters—Callière has encouraged our brothers, the Wyandotte and the Ottawa to move with Cadillac to his new post at Detroit. The Black Robes do not want them to move. This has caused great division among them. This must not happen to us.

Brothers and Sisters—our father the Governor wants to block the English from trading in the upper lakes and so moves the trading post.

Brothers and Sisters—everyone here knows of my dream and how it baffled both our holy men and me. While at Montreal for the Great Peace Conference my spirit helper gave me the interpretation. Again I dreamt of the territory I call Aamjiwnaang. This time I saw our people camped along the Black River and at Round Lake.

Brothers and Sisters—we are to move our lodges to Aamjiwnaang. It makes sense to move to our new territory. It is a good land. The winters are short. The fields are lush and the forests full of game. The rivers teem with fish. Brothers and Sisters; we would not only be closer to the French trading post but also to the English post at Albany.

Brothers and Sisters—the Boweeting Ojibwa must obey the dream and move to Aamjiwnaang territory at the foot of the Great Lake of the Huron. It is good ground for hunting, fishing and trapping. The white fish at its great rapids are as plentiful as at Boweeting.

Brothers and Sisters—this is all I have to say."

The Grand Council broke and the Three Fires returned to their dwellings to wait out the winter. The villages of the Saulteux Ojibwa prepared for their move to Aamjiwnaang the following year.

3

The move had been successful and Young Gull's village was strung out along the shores of the Black River. Small Kettle was appointed a chief by the council and had taken some of the Saulteux Ojibwa to the north end of Round Lake. They set up villages on Swan Creek and Saline Creek.

The sultry summer heat had made for a lazy day and now the sun was a huge red ball hanging above the western horizon. The children of the village were playing games as some of the adults readied the evening fire. It was set up in the middle of the village and only needed for light when the people gathered round to listen to the storyteller.

The village began to buzz with excitement as night fell and the flames of the community fire shot high into the darkness. There was no moon that night so the black sky twinkled with an abundance of tiny points of light. The community gathered, children sitting closest, and the crowd began to quiet down. Old Corn Woman began to speak.

"Long ago there was a little boy who was left an orphan and so his grandmother took him in. But his grandmother was unkind and began to torment the little boy. The little boy wished Nanabozho would turn him into a bird and Nanabozho granted him his wish. He immediately flew up to the limb of a nearby tree and started to laugh. His grandmother begged him to come back but the little boy would not and so we have the robin still hanging around the lodge."

The old storyteller continued. "Nanabozho was on a hunting trip and came upon a large flock of geese on a small lake. He wondered what he could do to get a large number of them. The idea came to him to get some basswood bark in strips to make rope and with this rope he crept to the edge of the lake. Nanabozho slipped into the lake and swam underwater to the geese. He began to tie their legs together. When he got near the end of the rope he rose out of the water and frightened the flock and they started to fly away. With their combined strength they lifted Nanabozho, who was hanging onto the end of the rope, high into the air. As they flew over the woods Nanabozho let go of the rope and fell into a hollow tree. There was a bear sleeping in that hollow tree so Nanabozho ask the bear to take him out of the tree, so the bear did. Now geese have been flying the way Nanabozho tied them ever since."

The adults in the assembly smiled with approval while the children chuckled with delight at the telling of the old stories. Corn Woman continued her story telling.

"Nanabozho once found himself on a large raft of logs floating on a vast sea of water and in the company of all kinds of animals and fowl of the air. He could talk to all the creatures. There was no land so Nanabozho called a council and all the creatures decided that Nanabozho should use his great medicine to form land. So of all the creatures he chose Loon to dive down to the bottom of the water and bring up a small quantity of earth.

Loon dove down into the water. Down, down he swam. The water became darker and darker. He used up all his energy but could not reach the bottom. Loon ran out of breath and so returned to the surface. "I couldn't reach the bottom. I don't think there is one," he gasped.

Next Otter was chosen to try. He jumped off the raft and dove down into the water. Down, down he swam exerting all his strength to reach the bottom but he became exhausted before he could. After a long time Otter's body floated to the top and Nanabozho examined his little paws to see if there was any earth. Sadly, there was none.

Beaver then volunteered to go down and get the earth. Nanabozho accepted his offer and granted him permission to try. Just like Otter, Beaver became exhausted and couldn't reach the bottom. When his body floated to the top Nanabozho examined his paws but found no earth. It was beginning to look very bad for the creatures of the earth.

Nanabozho called all the creatures together and asked if there was any who could swim and dive better than Otter or Beaver. Muskrat stepped out and volunteered to get the earth. All the creatures began to chuckle and poked fun at Muskrat. Nanabozho looked at the tiny little animal and said to him, 'How can you, being so small, have the courage to say that you can do what Otter, the swiftest of swimmers, and Beaver, the strongest of swimmers could not do?' Nevertheless Nanabozho granted him permission to try.

So Muskrat dove down into the water. Down, down, down he swam till he was almost exhausted. He reached the bottom, scratched the bottom with his little paw then, just like Otter and Beaver before him, Muskrat passed out. When he floated to the top of the water Nanabozho examined his paws and to his amazement there was a tiny morsel of earth in one of them.

Turtle swam up to the raft and said, 'Put the ball of earth on my back and I will use it for support.' Nanabozho did this and greatly rejoicing he sang and chanted his incantations and the four winds began to blow. The little piece of earth began to grow! Bigger and bigger it became. As Nanabozho sang his song all the animals began to dance in a circle. Round and round the growing island they danced. Finally Nanabozho stopped singing. The winds ceased and the waters became still. The little ball of mud that Muskrat had given his life for had become a vast island in the middle of the great water. Today we call this land Turtle Island."

Corn Woman, who told many more stories much to the delight of all the assembly, carried the warm summer evening far into the night.

4

Summer turned into fall. The crisp autumn air changed the landscape from a variety of shades of green to a myriad of vivid colors from yellow to orange to bright red. Young Gull was satisfied with the move. A trading trip to Detroit could be made in less than a week compared to the month it took to trade at Montreal. And there were no portages. Fishing camps had been set up at Kettle Point on Lake Huron and at the mouth of the Ausable River. The hunting and fishing more than amply supplied the needs of the several hundred families that lived along the Black River.

Yes, Young Gull felt good, but yet he was worried about Chenoa. He had noticed lately that her mind had become dull. She had become forgetful of even the most recent events. She even had difficulty remembering names.

"Chenoa" he called as he poked his head into their lodge. She was lying on their mat looking very distant. "Chenoa" he called again. She slowly turned her head and looked toward Young Gull. Her eyes were swollen and red.

"My eyes hurt so," she told Young Gull.

Young Gull left their dwelling immediately to search for Young Bear. He found him up river attending to the elder Gabanquè who had also become sick. Young Bear had finished his apprenticeship in the Mdewnini Society of Medicine and had become a nanandawi curer of the fourth degree. His particular craft of healing was known as nanandawi iwe winini or tube sucking and he had become quite adept at it.

Gabanquè's grandson The Fork was drumming outside Gabanquè's lodge. His drumming was intended to assist in the healing. Inside Young Bear prepared the ceremonial instruments of his craft. Gabanquè lie on his side as the young nanandawi laid his tubes, bowl and rattle neatly on the ground. The tubes were small hollowed out bones about two inches long and the bowl contained a little water in it.

He began the ceremony by telling Gabanquè the dream he received while fasting for this rite. He spoke so fast that his words were mostly indistinguishable but his patron spirit was understood. It was thunderbird.

Young Bear began to shake his rattle and chant. After singing a healing chant Young Bear bent over the two bones, which were lying flat on the ground. His medicine was so great the two tubes moved on their own across the ground toward his mouth. He picked them in his mouth and swallowed them. Then he coughed them up.

Young Bear then picked up one of the tubes with his mouth and pressed it hard on Gabanquè's chest. He began to suck. He sucked hard and the skin pulled back. Gabanquè cried out in pain. He sucked hard on his patient's chest again but this time he drew out some dark reddish fluid, which he spat into the bowl. He showed this to Gabanquè then threw the contents into the fire. Young Bear said that if left the blood would turn to pus and sometimes this pus would burst and the patient would die. The he rattled and chanted some more before repeating the procedure. He did this four times. The last time there was very little fluid.

He came out of the lodge and spoke to The Fork. "Your grandfather will recover. His sickness was due to his worrying and fretting over an argument he had with you last year. My dream revealed this to me during the fast." Then he turned to Young Gull.

"Chenoa is getting worse!" Young Gull exclaimed with an anxious tone in his voice. He described her symptoms to Young Bear. The two left at once for Young Gull's lodge.

When Young Bear and Young Gull arrived they constructed a sweat lodge for the nanandawi healer to seek the help of his patron spirit and the reason for the sickness.

Young Bear prepared for the vision quest by fasting and chanting. Others from the village drummed and danced. Two more days passed and Chenoa's condition worsened. She had lost all appetite and if she forced herself to eat she couldn't hold down the food. There was a great pain in the pit of her stomach and she was continually nauseous.

Young Bear entered the sweat lodge and began to utter his initiating dream in repetitive fashion. He continued all the while grimacing, rolling his eyes, thrusting his lower jaw out then in and spitting up blood. He would stretch his neck then sink his head into his shoulders, propel his arms high into the air with fingers outstretch beyond endurance. He did these things to induce the trance that would enable his thunderbird spirit to communicate to him the cause and cure of Chenoa's illness.

Overnight Chenoa's condition continued to deteriorate. She now suffered from diarrhea and her watery stool was mixed with mucous and some blood. She had a high fever and began to shake uncontrollably as she drifted in and out of alternate periods of chills and hot spells.

Young Bear finally emerged from the sweat lodge. His face was grimaced as he began to talk with Young Gull. "This illness contains the most power that the Evil One can instill. It is almost never to be overcome. There is no cure for this occurrence and there is no cause. It is Chenoa's time to cross over." Young Gull was devastated. He began to wail. The whole village joined in and the drumming, chants and dancing changed from the ceremonial evoking of the helping powers of the spirits to the resigned chanting of the dirge. After two more days of lamenting Chenoa passed.

5

Winter approached covering the landscape with a blanket of deep white snow. The days grew short and the rivers and ponds froze solid. The village had broken up into small winter hunting camps dispersed throughout Aamjiwnaang territory. Young Gull had moved to a previously used camp a few miles up the Ausable River. The hunting was good in that area and it was close to a sugar bush where they would move to in the early spring.

Young Gull's heart ached with grief for Chenoa. He missed her companionship. The unobtrusive way she gave him counsel when he had an important decision to make. She had a way of making her opinions seem as if they came from him. He missed her warm soft body next to his during a cold winter's night. This made the long winter nights seem even longer. He grieved for her constantly, pining for her return. Of course she would not. Even the arduous hunting through the brief daylight hours could not ease his pain. He missed her so.

After the gathering of the maple sap during the Sugaring moon the small group moved to the fishing camp at the mouth of the river for the spring run. The Flower moon arrived and it was time for all the small hunting groups to congregate back at the base camp on the Black River. Young Gull's canoes, ladened down with dried fish and sugar products, made their way down the eastern shore of Lake

Huron to the great rapids. The hunting had been so good that they even had a quantity of dried meat in their provisions.

A week after Young Gull set up his summer lodge The Fork arrived from his winter camp on the Flint River. Old Gabanquè was not with him. He had died on the Flint. Others arrived from the many scattered winter camps including Young Gull's nephew Wahbahnoosay or Morning Walker. He had been wintering at the eastern boundary of Aamjiwnaang near the mouth of the Maitland River.

The summer months that would follow would be spent trading at Detroit. Meanwhile, Young Gull, Small Kettle and Morning Walker along with two other warriors prepared to travel to Albany. The purpose was to meet with the new Governor of New York, Lord Cornbury, to confirm trade agreements made with Earl of Bellomont. The trip was uneventful except for one particularly demanding portage and the small party arrived on a sultry July evening. They would meet the new governor in the morning.

Young Gull spoke for the Ojibwa. "Brother Corlaer—please consider our words even though they are few. By this calumet given in peace we give you a hearty welcome on your arrival to take up your new post of governor of New York. We have come to Orange sent by our Sachems and given leave to speak for our Nation by them. We Ojibwa have removed and come to live by the new French fort at Detroit where we now trade. We have come to see you and to find out if our agreements with your Earl remain in place or if they have passed with him. He treated us kindly when we were here before and we are in a desire to begin a trade with your English. Here is a necklace given to one of our great chiefs by one of your Seneca who is a chief among his people. The English governor inviting us to come and see him sent it to us by him. We now come with our bales of beaver and various pelts as our Sachems wish to see if prices be cheaper here than at Detroit. If they be then we should come here to trade. If we do we ask now that you put in place a commandant in your Seneca's country so that we may pass through freely and not be prevented from continuing here to Orange.

Brother Corlaer—by this fur coat we ask but one more thing of you. We are strangers here having only come this way but once before. We were at a loss when we came upon the carrying place of the Oneida. The creek has since filled up with fallen trees so we ask that the governor at Orange give orders that it should be cleaned out as it hinders much the passing of canoes and this should also make it far easier to come to your English for trade.

We should like to acquaint you also with this knowledge that we Ojibwa have gone to war with a people called by you Sioux and by us Naadwesioux who live to the west toward the Spaniards. They are a craven people and when their lessons be learned from our warring our young men will return and our trade will prosper." Young Gull ended his speech and retired until the next morning when Lord Cornbury would give his reply.

"I am glad to see you and I wish to bid you a very warm welcome. I also wish to thank you for your kind congratulations. I am appointed by Her Majesty's royal commission to succeed the late Earl of Bellomont as Governor and therefore assure you in the name of Anne Queen of England that your previous agreements remain in place and you will always be treated kindly and fairly on your trading journeys here.

I am dispatching my servants, Mr. Abraham Schuyler and Jean Baptist to go with you to see that our traders treat you civilly in the disposal of your beavers and peltries.

In the matter of placing a commandant in the Seneca's country I cannot do so but it be approved both by our Trade Board and the Seneca council. If our trade should prosper I will take this matter up with them.

In the matter of the carrying place of the Oneida I shall confer with them about a clean up at our upcoming council and if need be will supply men enough to effect a solution."

The council with Lord Cornbury ended and the following day trade was completed. The Iroquois had been truthful. Prices were cheaper and the goods of better quality. The Aamjiwnaang Ojibwa were pleased because this gave them the option of trading at Detroit or if time was not an issue trading at Albany.

6

A few more seasons came and went and another annual great fall gathering was about to commence. All the preparations had been completed and the participants were beginning to arrive from all over the territory. There were Wyandotte and Ottawa coming from Detroit as well as Michilimackinac. Potawatomi from Detroit and St. Joseph were expected as well this year. The Mississauga had established two villages on the east side of the St. Clair. They were now part of the host Saulteux Ojibwa of Black River and Swan Creek. Chichikateco, chief of the Miami would be there with many of his nation as honoured guests.

The Ojibwa had settled into their new territory and now the great gatherings were being held on the islands of Aamjiwnaang where the Great Lake of the Huron empties itself into the Straits of Detroit. There were several channels at the mouth of the river forming these islands with one channel in particular that was very deep, very swift with great rapids. The east shore of this channel was also the west shore of a particularly large island where the great powwows were held.

The resonance of drumming filled the air surrounding the great island where the gathering would take place. The sound, being carried on soft gentle summer breezes, could be heard at Young Gull's village. Guest lodges were constructed along the Black River beside the village and Young Gull's old friend Sahgimah was staying in one of them.

"Boozhoo" Sahgimah greeted Young Gull as he strolled up to meet his old comrade.

"Aanii" replied Young Gull. "Are you ready to go over to the gathering grounds? They have been set up and my stomach tells me to hurry," he said grinning.

"En," was the short reply and the two left for the gathering grounds by canoe. After crossing the greater blue river they beached their craft on the south end of the island. After eating their fill of the great assortment of food spread out for the community they moved off to a less populated area near the north end of the island, near the great rapids, for conversation.

"Many have arrived for the gathering and yet there are many more to come," said Young Gull. "A little bird told me you have moved your lodge near Detroit. Tell me of things there."

"Lamothe Cadillac invited all the nations around to move near the post. First he invited the Wyandotte and Ottawa from Michilimackinac but they refused to relocate. Later, after Governor Callières invited them Governor Vaudreuil implored them to move and they did so."

"When I was in Albany I heard that Callières had passed over."

"Many chiefs sent envoys to Montreal to bewail him. They met the new Onontio appointed by the French King. His name is Vaudreuil. The envoys report he is like Callières, a man to be much loved."

"How many surround the French post. Our young men tell us there are many villages."

"There were about 2000 souls living there. Ottawa, Mississauga, Wyandotte, Potawatomi and the Miami from the St. Joseph River moved there along with some Wyandotte from Michilimackinac who were living with them. Quarante Sols was sent there by Cadillac to entice them and he succeeded."

"Kaa. That is too many! They shall all starve or die quarrelling with one another. It is not good to dwell to close to French. I only see trouble ahead."

"Not enough game to support all the people is what the Miami feared. They refused to go at first but the lure of cheap trade goods was too much. Even worse Cadillac has invited the Fox from Wisconsin and they came with 1000 men, women and children."

Young Gull could only grunt an unintelligible response. "I look forward to seeing old allies like Hassaki and Ouenemek, La Pèsant—and Outoutagan!"

"Hassaki passed over last winter."

"Gabanquè as well. They were both full of years and the Master of Life had treated them kindly. Perhaps it is time to join in the festivities. There is a game of lacrosse to start at any time," Young Gull said.

The two moved into the main grounds to intermingle with old friends and allies. The Great Gathering was a huge success and enjoyed by all who attended especially the Miami who were new to the territory.

Chapter 9

Murder at Detroit—Onaskin's Appeal—Vaudreuil's Confidant—
Outoutagan goes to Quebec—Crisis Resolved

1

The following year Sahgimah came to visit Aamjiwnaang again.
There had been trouble at Detroit just as Young Gull predicted.
The two chiefs met on the island where the Great Gatherings
were held, as Sahgimah could not stay. He was on his way back to
Michilimackinac. Sahgimah spoke first.

"Boozhoo," he greeted Young Gull. "I have been in the south
at war with the Flatheads. I was there some time and when I
returned I found there had been much trouble at the French Post.
The Wyandotte Grand Chief Michipichy plotted with the Miami
to attack us. The Wyandotte Tionontati have become strong allies
with the Miami but the Wyandotte Arendahronon remain allied to
the Ottawa. So we attacked them first. A French soldier and a Grey
Robe were killed."

"Kaa" exclaimed Young Gull!

"The French fired upon us during a peace settlement and
wounded Jean Le Blanc but he survived. The French have disowned
us as their children and most have moved back to Michilimackinac.
I have called for a Three Fires Council to be held at Boweeting," he
said. Details of what happened will be given at the Great Council.
It is to be held on the next new moon."

"Kaa! This is not good." Young Gull thought for a few seconds
searching for the right words. "The Miami have always been instigators

of evil doings. Our old allies, the Wyandotte Tionontati have sided with them before. This spring there was trouble between them and the Mississauga who have villages at Detroit. How quickly they have forgotten our hospitality when they suffered great calamities brought on by the Iroquois" said Young Gull. They have forgotten the late war and who their allies are and the strength of the Three Fires. It can only be to their loss."

The two old allies and friends talked some more then Sahgimah continued on to Michilimackinac. Young Gull, who had become a leading elder in the Three Fires Council, returned to his village where he sent runners to the other chiefs and principle men in the villages throughout Aamjiwnaang. In a few days eight canoes arrived from Swan Creek. They arrived to link up with the six canoes from the Black River band. The flotilla left the mouth of the Great Lake of the Huron and headed north. There were seventy Ojibwa in all, chiefs, principle men and warriors, conferees of the Great Three Fires Council.

After the opening ceremonies, when the Council was convened, Jean Le Blanc or Outoutagan stood to give a full account of the unfortunate events at Detroit.

"Brothers and sisters—let me tell you of the bad events that occurred of late at Detroit. The Ottawa Nations living there, the Kishkacon, the Sinago and the Sable, were preparing to go off to war with the Sioux. Before we left a Potawatomi who is married to a Miami woman informed us that Michipichy, the Wyandotte Tionontati, the one the French named Quarante Sous, conspired to destroy us by giving the wampum to the Miami privately. Their devious plan was to allow us to leave for war and travel three days at which time they would attack our villages and eat our women and children. Upon hearing this news we informed the French commandant, Sieur Bourmont, of their scheme. Then the three nations of the Ottawa hastily called a council. It was decided at this council that we should not deliberate on an affair of this consequence without the direction of Le Pèsant and me. We were the principal chiefs and they sent for us at once.

Brothers and sisters—when Le Pèsant heard what the Miami were planning to do he was enraged and said that since the Miami had determined to kill us and boil us it was necessary to forestall them by striking first. I was the first to see that he was about to do an evil thing and counseled against it. But it was impossible for any to contradict him because of his influence with the nations and to do so would have made us contemptible in the eyes of our young men.

Brothers and Sisters—my brother Chief Miscouaki and myself inquired of Le Pèsant his thoughts on attacking the Miami when our people were divided. Some were at Montreal and some were away at war with the Wyandotte Tionontati and Miami. And what would the French Commandant at the Fort think of us attacking at his gate. But he would not listen. Le Pèsant alone is responsible for causing all the trouble.

Brothers and sisters—we were on our way, according to our resolve, from the French fort to our own when we had to pass by the fort of the Wyandotte. As we did we met eight Miami chiefs going there for a feast. When Le Pèsant saw them he said 'Here are our enemies, the ones who would kill us. Here are the leaders. Now let us rid ourselves of them.' With this he gave a great cry, but no one moved. He gave a second cry and we began to fire upon them. Only Pacamkona escaped to the French fort. The other seven were killed.

Brothers and sisters—after the seven were killed our young men went up to the Miami village to kill those which remained in their lodges as the Miami were encamped near their fort. But when they arrived they discovered that the Miami had retreated into the fort of the French. They rushed to the French fort determined to burn it but Miscouaki threw himself in the midst of them, snatching the flaming arrows from them, and imploring them not to do the French any harm as they were not connected to any of the difficulties we had with the Miami. At this time there was a Gray Robe outside the French fort and I said to him, 'Go into your fort quickly and tell the commandant neither to fire upon us nor to give the Miami any powder or shot.' I did not learn until the next day that he and a

French soldier did not make it into their fort but were killed by our young men who were furious at the killing of two of our chiefs.

Brothers and sisters—the next day I took a flag the governor had given my brother and we approached the French fort. I asked to speak to the commandant to give our reasons and those with me had their arms all turned down. He said he had no reply for me and that Sieur de la Forest was expected early in the spring and I could explain our reasons to him. Seeing that he would not speak with us we returned to our fort. When our young men heard of this they again determined to burn the French stockade. Our old men were embarrassed and so to stop the young men spent three whole days in council. It was at this council that I said to Le Pèsant that it was all his doing. How foolish it was it was to attack the Miami at the gates of the French fort. Now we are all dead and we have killed ourselves.

Brothers and sisters—we knew there would be trouble when Sieur de Tonty left. Sieur de Bourmont could have settled this matter early but refused to parlay with us always wishing us to wait until the arrival of Sieur de la Forest. Meanwhile, he gave us certain signs that he wished to fight with us for he put swords at the end of his poles.

Brothers and sisters—we then went to the Wyandotte fort thinking they were our allies. They showed us a wampum belt that signified that they were allies with all the nations around them, the Ottawa, the Potawatomi, the Ojibwa, and the Mississauga and that it would give life or death to those they spoke with. They gave us this belt along with the French words that they wished to speak with us and would do so at the day of our feast. They said the French did not want us to be fearful about meeting in our lodges so they would meet with us on the open grassland at a place where they would plant the French flag.

I had my garden at a place near where the French planted their flag and as I was walking there I saw the French come and spread out large blankets near their flag and place upon them a large quantity of grain. I saw the Wyandotte women do the same. Fearful of treachery we sent out four young men as scouts and they reported back that they saw trails leading to the deep woods that encircled the open grassland where the French flag was planted.

Brothers and sisters—the next day was our feast day but fearing a trap we determined not to go to meet with the French. Some of the Miami, the French and Wyandotte were hidden in the glades near the flag waiting to leap upon us. The greater part of the Miami were concealed in the deep woods near our fort and thinking we had gone to the flag they rushed upon our fort to seize and kill our women and children. They had two bands and one came along the water and destroyed our canoes thinking it would prevent our escape. But they were surprised when they were met with the gunfire of our young men. We lost one young warrior and we don't know how many Miami were killed. They returned that night and on their way they met Katalibou and his brother. They killed and scalped them.

Brothers and sisters—the next day the Wyandotte joined the Miami and the brother of Michipichy called insults to us, calling us women and telling us that the French Governor had long ago abandoned us. This riled our young men so we attacked the Wyandotte and the Miami outside our fort and many more of them were killed. The Wyandotte held their ground but the Miami fled even though there were 400 of them. The next day they came and attacked our fort again but were unsuccessful. They were apparently angered over losing someone of high consideration to them so before they left they shot a prisoner who was one our allies.

Brothers and sisters—on this day some of our young men and two of our Mississauga allies who were returning from fighting the Flatheads were captured by the Wyandotte. They were bound and held in the French fort except the two allies who were taken to the Wyandotte fort. They were later released to their own village.

One of the captives held in the French fort was released to us with a message that they remembered well what we had done to them and for this reason they were bound. They did not wish to kill them but we only had to cover them according to our tradition to secure their release and end the hostilities.

Brothers and sisters—we carried presents, all that we had, to the appointed place at the gates of the French fort. We acted in good faith believing that we would receive the protection of the French. We arrived unarmed with ten pieces of porcelain beads, twenty kettles, two packs of beaver and everything else that we had. At this point Michipichy gave me his hand and as he did a shot rang out from the French fort and grazed my shoulder. As we were unarmed we were forced to flee the Wyandotte and Miami who had taken up the chase. Our young men that had remained in our fort came out to our assistance and the remainder of the day was spent fighting.

Brothers and Sisters—through this treachery we lost two killed and five wounded. Their young men attacked our lodges and took prisoner a young woman. We went after them to find out what they would do with her but it was too late as we heard her screaming from inside the French fort where they burned her.

Brothers and sisters—this war went on for two moons and we were tired and short of food. We were also short of shot and ball. Our council decided to send Onabemamtou, one of our chiefs, to parlay with the Miami. This man had danced the calumet peace dance with them in previous times. He reported that he said to their chiefs, 'Why do you attack and kill us? Do you not tire of this war? Do you not kill yourselves as well? Do you have no consideration for your young men?' They replied, 'It was not us who did that but the Wyandotte and French who wanted us to stay until autumn when you Ottawa would have perished in your stockade from hunger.'

Brothers and sisters—the Miami agreed with Onabemamtou to withdraw and return to their own lands on the St. Joseph and so they divided their prisoners. Two of our young men the Miami kept and two they gave to the Miami of the Wabash River who kept them in the French fort. One was shot and the other they burned but the French commandant intervened to secure the release of the son of Koutache, a Mississauga chief. The other two were being taken to the Wabash, but escaped and they made their way back to us. They reported they were treated well but that the Miami has lost fifty killed and wounded. We have lost twenty-six including one man who has not been heard from who was married to a Delaware woman.

Brothers and sisters—our old men being afraid that they would be unable to control our young men if we remained at Detroit have withdrawn to Michilimackinac where we remain today. I shall now advise you of my brother's voyage to relate these treacherous affairs to Onontio.

Jean Le Blanc continued. "Brothers and sisters—while recovering from my wound I sent my brother Miscouaki and Maurice Menard down to Quebec to parlay with Governor Vaudreuil. They gave him all of our reasons just as I have related them to you and asking him of his thoughts and for his permission to fight Quarante Sous and his Miami allies. The governor gave Miscouaki his reply the following day.

Brothers and Sisters—Governor Vaudreuil said he did not accept that Miscouaki spoke for all the lake nations but for me alone. He said that if Le Pèsant and I had not undertaken the attack upon the Miami without knowing his wishes we would not be in the distress and misery that we now are.

Brothers and Sisters—this is true for we are all now residing at Michilimackinac and have no provisions for the winter. The governor has also said that he cannot forget that a French soldier and a Grey Robe were killed and that the blood of such has much value to him, especially the Gray Robe. He has said that unless the Ottawa of Detroit make reparation proportionate to the offence we have committed against him, he will spare nothing to avenge himself.

Brothers and Sisters—Vaudreuil refused the belt offered to him by Miscouaki because it came from him personally and not from all the nations. He has said he would consider the words of our chief over the winter and would hear more from De La Mothe who has returned to Detroit. The governor must hear from all the nations. We must remain on our mats and not go off to war with the Miami or anyone but must fight for defensive reasons only. In the early spring we may return to the governor to receive his thoughts but he wishes to see all the Ottawa chiefs. If we are truly repentant we may resume trade for the goods we need.

Brothers and Sisters—Vaudreuil also says the blood of Frenchmen cannot be paid for with bales of fur but the making right of this wrong done to him will be decided upon in the spring. These were the words of Governor Vaudreuil.

Jean Le Blanc sat down and Young Gull rose to speak for the Saulteux from Aamjiwnaang.

"Brothers and Sisters—this is a very serious matter. Le Pèsant has put the Three Fires and our allies in a place of some discomfort. We have good trade relations with the French at Detroit and we have begun trading at Albany with the English. They are very desirous to have our pelts and we are in a most excellent position. We do not want to squander this situation on an affair that got out of control.

Brothers and Sisters—the Ottawa are our brothers and we must stand with them even to every limit. It has been reported that the Iroquois have been to Quebec to parlay with the governor. They have encouraged him to take up the hatchet in a war against our brothers the Ottawa. A war with our father the governor would be long and costly. With English supplies we would win but that would leave us in a poorer trading place with only the English to barter with. This should be our very last option.

Brothers and Sisters—Vaudreuil is right. It is up to the Ottawa from Detroit to settle this matter to the governor's satisfaction. The Ottawa from Michilimackinac were not involved except to go to Detroit to restore their brothers to Michilimackinac. This affair should be settled in the spring. Jean Le Blanc has recovered from his wounds and he and the other Ottawa chiefs should go to Quebec to discover what the governor would have to make this right. The Ottawa must do all that is in their power to avoid a war with the French, even to the handing over of Le Pèsant. This is what I have to say on this matter.

Young Gull sat down and many other chiefs and conferees spoke in turn all nearly unanimously agreeing with Young Gull's assessment of the situation. It was decided that twelve chiefs, three from each of the four nations of the Ottawa, would leave for Quebec after the winter snows had melted. Ontonagon or Jean Le Blanc as the French called him would be their spokesman.

2

The autumn leaves were falling to the ground in Quebec when two canoes arrived from the Sault Ste. Marie mission. Among them were two Ottawa chiefs from Michilimackinac and Sieur Boudor, a Frenchman attached to Father Marest of the mission. He delivered a letter from the Father to the Marquis de Vaudreuil about the affairs at Detroit. The two chiefs were there to deliver the words of their head chief who could not come due to age and illness. The old chief's words were penned on paper by Father Marest and attached his letter.

After Sr. Boudor delivered the letters and was dismissed the governor reclined in his chair by the fire and began to read:

Monsieur, I take the honor to write to you concerning the bad news we heard from Detroit. We have learned of the events from a Sinago Ottawa named Merasilla. He has proven himself to be loyal to the French and spoke in a most eloquent and sensible manner. He said there really was cause to fear for the French at Michilimackinac as well as the French here. The French at Michilimackinac had been living in great fear as the Ottawa there have held them as if holding a tomahawk over their heads while waiting for news from Detroit. This went on for eight days. When news arrived that the French had not been involved in the second attack on the Ottawa affairs at Michilimackinac became quieter.

Then all the Ottawa at Michilimackinac left for Detroit to withdraw their brothers from the situation there and return them to Michilimackinac. The next day the French that were at Michilimackinac left to join we here at the mission where we are now all located. If the French should take any part in the difficulties between the different tribes there would be all the more reason for the French here to fear for their safety.

The old men in council have condemned the departure of their tribe to Detroit, but say they could not restrain their young men after they had learned of the treachery of the Wyandotte. Since their departure for Detroit a few canoes have returned and I am permitted to give you their report. The chiefs of Michilimackinac, who remained at home, have always maintained that their young men did not go to Detroit to fight, but to withdraw their brothers.

Many, including Jean Le Blanc and Le Pèsant have been delayed by heavy winds. Those who arrived say a great battle was fought at Detroit, and that the French had gone out with the Miami and Wyandotte to attack the Ottawa in their fort. The Ottawa fear they may have killed some of the Iroquois of Sault Ste. Louis, if any were with the Wyandotte. The savages all say that the Miami were masters in the French fort, stealing their corn and other provisions. It was also reported that they burnt an Ottawa in the fort and the Wyandotte also burnt an Ottawa woman in their fort. Four Ottawa captives were sent to the Miami of St. Joseph but two of them escaped on the way. They have reported the Miami had not ill-treated them. They say the blame for the whole affair must rest on the Wyandotte chief Quarante Sous. Most of the fields at Detroit had been ravaged and all but a few Miami have left for St. Joseph. The Sacs that were there have also left. We anxiously await the return of Sr. Boudor and the Ottawa chiefs.

The letter closed with compliments to Vaudreuil and the confidence in his ability to resolve the whole matter amicably. Vaudreuil leaned back again, closed his eyes and wondered about his skill as a diplomat. The events at Detroit had been allowed to escalate into a perilous state of affairs for the colony.

At the council the next day Vaudreuil read Onaskin's letter in the presence of the two Ottawa chiefs Companissè and Le Brochet. Onaskin had sent five Iroquois prisoners from the late war to be returned as part of their treaty agreement. He promised to send four more the following year. He reported that his people had no involvement with the evil doings at Detroit and that he had sent his men to withdraw the French at Michilimackinac to his village to stay under his protection until the danger to them is over. Vaudreuil answered Onaskin through his two chiefs.

"I have seen, O Companissè and Le Brochet, what Onaskin has sent to me in writing. I am well acquainted with the news of what took place at Detroit and I have confidence that the Ottawa of Michilimackinac had no part in the evil that was perpetrated there last spring. However, you ought not to have withdrawn my French people to your village and held them there as if they were prisoners.

Instead, in order to show your proper sentiments, you should have helped them to come down here, even helping them bring their furs. This is the way you can give me confidence in your sentiments and this you ought to do even now. The French people up there are my children and I love them dearly and will not suffer them to come to any harm. If they do I will spare nothing to avenge them.

I thank you for the five Iroquois prisoners to be returned to their people and I have confidence you will keep your word by sending four more next year. As for your complaints about my commander at Detroit I am very surprised. After all it was the Ottawa of Detroit that attacked the Miami and they did this at my very door. He received them into his fort only to protect them, as they are my children also. If it were the Miami that attacked you would you not expect him to do the same for you? You complain that he fired upon your brothers but it was they that first fired upon the French, killing one of my soldiers and one of my missionaries and they are highly valued among us. I think you Ottawa of Michilimackinac are too wise to get involved in such despicable business. It is the Ottawa of Detroit that will have to make reparation in proportion to the offence they have committed. Unless they do I will spare nothing to avenge myself.

But as for you, remain in peace quietly on your mats. Last year you asked me to send you a man to guide you. I sent you Father Marest. You will do well to listen to his advice. As long as you do not involve yourselves with the affairs of your brothers of Detroit you will be welcome to trade here for all your necessities and you will prosper. But if you offer the slightest insult to my people up there I will not only refuse you the things you expect of me but I will declare war on you and that will only lead to your destruction.

Remember, O Companissè and O Le Brochet, all that I have said to you so that you will be able to repeat it to your people when you return. In order that you do I am putting it in writing to Father Marest that he may put you in remembrance of it." The conference concluded with the speech of Vaudreuil and he returned to his apartment for supper.

3

The Marquis de Vaudreuil was a military man through and through. He was of average intelligence but his formal education was limited. He had found it next to impossible to advance his career in France because ranks higher than captain were purchased and they were very expensive. So he turned to the new world where he worked hard to further his political career in New France. It was here that a beautiful young women, thirty years his junior, caught his eye and she became the Madame la Marquise de Vaudreuil. Fifteen years and eleven children later the crisis at Detroit had broken out.

Louise Élisabeth de Joybert was born in Canada the daughter of Pierre de Joybert de Soulanges et de Marson an officer in the Carignan-Salières regiment and she was well acquainted with the intrigues of Indian relations and new world politics. She was astute, highly intelligent and the Marquis depended on her continuously reliable advice.

On this particular night the nuns of the convent had joined the Marquis and Marquise to dine, a custom started by the Governor's wife as Louise was more inclined to unconventional behavior then adverse to it. After the meal and some frivolous conversation their company left and the Governor and his wife relaxed by the fire for tête-à-tête over a glass of wine.

"There is no end to the grief these wretched Indians cause the colony," Vaudreuil complained. "First there was trouble between the Mississauga and the Miami and now the Ottawa have not only attacked the Miami and Wyandotte but have attacked us killing one of our soldiers and even a missionary. Sieur de la Mothe declares that it was the Ottawa that bore ill will against both the Miami and the French and the Mississauga were not involved."

"My dear Philippe, you know that de la Mothe only wants to minimize the troubles there to save face on his plan to collect all the Indian nations in one place. He wants to maliciously lay all the blame at the door of the Ottawa. He says the Mississauga was not involved and that their disturbance with the Miami had been settled by the commandant of the post. But the councils held by

Sieur Bourgmont following the attack prove that the Mississauga affair was not settled. Monsieur de la Mothe contradicts himself as well by reporting later that the Mississauga came to the aid of the Ottawa to the number of one hundred warriors. This also agrees with Father Marest's report.

We can also tell by the soldiers that came down to report this news that they all agreed that the Ottawa called to the French not to fire and that although the Father and the soldier were killed, it was only after there was firing on both sides from both within and without the fort. This is not to excuse the Ottawa in any way but it does prove that initially they had no intention of attacking the fort.

I believe it was Miscouaki that reported the real facts, that the Ottawa did not attack the fort after the unfortunate deaths of our people and that any fighting that went on after this affair was instigated by the Wyandotte and Miami who attacked the Ottawa. The Iroquois interpreter, Maurisseau, as you know, also confirmed this. Yet, Monsieur de la Mothe says only that the fighting went on for forty or fifty days and gives no details so as to leave the impression that it was the Ottawa that kept coming to attack the fort."

"Now, as you know Louise, the Seneca and other Iroquois villages have sent their envoys to entice us to war against the Ottawa. They want to take up the hatchet against them for all the dead they suffered in the late war. And they want the French to provide arms and supplies. At the same time they came to Quebec they sent envoys to the English to advise them of their resolution. I am so disturbed and pent up with the feelings of vengeance that I am inclined to oblige them."

"Pierre, you must remember the Ottawa of Michilimackinac had no hand in the affairs at Detroit. But now they are consolidated at Michilimackinac. If the Wyandotte, Miami and Iroquois are united they will destroy a nation that had served us well in the past, or at least force them to abandon Michilimackinac. If that happens then the war will not stop there. They can be supplied by the English through the head of Hudson's Bay and will continue fighting as long as the memory of what they have suffered at the hands of the French dwells among them.

Remember that according to the words of Miscouaki they do not want war with us. But they do not fear it either. They are members of a powerful Indian confederation and to make war on them could draw in eight or ten of their allies. The tranquility and prosperity of the colony depends on peace with these tribes.

It would be better to temporize until next spring and let them anxiously await your conditions for peace. This will show the English that you have more influence than they have over the Iroquois because you can take the hatchet out of their hand. Next year, when they come to sue for peace, we cannot show any weakness. Insist on the head of Le Pèsant, but give the problem to de la Mothe. Send them to Detroit. After all it was Sieur la Mothe who insisted on consolidating all the Indian Nations around his post. Let him find some way of consolidating all of the parties while still insisting they turn over Le Pèsant."

Vaudreuil smiled at his lovely wife and thought how right she was and how fortunate he was to have such a beautiful young woman and with such perceptive observation. "You know, I have to send a report to Count de Pontchartrain updating my report of last spring. This needs to be done quickly in order to reach the ships at Placentia before winter sets in. I must thank you for your thoughts as they have brought clarity to the whole affair." Vaudreuil poured another glass of wine and their conversation turned to more domestic issues.

4

The long cold Canadian winter finally turned to spring and the buds on the trees had turned to leaves when a fleet of Ottawa canoes arrived at Quebec. It was Jean Le Blanc and the other chiefs, twelve in all, four from the Kiskakoua, four from the Sinago Ottawa and four from the La Fourche Nation.

Jean Le Blanc spoke for the whole Ottawa Nation giving his sincere regrets for the Detroit affair and repeated their explanation of what had happened even offering his own body as payment for the whole unfortunate incident. He was well aware that their custom of offering bales of furs or other goods as retribution for a death would not satisfy the French. They had been told that French blood was very valuable and could only be paid for with the blood of the person responsible. Le Blanc offered instead two men that they had adopted into their village for the Governor to do with as he wished.

Two days later the Marquis answered. "I am not surprised, Jean Le Blanc, that you are embarrassed to speak with me after what has taken place at Detroit. The reason I did not receive you immediately upon your arrival here as I did Companissè and Le Brochet last fall as I regard them as obedient children who always follow their father's instructions, but you O Le Blanc are a disobedient child. I know all that took place at Detroit and how it took place. I have been informed by Monsieur de la Mothe, by Monsieur Bourmont, by Father Marest, by Miscouaki and by you.

The Miami are my adopted children and also are under my protection. You ought not to have attacked them but should have come to me with your complaints. You have taken the lives of my own children, the French soldier and the Recollect Father. They are my blood, my own blood. The two you have offered although adopted by you are of foreign blood. The one you should have brought to me is that evil bear up there Le Pèsant. He is the sole cause of all your misfortunes. Reflect on what I have told you and give me your answer tomorrow."

The following day Outoutagan met with the Governor to give him his reply. "My father, my father, I am deeply grieved that I am unable to make amends for what I have done. I have nothing to offer you but my own body to do with, as you will. I am in despair that I am not able to repair the wrong done at Detroit.

My father, you have demanded of me the head of Le Pèsant and it is true that he is to blame, but I cannot promise you the reparation. If I were to say to you, 'My Father, I will give you the head of that bear up there' it would be impossible for me to keep my word, for he is a great chief and has many relations and allies among the nations around us. His influence is great and there would be much unrest among all the nations even to the turning on the French who are among us. For these reasons I cannot promise his head."

The next day the Governor gave his determination to Le Blanc. "I have considered the reply you gave to me yesterday and I am willing to accept that it is impossible for you to give up the head of Le Pèsant. I must however have blood to content me. The death of a missionary cannot be paid for except by blood.

Because all of this evil business occurred in Detroit and it was there that you killed the Recollect Father and my soldier I am sending you to Monsieur de la Mothe to make reparation. Take the two lives you offered me to him. Remember, O Le Blanc that Monsieur de la Mothe and I are of one mind and he has full authority in my name to make any decision that will secure peace among the Indian Nations." The next day Vaudreuil's courier left for Detroit with instructions by letter to Cadillac. In it the governor sent word that he was turning the whole matter of the disturbances at Detroit over to him to settle. He would be given a free rein to resolve things among the nations there with the only stipulation that Le Pèsant must be handed over as retribution for the French killed the previous year. The following week four of the chiefs including Outoutagan left for Detroit via the lakes while the others returned to Michilimackinac via the Great River.

5

The courier arrived at Detroit four weeks later with his dispatch and the news that the Ottawa delegation was only days behind him. Cadillac immediately sent a courier up river to request a parlay with Young Gull. He asked if he could come to Detroit immediately. He wanted to know the sentiments of the Saulteux Ojibwa if war the broke out between the French and the Ottawa. He knew they currently could muster six hundred warriors and they were right on his doorstep. He was also aware that if the Ojibwa threw in their lot with the Ottawa the Three Fires Confederacy with their allies would quickly follow. He then quickly arranged for a council with the Wyandotte and Miami to inform them that a delegation of Ottawa chiefs would be arriving at the post and to assure them their dead would be avenged with the head of Le Pèsant.

Young Gull arrived at Detroit with his entourage just before Outoutagan and de la Mothe received him alone in his quarters. He informed Young Gull of the contents of Vaudreuil's letter and reinforced the French position that only Le Peasant's blood would purchase forgiveness for the Ottawa of Detroit. He asked Young Gull what his sentiments were and what he thought the Great Council's reaction would be if Outoutagan refused to give him up.

Young Gull knew they had already suggested the Ottawa go that far to avoid war but he wisely kept that to himself. Instead he said that he felt the Ottawa could not give up such a great chief and that if war broke out the Saulteux would send their young men to join the Ottawa and the Confederacy and their allies would likely do the same.

Cadillac was filled with apprehension at the thought of such a wide-ranging war. He knew the English would jump on the opportunity to help remove the French from the scene by supplying their enemies with munitions. Such a war would be long and costly for France and he was not at all sure they could even win. On a more personal note he also knew that such a war would end all his plans for a pan Indian trading alliance with his beloved Detroit at the center. It would also bring an abrupt end to his career and he would have to shoulder all of the blame for not being able to execute his governor's instructions.

"O Young Gull, you must know that the blood my soldier and of the Recollect Father must be paid for by blood. This is the French way and there is no alternative. Governor Vaudreuil has placed the whole matter in my hands and will abide by any decision made by me. However, I must insist that the life of Le Pèsant be handed over to me to do with what I will. If I wish him to die he should or if I wish him to live and be my slave he should. I have the power to kill him or let him live. Besides, our stockade is not so secure and our palisade not so high. It is only peace that I wish for."

Young Gull understood Cadillac's inference to the fort being not so secure and its wall not so high. It was an offer to eventually let Le Pèsant escape. So Young Gull made camp outside the French fort to await the arrival of the Ottawa. When Outoutagan and the other chiefs arrived he told them of Cadillac's words and then left for Aamjiwnaang.

At the first council Cadillac spoke. "Outoutagan, Kinonge and the rest of you, listen to me well. I will not repeat the words of the governor, as you know them as well as I do. Monsieur de Vaudreuil writes to me that you have with you the two slaves you offered him. He writes that he gives me the power to make peace and I may take whatever measure I deem reasonable to procure it for you. When I first heard of the evil business you Ottawa were engaged in last year I was wounded in my heart. My anger boiled over and I was determined to destroy you. But as my anger cooled and my senses returned I said, why should I destroy my eldest child when it was that evil bear, Le Pèsant, that was the sole cause of it. It was this drunken bear that intoxicated his young men and made them lose their wits. Therefore Outoutagan, hearken to my final decision.

I demand that you hand over Le Pèsant to me here, where he committed his offence. I wish him to be in my power, either to grant him his life or to put him to death. If he refuses to come down here, I demand you slay him in his village. It is not I who kill him but he who kills himself. Think of your wives and fear for your children. Nothing can make me change my mind. It is your affair to consider. Think it over well and determine the course you have to take and give me a reply a little before sundown."

At the second council Jean Le Blanc, or Outoutagan, gave his answer. "My Father, the demand you make of us is surprising. The bear you ask for is very powerful in our village. He has strong alliances among all the lake tribes. It is a great tree that you ask us to uproot. It is very difficult.

We have thought over this matter and since nothing can soften you and your heart is hard as a rock we must obey you. Only we beg of you to spare us the grief of having to bring him to you ourselves. We ask that you send a boat with us to Michilimackinac where we will turn him over to you to be the arbitrator of his life or death. If he refuses to embark we will slay him in his village. He our brother and of our flesh, but what can we do? We must obey you. This is what you have demanded and this is what we have decided."

Cadillac replied, "By this means you will obtain peace. Your wives and children will rejoice at it and I will forget the wrong that you have done me."

The council ended and the group left for Michilimackinac. When they arrived they called a council among themselves and discussed all that had occurred and their belief that if they turned over Le Pèsant he would not die but live; even free. The next day they handed over Le Pèsant to the French soldiers that had traveled with them to the head of the Lake of the Huron. They took him back to Detroit along with a message that the old men begged for his life to be spared.

When he arrived Cadillac put him in the stockade but placed no guard over him. That night Le Pèsant escaped disappearing into the darkness of the new world wilderness. He escaped with his life but his power as a chief was greatly diminished.

Now Cadillac had only to appease the Wyandotte and Miami to defuse the crisis. He called a council with them the day after Le Pèsant escaped and gave them the two slaves Outoutagan have given him as partial payment for the deaths of their chiefs. He also inferred that the Ottawa had been humiliated and that Le Pèsant would probably not survive in the wilderness alone as he was now a fugitive. If he died it would only be he that killed himself. The Wyandotte and Miami were not totally satisfied but it was enough to avoid further bloodshed and it avoided a very costly war with the Three Fires Confederacy, a war the French could only lose.

Chapter 10

Young Gull's New Companion—Annihilation of the Fox—Birth of Little Thunder—The Windigo from Nepissing—Little Thunder and the Fox War—Death of Young Gull—Who was Mr. Nanabush?

1

Hunting seasons came and went, the cycle of life continued, yet Young Gull felt overwhelmed by emptiness in his life. He could deal with the loss of his life's companion and accept the role of widower, but he had no progeny. He was on the council now, an elder, and the emptiness weighed more heavily with each passing moon.

A single canoe entered the mouth of the Black River and approached the village. Young Gull could see that it was Small Kettle and his son from his vantage point at the entrance to his lodge. He always enjoyed a smoke and conversation with his old friend. Small Kettle beached his canoe and climbed the small knoll to Young Gull's lodge. "Boozhoo, he called out.

"Aanii", replied Young Gull. He retrieved his pipe from his lodge and the two old companions sat down together. After a smoke and a time of reflection Small Kettle began their talk with news of the villages at Swan Creek and some of the goings-on at Detroit. Young Gull countered with reports of recent events at Aamjiwnaang. Up to this point their conversation had been only casual chat.

"Aanish naa?" Small Kettle asked wanting to know how his old friend had been. The conversation took a serious turn when Young Gull unloaded his burden on his younger friend and confidant. Small Kettle listened intently as his mentor described the barrenness of his days. They smoked some more and sat in silence for a long time reflecting upon Young Gull's problem.

Small Kettle returned to his village. After a moon passed by he related his old friend's concerns to his wife. "I have thought on our good friend's feelings for some time now and I ask you for your wisdom. Eagle Feather has been with us now since she lost her husband. What do you think about a match between them?" Eagle Feather was their daughter and her husband was killed in the skirmish with the Miami at Detroit several years earlier.

"I think it is a good idea. You should talk to her. See how she feels about it" Small Bird Woman said.

Later that evening Small Kettle and Small Bird Woman talked to their daughter about Young Gull. She said she thought it would be a great honor but she would still like to give the matter more thought. Eagle Feather promised to give them an answer in a week.

Meanwhile, the days passed rather routinely for Young Gull. There was some news that some Mascouten warriors had insulted Sahgimah by calling him a coward and that he had gone off to redeem his good name. He also heard that the Potawatomi chief Makisabi was with him. The Mascouten were allies with the Fox and Young Gull could sense turbulent times approaching. There were many Fox at Detroit and they were always a troublesome people.

Young Gull was fishing on the great lake of the Huron and when his canoe was loaded with whitefish he returned to his village where Small Kettle was waiting for him. When they greeted each other the affection and respect they had for one another could be seen etched on their faces. The two old friends sat for a smoke and their conversation soon turned to the purpose of Small Kettle's visit.

"You know my daughter and young boys have been living in my lodge since her man was killed at Detroit."

"Yes" confirmed Young Gull.

"She has become restless in spirit and lonely in heart. She misses the independence of her own lodge and the comfort of a companion on the path of life. It seems to Small Bird Woman and me that you each may hold the fulfillment to each other's emptiness. What are your thoughts?"

Young Gull smiled at Small Kettle, reflected a while then spoke. "Eagle Feather is a fine looking woman. She has a two fine sons and I think if she would have an old warrior for a husband it would please me very much."

The quick response by Young Gull was uncharacteristic. Usually such an important decision was smoked upon and contemplated for a long time. But recently Young Gull has found himself thinking of Eagle Feather more and more often. He had not really understood why, at least not up until now. So when the opportunity arose there was no need for reflection. Small Kettle was surprised but well pleased.

"I will talk with Eagle Feather and will return with her answer on the new moon" replied the Swan Creek chief. He didn't tell Young Gull that he had already talked to her and she had already given an affirmative reply. After all, these things must be done properly.

Small Kettle returned as promised. The arrangement was struck and the couple was formally introduced even though they had known each other since Eagle Feather was born. The courting began.

Young Gull traveled the one-day journey to Swan Creek many times spending the idle summer days with Eagle Feather. They grew closer and closer with each visit. Eagle Feather was a quiet, sensitive woman and oh, how she loved to hear Young Gull talk. She loved to hear the stories of his youthful escapades many of which included her father. She also learned to appreciate his playful teasing and subtle humor.

On the other hand, Young Gull began to recognize the value of Eagle Feather's sense of commitment. He could see that she would make a good companion. Small Bird Woman's training was evident as she was a good cook, knew how to mend clothing and did most of the chores around the lodge. Young Gull's feelings of attraction very quickly changed to feelings of deep love. These were emotions not felt for such a long time that Young Gull did not expect to ever feel them again. This match so cleverly orchestrated by Small Kettle and his wife seemed to satisfy the two lover's needs to the fullest.

Shignebeck and Onsha, her two young sons idolized Young Gull. They too loved to hear his stories as well as the times spent hunting and fishing in the territory around Round Lake. As the boys began to realize what the courting meant they bristled with excitement. Having Young Gull as a new father was most pleasing to them. And the prospect of having two new sons was just as pleasing to Young Gull.

Young Gull and Eagle Feather would marry in early autumn, before the winter hunt. Word went out via runners to all the surrounding villages. Relatives at Boweeting were informed, as were those who had intermarried with the Miami and Shawnee in Ohio. The celebration would be large but not as large and Young Gull's marriage with Chenoa.

2

The winter hunt had ended and The Fork and Morning Walker led a flotilla of trade canoes loaded with pelts to Detroit for trade. Sieur Du Buisson had replaced Lamothe Cadillac as commandant of Fort Pontchartrain and they were anxious to ascertain his manner and fairness in trade. They were joined by Small Kettle and several more barks as they passed Swan Creek. When they approached the French fort their ears were greeted with the sounds of volleys of musket shot. The Ojibwa convoy immediately pulled up and hid their goods in the underbrush of a large island in the Detroit River just north of the French fort. Then the intrepid band of Ojibwa stealthily glided their canoes just out of sight of the stockade.

Two Ottawa villages were located across the river from Fort Pontchartrain. When the Ojibwa warriors arrived there were only eight men there.

"Aanii" greeted Small Kettle. "What is this disturbance we hear at the French fort?"

A young Ottawa woman answered, "The Mascouten and Fox have set their two villages within a shot's range of the commandant's castle. Commandant Du Buisson objected bitterly, but the Fox only hurtled insults at him telling him they are the true owners of this country. They are liars, agitators and always disturbers of the peace.

Their villages are large to the number of one thousand while the French are inside their fort with only thirty Frenchmen and eight Miami warriors. They burned the French church and a house outside the stockade and tried to set fire to the fort. These craven people shot fire tipped arrows inside the commandant's castle setting fire to the grass roofs, but the French soldiers put them out. They have been shooting at each other like this for days. We now await the arrival of our young men to return from the hunt. The Wyandotte and Potawatomi also await all the young men."

"We will wait here as well", retorted Small Kettle, "then we will come to the aid of our French father." The small band of Ojibwa warriors settled in to await the main force. Two days passed when a Wyandotte runner arrived all out of breath.

"I was with Sahgimah on his mission to avenge his name. We left Detroit with one hundred warriors to seek out the Mascouten main village. We found two hundred of their warriors camped along the river's mouth at Lake Michigan and slaughtered them all except for fifty who escaped and have fled to their kinsmen at Detroit." These refugees arrived about the same time as the Wyandotte runner and the news of the massacre on the St. Joseph agitated the Fox and Mascouten greatly. Volleys of gunshot could be heard for two more days, and then Sahgimah and the great Potawatomi war chief Makisabi arrived with their warriors.

As the two redoubtable chiefs returned from Lake Michigan as many as six hundred warriors joined them. Young men from the Illinois, Missouri, Osages, Sacs, and Menominee were all intent on destroying this troublesome nation and their allies the Fox. Sahgimah wished to council with the French so Du Buisson sent Mr. De Vincennes to parlay with their allies. Makisabi spoke for the nations.

"We are here to help our French father and to eat those two miserable nations who have troubled all the country. Keep you guard against them for they may learn of your aid that are now arriving."

"Great Chief, would it be acceptable to you to not exterminate the Fox and their allies, but instead to drive them away to their former villages?" queried De Vincennes.

This greatly agitated the chiefs and principle warriors that attended the council causing Makisabi to reply, "These wearisome nations are liars who never keep their word. They have caused nothing but turmoil throughout all the country and we have, since the fall hunt, determined to destroy them. We will do nothing else. Do you no longer wish to live knowing their evil intentions? These wicked men never keep their word and their fires must be extinguished. It is our French father's wish that they perish. We learned this from him last year at Montreal." Makisabi was adamant and De Vincennes could see that such a proposition only irritated their deliverance so he promptly dropped the subject.

When the full compliment of warriors arrived they all proceed to the Wyandotte fort where Sahgimah gave a speech of encouragement.

"You must not encamp. Affairs are too pressing. We must enter immediately into our father's fort and fight for him. He has always had pity on us; always loved us and we ought to die for him. And don't you see that smoke also. They are the women of your village burning there and my wife is among them!"

Then there arose a great cry and all the warriors rushed the Fox fort with the Ottawa, Wyandotte and Small Kettle with his small band at their head. The Fox and Mascouten responded with a loud war cry and forty warriors issued out of their fort. When they saw the superior number of their enemy they retreated immediately back into their fort. Sahgimah attacked their palisades with flaming arrows then they all returned to the French fort.

"My children!" Du Buisson called out. "Encamp at the wood's edge and I will council with your chiefs inside the fort." But the young men where too highly agitated so they flung open the gates and the whole company of warriors came in. The chiefs sat in the middle of the parade square along with Du Buisson and De Vincennes. Makisabi spoke first.

"My father, I speak to you on the part of all the nations, your children, who are all before you. What you did last year in drawing our flesh from the fire, which the Fox were about to roast and eat, well merits that we should bring you our bodies to make you the master of them, and do all you wish. We do not fear death whenever it is necessary to die for you. We request only that you would pray that the father of all the nations have pity on our women, and our children, in case we should lose our lives with you. We beg you to throw a blade of grass upon our bones to protect them from the flies. You see, my father, that we have abandoned our villages, our women, and our children, to hasten as soon as possible to join you. We hope that you will have pity on us, and give us something to eat, and a little tobacco to smoke. We have come a distance and are destitute of everything; we hope you will give us powder and ball to fight with you. We don't make a great speech as we perceive that we may tire you because of the great length of the fight you have already endured."

Then Du Buisson answered, "I thank you, my children, and the determination you have taken, to offer to die with us, is very agreeable to me, and causes me much pleasure. I recognize you as the true children of the Governor General, and I shall not fail to render him an account of all you have done for me today. You need not doubt, that when any question arises respecting your interest, he will regard it favorably. I receive orders from him every day, to watch continually for the preservation of his children. With regard to you necessities, I know you want everything. The fire, which has taken place, is unlucky for you, as well as for me. I will do all I can to provide you with what you want. I beg you to live in peace, union and good intelligence together, as well as among your different nations as with the French people. This is the best means of enabling us to defeat our common enemies. Take courage, then; inspect and repair your war clubs, you bows and arrows, and especially your guns. I shall supply you with powder and ball immediately, and then we will attack our enemies. This is all I have to say to you."

The whole throng gave a loud cry of joy and thanks and Makisabi said in a loud voice, "Our enemies are all dead from this present moment. The heavens begin to grow clear, and the Master of Life has pity on us!"

All the old men gave long harangues encouraging the young warriors to listen to the commandant's words and obey his every command. Then ball and powder was distributed and they all raised the war cry. The Fox and their allies responded with their war cry at the same time, then guns were discharge on both sides and the balls flew like hail.

The Fork and Morning Walker led a large contingent of warriors to the forested area just west of the Fox fortress. Small Kettle, Sahgimah and the Wyandotte war chief encircled the enemy's stockade to attack them from the south and also to prevent them from getting water from the river. Makisabi stayed inside the French fort with Du Buisson and their men staffed the scaffolds. Together they kept the Mascouten and Fox under siege for nineteen days.

Makisabi and Du Buisson fired upon the Fox fortress continually while Small Kettle and Sahgimah captured many Mascouten and Kickapoo prisoners. They kept arriving in small groups to join their brothers not realizing they were besieged. The heat of the battle excited the young men and they made sport of killing their prisoners by shooting them with arrows and burning them. The enemy was running out of food and water so many began to die of thirst and hunger. They were forced to send their women out to retrieve water from the river. Most never made it back.

Whenever lulls in the fighting occurred the opponents would hurl insults at one another. The Fox covered their palisades with scarlet blankets and shouted, "We have no father but the English. We wish the ground to be covered with your blood. These red standards are the mark of it. Brothers, you would do much better to quit your French father and join us in serving our English father."

When Makisabi heard these words he bristled with anger.

"I, Makisabi, the great Potawatomi War Chief speak in the name of all the nations that surround you. Wicked nations that you are, you hope to frighten us with that entire red color you present on your walls. Learn that if the earth is covered with blood it will be yours. You speak to us concerning the English. They are the cause of your destruction because you have listened to their bad councils. They are the enemies of prayer, and this is the reason the Master of Life chastises them as well as you, wicked men that you are. Do you not see that the Father of all the Nations, who lives at Montreal, sends his young men to make war upon the English and takes so many prisoners that he does not know what to do with them? The English are cowards who only defend themselves by that strong drink that kills their enemies immediately after drinking it. So, we shall see what happens to you for having listened to them."

In the middle of Makisabi's harangue Du Buisson noticed that the Fox were only using the verbal abuse as a distraction while they went for water. He immediately ordered the firing to recommence killing some thirty of their enemy including some women. During this skirmish the Fox captured a house situated between the two forts and constructed a scaffold on it. This enabled them to fire upon Fort Pontchartrain from a closer vantage point. Du Buisson set a large cannon in place and fired upon the Fox scaffold destroying it and killing all. This frightened them and after uttering cries and groans they called out for a truce to parlay. Du Buisson called the chiefs together to get their thoughts on the matter.

"If we allow them to come and talk to us we may be able to devise a stratagem to rescue your women whom they hold prisoner", advised Small Kettle. Sahgimah was quick to agree for one of the women they wished to rescue was his wife. The rest of the chiefs agreed as well. Du Buisson sent Morning Walker as a messenger to the Fox fortress.

"My French father sends these words. You may come in peace in the morning to speak with him. He guarantees your safety while you parlay as well as your safe return. He is willing that you have that satisfaction before you die", Morning Walker called out.

The next morning the red banners were nowhere in sight. Three men emerged from the Fox fortress, one carrying a white flag. It was the great chief Pemoussa. He was escorted to the center of the parade grounds where all the chiefs were assembled.

"My father, I present you with this wampum and to the nations these two slaves to do with as you wish.

My father, I am a dead; I see very well the heaven is clear and beautiful for you only and for me it is altogether dark. I demand of you, my father, by this belt, which I lay at you feet, that you have pity upon your children, and that you do not refuse them the two days that we ask of you and the chiefs that are with you, that there be no firing by either side in order that our old men may council to come to a solution that will turn aside your wrath.

To the great chiefs that are before me I say, this belt that I present is to recollect that we are kindred. The blood you spill is your own. Soften then, the heart of your father, whom we have often offended. These two slaves are to replace, perhaps, a little of the blood that you may have lost. I do not speak many words until our old men can council, if you grant us those two days that we ask of you." When Pemoussa finished speaking Du Buisson answered him.

"If your hearts were properly moved, and if you truly considered the Governor at Montreal your father, you would have begun by bringing with you the three women you hold as prisoners. Not having done so, I believe your hearts are yet bad. If you want me to listen to you, begin by bringing them here. This is all I have to say."

The chiefs all shouted in unison and Makisabi said, "My father, after what you have just said, we have nothing more to say to this ambassador. Let him obey you if he wishes to live."

Pemoussa then said, "My father, I am but a child. I shall return to our village to render an account of what you have said to our old men."

"These four French soldiers will conduct you back to your village and we will not fire upon you this day, unless you attempt to go for water. If you do the truce is broken and we will fire upon you" Du Buisson promised.

No more than two hours passed and two Mascouten and one Fox came to the French fort bearing a flag. They had with them the three women prisoners. All the chiefs assembled again and the Fox messenger spoke.

"My father, here are the three pieces of flesh that you have asked for. We did not eat them thinking you would call us to account for it. Do with them as you wish. You are the master.

Now, we Mascouten and Fox request that the chiefs of all the nations that surround us, that you retire while we go out to gather provisions for our people. Many die every day of hunger. Our entire village regrets that we have displeased you and your father. Remember that we are your blood and brothers. Good father, if you are a good father, you will allow us this favor that we, your children, may not perish."

"If you had eaten the flesh, which you have brought me, you would not be living at this moment. We would have buried you so deep in the ground that your names would no longer have been spoken of", retorted Du Buisson. "Now, as to your request, I leave our great chiefs to answer you." Du Buisson deferred to the chiefs and Makouandeby, the head chief of the Illinois was appointed to speak for them.

"Now listen to me, you nations who have troubled all the earth. We clearly perceive by your words that you seek to only to deceive and to surprise our father in demanding that we retire. We would no sooner do so and you would again torment our father and this time you would kill him for certain. You are dogs who have always bit him. You have never been sensible about all the favors you have received from the French. You have thought, wretches that you are, that we did not know of all the speeches that you have received from the English governor, telling you to cut the throats of our father and of his children, and then to lead your English father's children into this country. Go away then. As for us we will not retire nor stir a step from you. We are determined to die with our father and not to disobey him because we know your bad heart, so we will not leave him alone with you. We shall see from this moment whether the master will be you or us. You have now only to retire, and as soon as you have entered your fort we will fire upon you."

The ambassadors were escorted back to their fort and the firing resumed. For four more days the fighting continued unabated. During this time the chiefs conferred and the decision was made to send a runner to invite the Ojibwa at Swan Creek and Aamjiwnaang to join in the war. Morning Walker left immediately.

A council was called as soon as he arrived. The old men decided that they should support their brothers and the French fort as this trading post was close by and should not be allowed to fall. Besides, The Fork and Small Kettle, who was now Young Gull's father-in-law, were already there with a small band of warriors. Young Gull, being one of the Three Fires most prominent war chiefs, was asked to raise as large a force as possible and to accompany them to Detroit so that he could conduct their affairs in the war. However, this would be the last time he would do so. His bones were now beginning to ache with age and he had seen more than seventy summers. Runners were sent to Saginaw while forces gathered at Swan Creek and Aamjiwnaang.

Again the Mascouten and Fox chiefs demanded to speak to their adversaries. Again they were given permission. Four of their great chiefs, Pemoussa, the great Fox war chief, Allamina, a Fox peace chief, and the two Mascouten chiefs Kuit and Onabemamtou arrived painted entirely green. They had with them seven women slaves. Two of the chiefs continually beat upon their small medicine drums, which they carried with them. They entered the French fort singing the death song. Then they were placed in the midst of all the nations and Pemoussa spoke.

"My father, I speak to you, and to all the nations that are before you. I come to you to demand life. It is no longer ours. You are the master of it. I bring you my flesh in seven slaves, whom I place at your feet. But do not believe that I am afraid to die. It is the life of our women and our children that I ask you for. I beg you to allow the sun to shine, the day to be clear, that we may see the day and that hereafter our affairs may be prosperous. Here are six belts that we give you that bind us to you like your true slaves. Untie them, we beg you, to show that you give us life.

Recollect, you nations, that you are our great nephews; tell us something, I pray you, which can give pleasure on our return to our village."

Makouandeby again spoke for all the nations. "You are dogs that are abandoned by even you allies. See, the few Sac that were with you have come over to our side. We know that eighty of your women and children have perished from hunger and thirst and now lie in you village with your young men that have been killed in battle. We know you could not inter them because of our heavy fire upon you and that this has caused an infection in your camp to further weaken you. If you had not returned our three women, one of who was Sahgimah, the great Ottawa war chief's wife, you should all be dead long ago. If you four chiefs were not here under our French father's protection, we should crack you heads open that your people should be without their leaders. Return to your village. We have nothing to say to you that would give you any reason for delight."

The firing recommenced all the more violently pinning the Fox and Mascouten in their villages. Their only recourse was to wait until a dark night obscured by rain, which would enable them to effect their escape. That night arrived on the nineteenth day of the siege.

All through the night the rain relentlessly pelted the two forts. The gloomy darkness of the night and the persistent stinging of the gale driven downpour gave the French sentries a sense of apathy. The Fox and their allies took advantage of this to make their getaway. Sometime after midnight they stole out the rear of their fortifications and made their way to the river. The howling gale force winds and the strong current hindered their progress up the river. The hunger, dehydration and lack of rest had also left them in a state of exhaustion and they knew their adversaries would be hot on their tail as soon as they discovered their escape. They would need to find a suitable place to renew their strength and to make their stand.

By the break of dawn the wind had died down and the rain changed from a pelting downpour to a gentle drizzle. Once again the French began to fire volleys of shot at the Fox fort. Their First Nation allies joined in firing from the forest's edge. But this time there was no return fire. Small Kettle sent two scouts to reconnoiter the enemy's fortifications. The breakout was discovered and this incensed the chiefs and all their young warriors. De Vincennes and a few French soldiers joined them in hot pursuit.

About the time their flight was discovered the Fox had entered Lake St. Clair and had found a point of refuse that suited their needs precisely. It was a peninsula that jutted out in the lake called by the French Grosse Pointe. The point was lush with herbs and other edible plants. Wild game birds abounded and it contained a spring for fresh water. The glen they had chosen was well protected and had only a defile by which they could be assailed. They guarded this entrance closely building a rampart there and dug in for the siege they knew was to come.

Sahgimah and Makisabi arrived with their forces settling in to take pot shots at the Fox rampart. De Vincennes arrived a short time later with his small company and two small cannons. For three days the battle raged. Combatants on both sides began to weary, but reinforcements were on the way.

Young Gull left Aamjiwnaang with his warriors as well as men from Saginaw. As they glided into Lake St. Clair and past Swan Creek more young men joined them. They arrived at Grosse Pointe on the fourth day fresh and yearning for action. They attacked the enemy with a vengeance killing many good warriors. Pemoussa knew the end was near.

During a lull in the fighting the Fox and Mascouten began to sing their death chant. De Vincennes took advantage of the opportunity sending an envoy carrying a white flag to the Fox fortification.

He called out, "You are all dead men! Save your women and children and surrender now. You will be escorted back to Fort Pontchartrain to discuss terms with Sieur De Buisson". Pemoussa agreed, but De Vincennes forgot to get his allies consent. The Fox laid down their arms so Young Gull set all his young men on a frenzied attack. All the Fox and Mascouten people died except for forty warriors, sixty women and one hundred children. They fled as a group to Grand Rapids on the Grand River where they were overtaken by Small Kettle and his band of Ojibwa warriors. They were in a heightened state of excitement so they expended their energy by annihilating all the Fox fugitives. This poor group of escapees met the same fate as their relatives at Grosse Pointe.

Thus ended the Fox sojourn to Detroit to trade with the French. Du Buisson was forced to explain the slaughter of over one thousand Fox and Mascouten people to the Governor General and worst of all the wheels were set in motion for years of fighting that became known as the Fox Wars.

3

Several years went by since the Fox debacle at Detroit. Despite the difference in age the more time past the closer Young Gull and Eagle Feather became. She was reaching the end of her childbearing years and Young Gull worried that no protégé would be his fate. However, he kept that nagging feeling deep inside determined to take his secret to the land of souls.

"Aanii", she exclaimed as she returned from the river. She had been washing clothes. "We shall have a special supper tonight, venison stew, just the way you like it. You know with extra maple syrup."

Young Gull rose from his mat grinning like a five year old. "How soon before supper", he asked.

"I'll put it on now. I have news that I know will please you."

Eagle Feather began to prepare the stew.

"What news?"

"You will just have to wait. I want to tell you after supper, you know, when the sun is stetting. It's so beautiful then." Eagle Feather was a romantic.

"But you could tell me now", he said impatiently. The little boy inside burst forth. Eagle Feather loved that quality.

"You can wait", she said wanting to drag it out.

When supper was over they sat outside their lodge overlooking the river. The autumn sun was a large red ball hanging in the western sky. For a long time they said nothing. Silently they immersed themselves in the richness of the Creator's goodness just enjoying each other's companionship. But poor old Young Gull could no longer contain himself.

"What was your news?"

"What news?" Eagle Feather loved to tease Young Gull. He was getting frustrated.

"You know—the news you said you had when you returned from the river."

"I have missed my time for the last three months. You are going to be a father", she blurted out.

Young Gull face broke out in the grin of all grins. His heart began to pound. "I love you", he whispered as he tenderly drew her close.

The moon went through its cycle again and again. Young Gull excitement about the pregnancy kept him from sleeping properly, but that didn't affect his health at all. In fact he was feeling strangely young again. The time for birthing was fast approaching and he wondered, "Would it be a boy, a girl—who cares".

Then, one hot summer evening as the sun was setting a thunderstorm could be seen to the south. There was a lot of heat lightning but little thunder. Eagle Feather was moving awkwardly around the lodge, you know, the way a woman at the end of her trimester does. Suddenly she stopped seemingly frozen in time.

"It's time", she exclaimed. Young Gull moved like a man half his age. Out of the lodge he flew, returning with the same dispatch and with two midwives in tow. He could do no more but wait.

It didn't take long. The cries of a newborn could be heard throughout the village. Young Gull would again be a father. Shignebeck and Onsha would have a new brother.

Fish Hawk, Young Gull's old friend, had been chosen to name the new born. The name would be announced at the naming ceremony, which was scheduled for the following week. After all Fish Hawk had been given the name the night of the birth.

Great celebrations were held for seven days. Then the whole village along with many visitors gathered at the powwow grounds at the mouth of the river. At the climax of the naming ceremony Fish Hawk cried out, "His name shall be Animikeence!"

4

Little Thunder came running to the village. He was now a boy very near the right of passage to manhood. He was all excited, shouting "Canoe's are coming down river. It is The Fork!" Young Gull emerged from his lodge to watch his pride and joy bounding down the path that wound its way along the river bank toward the village. He was amazed at how quickly the dozen years had passed since Little Thunder's naming ceremony.

The Fork beached his canoe, greeted Young Gull and Little Thunder watched as the two chiefs entered Young Gull's lodge and closed the flap behind them. They are in there a long time thought Little Thunder. Then the two emerged and Young Gull went off to call a council for the following day. The Fork was taken to a newly erected lodge where he could rest. He was also provided with food and drink to replenish his strength. Later in the evening, around sunset, he called Little Thunder to his lodge.

"Come into my lodge" The Fork said. "I want to tell you a story". Little Thunder obeyed the older chief from the Flint. His lodge was dimly lit by the small fire in the center of it. The Fork took out his medicine bundle laying it in front of him. He took down his pipe, lit it, and then paused a long time as if collecting his thoughts. Little Thunder sat waiting cross-legged opposite the chief of the Flint River Band.

"There is a village half way between here and the Flint" The Fork began. "It is on the shores of a small lake called Nepissing and they had a young warrior named Black Cloud turn bad last winter. It was a hard winter and game was scarce. The people were down to eating bark and boiling their moccasins for soup. Black Cloud was so famished his thoughts turned from concern for the survival of the village to selfishly satisfying his own hunger.

Finally his selfishness led him to seek out a conjuror from the Society of the Dawn. They deal in magic and potions given to them by the Evil One. The conjuror gave Black Cloud a potion made of the roots of certain plants and told him to make a tea from it. He said it would enable him to find food but only for himself.

Black Cloud waited until early the next morning. When he arose he took the powder, made a tea and drank it all down. To his amazement he began to grow, taller and taller until he was twice as tall as any other warrior in his village. And such long strides he had. Deep snow was no barrier and he could out run even the swiftest of deer."

Little Thunder sat mesmerized his eyes as wide as saucers. The Fork continued.

"Black Cloud set out over hills, through valleys and across rivers until he reached the top of the hill which overlooks my village. I was away hunting in a nearby valley so I missed the horrid spectacle that was about to take place.

Black Cloud's appearance had changed. His skin had turned a gray, putrid color and gave off a rancid odor. It was the color and odor of death. This deathly skin was pulled tightly over his long, lanky skeleton and Black Cloud's eyes had become sunken giving him the grotesque appearance of a monster. Black Cloud had become a windigo!

Down the hill it bounded toward the village shouting all the way. Its voice had become like the crack of overhead thunder. The windigo was an awesome and fearful sight, so much so that a few people immediately dropped dead. The rest fled.

When the windigo reached the village it did not avail itself of the winter's supply of food stored nearby. Instead it found that the corpses which lay were they dropped had a strange appeal to its insatiable hunger. It began to eat the dead but they held no nourishment for it. Because of its selfishness the more of the lifeless flesh it ate the hungrier it became. When it finished it set off in search of more human flesh.

I returned the next day to find my village empty and the tell-tale signs that it had been visited by a windigo. Some of the dead that it had feasted on were my relatives. I was horrified and flew into a rage. I gathered my weapons and set out tracking the windigo. I came upon it resting in a valley near the Flint. It was in its habitual weakened state so when he saw me about to descend upon it, it begged for mercy. But I had none. I killed it on the spot and left its flesh as carrion for the vultures!"

Little Thunder left The Fork's lodge astounded by the story. The sun had set and the village was dark and he was sure there was a windigo hiding behind every tree and every lodge he passed. He made it back to his parents lodge in record time with the story of the windigo from Nepissing buried deep in his heart. It was a tale designed to teach morals about generosity and greed, moderation and excesses and it would serve Little Thunder well for the rest of his life.

5

The years came and went and Animikeence or Little Thunder had grown to manhood. He had his vision and with the confidence that only a personal spirit can bring. He longed to see action in battle. Little Thunder was destined to be a Great War Chief as his father was before him. But at this point he was a warrior with no credit. After all he had only seen sixteen summers.

It was late in the autumn and most of the men had left for the fall hunt. Shignebeck, Onsha and Little Thunder were at Detroit making one last trip to trade for supplies for the long winter. Suddenly the place was abuzz with excitement. A flotilla of barks could be seen making its way up the river. As they passed between Bois Blanc Island and the west bank they came into full view from the fort. Little Thunder ran to the bank of the river full of curiosity. Who were these strangely dressed warriors bedecked with trinkets and painted for war?

When they landed he discovered they were the fearsome warriors he had only heard about. Iroquois! They had come to join their Wyandotte brothers in a war against the Fox. He also learned that they were the Praying Indians from the Lake of the Two Mountains near Montreal. They were here at the instigation of the great French father but the timing for such a war was wrong! There would be a council held that evening and Young Gull's three sons would attend. Little Thunder's heart soared with excitement.

That evening the council fire was lit at the Wyandotte village. The old chiefs of the Ottawa and Potawatomi attended as did Laforest, the first chief of the Wyandotte. The French commandant was also there as an observer. The pipe was smoked then Laforest rose to speak.

"My brothers—with this calumet we greet you and are pleased with your arrival. We see that you are dressed for war and ready for battle. We are pleased that the Governor, our great father has approved of the expedition. The Fox are dogs that displease the

Master of Life and are therefore not fit to keep their lives. The Illinois have attacked them two moons ago and are determined to wipe them out. We Wyandotte are ready to join with you in setting these degenerates upon the path of souls. However, our Three Fires brothers have already sent most of their young men to their hunting grounds. Their old chiefs who are with us in this council have given us collars to ask if we can wait until their return in the spring. At that time they promise that all their young men will follow us. They await your answer" he said. Then Laforest sat down.

Nonatgarouche, the War Chief of the Praying Indians rose to his feet. He was a fearsome looking man, tall and muscular, fully armed and ready for the conflict. He laid down several beaver pelts.

"By these presents we thank you for inviting us to make war upon the Fox. They have done nothing but cause turmoil in the whole of the country. They have continued to not only agitate the nations around them but also have grieved our great father, Onontio and his master the great king. The time for teaching lessons is over and the time for extermination has come. We thank the Three Fires peoples for their generous offer and we appreciate their willingness but we cannot stay until spring and lose a whole winter's hunt. Nor can we return home without first going to seek our common enemy."

He then turned to the commandant Boishébert, presented him with a robe then asked, "Since we have come a long way to exterminate our common enemy and are in need of the munitions of war we ask that you supply us with the means of dealing with these Fox dogs. Also, we ask that you give us the most accurate way to find their homeland so that we may most expediently carry out our task." Boishébert agreed. With that the council parties decided to leave at daybreak and Little Thunder, Shignebeck and Onsha were anxious to join them.

The following morning the small army of seventy-four Wyandotte, forty-six Iroquois and three young Ojibwa warriors left Detroit heading west. Little Thunder's heart pounded with anticipation. Within a few days they came upon the main village of the Potawatomi on the St. Joseph River.

"Welcome!" greeted one of the elders of the village. "I see you are dressed for war. Who is it you march against?" the old man enquired.

"The remnant of the Fox dogs!" replied Nonatgarouche. "Are there any young men left among your people who would join us?"

"All our young men have gone off on the fall hunt. If you winter here with us and await their return in the spring we can double your force with our young warriors" suggested the Potawatomi elder.

"We cannot wait. We Iroquois are far from home and it would cost us a whole winter's hunting season. We will press on" replied the Iroquois chief dejectedly. They spent the night on the St. Joseph before moving on to Chicagou.

"Why are they building a fort here at Chicagou?" Little Thunder asked his older brothers. "We still have a way to go to Wisconsin. I wish I understood Nonatgarouche's speech." Little Thunder only complained because he had been full of anticipation for days and days.

"A few of the older Iroquois warriors have become sick. They are going to stay here and wait for our return" said Shignebeck to Little Thunder. Shignebeck had attended the council of chiefs called by Nonatgarouche. He had been invited being the elder of the three Ojibwa warriors. He understood enough of Nonatgarouche's language to make out was going on.

During their stay at Chicagou some Potawatomi chiefs arrived and begged them to wait until spring. "We will march with you in the spring" pleaded the chief's spokesman. "We chiefs and our entire nation will rise from our mats with you" But they received the same answer as the old man on the St. Joseph.

The warriors that were still healthy rose the next morning and traveled west into Kickapoo country. When the Kickapoo first saw them coming they became alarmed but after learning the purpose of the Iroquois' mission they made the same offer that the Potawatomi had made. They also received the same reply from Nonatgarouche and the intrepid group marched further west into Mascouten territory.

The Mascouten were very badly frightened at first seeing a large Iroquois war party enter their country. They remembered the ferocity of the Iroquois expansion a half century earlier and the terror it struck. Cautiously, reluctantly they welcomed them into their main village.

"We are on our way to annihilate the remnant of the Fox nation" announced Nonatgarouche. "If you have any warriors who wish to join us and share in the victory they are welcome!"

The head chief of the Mascouten declined saying that he thought it a foolish mission seeing that the Fox were very numerous and their warriors very brave. Nonatgarouche bristled at the old chief's suggestion.

"If you are too afraid to join the battle then supply us with guides to take us to your border with the Fox and point us in the right direction so that we may accomplished the task set before us without delay" ordered the Iroquois chief. The old Mascouten complied by providing ten guides.

When they reached the border they pointed the direction the war party should go saying "Go in this direction. Do not deviate from it and you will meet nothing but Fox warriors." Little Thunder watched as the ten Mascouten guides disappeared into the forest heading east.

They set up camp on the border content to strike out in the morning. Little Thunder looked to the west as nightfall approached and wondered if the dark, ominous, clouds on the horizon might derail the campaign. He could see that they were full of snow.

When the first light of dawn appeared the camp could see that the first of the winter storms had arrived. The wind was howling above the tree tops swirling first out of the north then the west. The snow flew passed their lodges horizontal to the ground. They wisely decided to stay camped and wait out the blizzard.

The next morning Little Thunder awoke. He listened intently but there was no howling wind to be heard. He threw off his blanket and poked his head out from behind the flap of his lodge. The sky had patches of blue but the ground was blanketed with snow as deep as a man's knees. He could see drifts in the distance as high as his chest. A council of chiefs was called and Shignebeck attended while Little Thunder and Onsha waited impatiently.

"What was decided?" Little Thunder blurted out when Shignebeck returned.

"Yes, tell us quickly" demanded Onsha of his older brother.

"The campaign will continue. Nonatgarouche was adamant. He said he has not traveled such a long distance not to strike a blow. Laforest spoke for our Wyandotte brothers. He said it was impossible that his warriors should come this far without killing some men. We are to continue on snowshoes" replied the elder Ojibwa.

The whole camp prepared for war each according to their tradition. The Wyandotte made medicine by preparing a kind of grease which they rubbed themselves with to protect them from the effect of bullets and arrows. The Iroquois disapproved telling them that they should depend entirely on the Master of Life. They spent their time in prayer while Young Gull's sons took out their medicine bundles and offered tobacco.

Little Thunder Onsha and Shignebeck then packed up their implements, donned there snowshoes and were among the first ready to proceed. The party trudged over the deep snow for several more days. Then some of the old men became too fatigued from hunger and the heavy toil of the march. Another council was called and the old men thought they should turn back. But the young men were not of the same opinion. So it was decided that the older warriors should return to Chicagou and the rest would press on. Of the old men only two Wyandotte said they felt strong enough to continue so the war party, now down to forty Wyandotte, thirty Iroquois and three Ojibwa marched forward.

Two days later they came across three men approaching them across a small prairie. They were Fox warriors. When the three saw them they turned and fled. They were quickly caught as they had no snowshoes being unaccustomed to them. The young warriors had so much anticipation for battle built up that they killed them immediately without first gaining any intelligence.

The war party picked up the pace following the Fox's tracks back across the meadow to a top of a large hill overlooking the Wisconsin

River. When they reached the top of the hill they were amazed to see the main town of the Fox spread out before them. It contained forty-six lodges. The small party from Detroit froze at the sight giving the Fox in the village time to spot them.

Laforest encouraged the warriors. "We have nothing to fear! The Fox are dogs that do not acknowledge the Master of Life."

Ninety Fox warriors seized their weapons and came pouring out of the entrance of their stockade to the bottom of the hill. They stopped and got off a volley but their enemy was out of range. Their volley was returned by two volleys in quick succession.

"Young warriors—do not let the volleys amuse you!" exclaimed Nonatgarouche. "Lay down your guns and take up your hatchet in one hand and your knife in the other. Let the Fox dogs come to us."

Little Thunder's heart pounded as he waited for the Fox warriors to make their way up the hill through the deep snow. The first Fox warrior to face Little Thunder was a muscular young man and half a head taller but winded. He swung his knife in a large arc. Little Thunder quickly stepped aside. His snowshoes enabled him to easily out maneuver his adversary and he buried his tomahawk in the larger man's skull.

The other warriors under Nonatgarouche and Laforest enjoyed the same success as Little Thunder and for the same reason. The hand to hand combat moved down the hill. By the time they reached the town's gates seventy Fox had been killed and fourteen were taken prisoner. The war party highly agitated by the battle moved into the town where eighty women and children were killed and one hundred and forty were taken prisoner.

After the battle a fox chief who was wounded in the thigh was brought before Nonatgarouche. Six Fox women were also brought before the Iroquois chief.

"Go with these six women and take this message to the rest of your nation. Tell your chiefs that the Iroquois and Wyandotte have just eaten up your main village. In two days we march back to Detroit with our prisoners. You may follow us if you wish but at the first sight of you we will begin by breaking the heads of your women and children. We will make a rampart of their dead bodies to hold you off and then we will pile the remainder of your nation on top of them." Nonatgarouche then ordered the Fox chief's wound to be dressed and he and the six women were released.

Nonatgarouche, Laforest and their warriors returned to Detroit with one hundred and fifteen Fox prisoners. Ten had escaped before they left the Fox town and fifteen were killed trying to escape during the journey.

Young Gull's sons had their first taste of battle. Their courage proved exemplary and Young Gull was proud of his boys who had all become redoubtable Ojibwa warriors. He was especially proud of Little Thunder who arrived home with three Fox trophies on is belt. A feat to be honored for the first time out and indicative of the future war chief's destiny.

6

More summers came and went adding to Young Gull's long and eventful lifespan. His mind was still alert and his wisdom exceeded the other council members. However, his eyes had dimmed and his body was all but spent. After all he had lived 1300 moons.

Little Thunder had added to his prowess as a warrior. Like his father he had added many victories to his credit especially during the Fox Wars. Now he had been asked to serve as a War Chief. He was still young but continually displayed wisdom beyond his years.

The sun had only risen an hour earlier and already it was hot. Little Thunder had been up for some time and was down at the river's edge busily repairing some of the village's fishing nets. Although this task was usually handled by the women of the village he always liked to help out. Besides, it gave his hands something to do before he traveled to Swan Creek to get his mother. She had been visiting her parents and was to return home today. About mid-morning his thoughts turned to his father.

"Have you seen my father?" he asked some of the young boys who were fishing off the bank of the river.

"No" was their reply.

Little Thunder thought it strange that his father was not out and about. After all, the morning was half spent. He began to get concerned and moved a little quicker towards Young Gull's lodge.

"Father" he called. As he reached the lodge he called out again, "Father?" There was no answer. Little Thunder threw open the flap and poked his head inside. Young Gull was lying on his mat looking very much asleep, but Little Thunder knew this could not be so. He moved closer to his father confirming the very thought he had been trying so hard to ignore. Young Gull had passed in his sleep. Now his spirit journey would begin.

The family of Young Gull met at once. Little Thunder was first to speak. "We need to do something special for father, something that would show his eminence as a warrior, chief and elder."

Shignebeck agreed asking "did you have anything in particular in mind?"

"I thought we should have the internment in the great burial mound on the Horn River—at the sight of his great victory over the Seneca."

Eagle Feather smiled. It was a tentative smile, but a smile never-the-less. Shignebeck and Onsha agreed whole heartedly and the four approached the council with their wishes that afternoon.

Runners were sent throughout the territory with tidings of Young Gull's death. And the news spread beyond Aamjiwnaang, north to Michilimackinac, south to Detroit and beyond. Dignitaries began arriving at the mound on the Horn River almost immediately.

Young Gull was taken down the St. Clair River to the mouth of the Horn or Thames River. The young warriors continued with powerful strokes up the Thames for a distance of twelve miles. As they rounded a bend in the slow moving river the great mound came into view. The entourage of young men accompanying the body placed Young Gull beside the great mound facing the area where the large Seneca town once stood.

Young Gull was dressed in his finest. All the implements he used in life, his gun, powder and shot, knife, tomahawk, blanket, bowl, spoon and medicine bag or bundle were place by his side. They would be buried with him as he would need their spirits to help him along his spirit journey to the land of souls.

Mourners began arriving from all of Aamjiwnaang's villages. Also the great chiefs of the Potawatomi, Ottawa, Miami and Wyandotte as well as other nations south and west of the lower lakes kept arriving with their families throughout the burial ceremonies. The sacred fire was lit and would be kept going until the end of the ceremonies.

The next morning Young Bear began the ceremonies by chanting instructions to Young Gull's spirit telling him what to expect on the journey he was about to take and the dangers he might encounter. When he was finished he left but the mourners stayed to lament the passing of the great man. A few of the young men left to dig the grave at the head of the great mound. They could hear the wailing and moaning of the women mourners as their shovels dug deep into the edge of the mound. The women lamented loudly but the men were silent.

Later that day Young Bear returned and made a long speech to the mourners explaining the origins of the burial rites. At the end of the day Young Gull was encased in a bark casket and four pall bearers moved it to the gravesite.

The next morning Young Gull's village brought huge quantities of gifts of corn, pelts and trade goods and placed them all around the casket. The gifts were so numerous they covered both sides of the great mound. Young Gull was slowly lowered into the grave then covered with earth by the attendants while Young Bear chanted a hymn of benediction. At this point a small grave house made of bark was placed over the grave facing west. It had a small entrance by which Young Gull's spirit would be able to leave on his spirit journey.

For four days the mourners lamented at the grave site while Young Gull's essence underwent the change to spirit. Little Thunder started by giving a long eulogy extolling the great deed of his father from his "capture" of the Huron warriors as a boy to his wise counsel as a member of the Council of Aamjiwnaang. When he was finished the women began to wail for a time then there was a great silence.

Then anyone wishing to speak got up and did so followed again by wailing and silence. Many gave eulogies including good friends like The Fork, Sahgimah and Jean le Blanc.

At the end of the fourth day Young Bear and the attendants were paid in trade goods. Then a great feast was given by Young Gull through his relatives for all the mourners who were friends. Each person took a small piece of food and placed it at the grave. The spirit of the food would sustain Young Gull on his spirit journey which he was now ready to embark upon.

Great quantities of food were consumed at the feast and the next day a period of celebration commenced while Young Gull made his journey. Games were played; races were run with drumming and singing that went on for several days. At the end of the celebration the rest of the gifts were handed out to the friends of Young Gull by his relatives. Thus the life of the celebrated Ojibwa Young Gull ended with one of the largest celebrations of life ever seen.

7

Karen and Brad had decided to confront Mr. Nanabush for an explanation for all the mysterious things that have happened over the last four weeks. They planned to go down to the lecture hall before his last session started but a meeting with the contractor on Brad's project interfered. They would have to wait until near the end of the day and catch him before he left.

The time arrived. Four o'clock and the two hurried down to the small auditorium where Mr. Nanabush told his stories. When they got there only a few people were left chatting in small groups about how interesting the stories had been.

"Has Mr. Nanabush left?" Brad inquired.

"Yes, about ten minutes ago" replied one of the patrons.

"I have an idea" Brad said to Karen. "Who did you say recommended him?"

"The Assembly of First Nations—they have an office on Bloor Street."

"We'll call them on Monday and find out what they know about this guy" Brad said rather forcefully. Karen agreed with a smile.

First thing Monday morning Brad called the AFN.'s office.

"Assembly of First Nations: How may I direct your call?" the receptionist sang out.

"My name is Brad White. I'm the Curator of Egyptian Antiquities at the ROM. For the last four weeks we have had a Mr. Nanabush here doing weekly story telling sessions. I wanted to talk to the individual who recommended him."

"I'll put you through to David Root's office" said the receptionist as she transferred Brad. Another woman answered saying that Mr. Root was away until Wednesday. She offered to have him call Brad back.

"On second thought could I make an appointment? It would be for me and my assistant Miss Blackbird" Brad asked. The appointment was made for Wednesday afternoon at one o'clock.

The AFN office was within walking distance from the ROM. Karen and Brad arrived right on time. The same singing receptionist let Mr. Root know they were here and he came out and got them.

"I did some checking but could not find anything out about a Mr. Nanabush. No one here seems have recommended him or even know him" said Mr. Root somewhat puzzled. "He has an interesting name. Can you tell me what you know of him?"

"We don't have any complaints" explained Brad. "It's just that there seemed to be these strange occurrences happening during his time at the museum."

Karen interjected describing the elder from Michipicoten. She told him of all the unexplained incidents from his disappearance from the outer courtyard to their rescue by the timber wolf. David listened intently. When Karen finished her story the three sat there in David Root's office and said nothing while David collected his thoughts. Finally he spoke.

"First of all let's deal with his name. Do you know who Nanabush was in Ojibwa lore?"

"No" replied both Karen and Brad.

"Nanabush is another name for Nana'b'oozoo. His father is said to be a Manitou or spirit being and his mother was a human woman. He had extraordinary powers and was a protector of his people. There are many stories of him in our culture and he is sort of a patron saint."

"I've heard of him" interrupted Karen.

"It is said that he began to disappear as we began to take on more and more of the white man's ways. But he promised to return when his people returned to the traditional ways. That is happening now.

Our gatherings, the way our different communities interact, are changing. Traditional powwows are on the up-swing and Christian camp meetings are on the wane. Many of our people are abandoning the church and returning to our traditional religion. It is also being chosen over Christianity by our young. There is definitely a return to our culture."

"As far as coming from Michipicoten goes—No one comes from Michipicoten. Our forefathers believed that island was the abode of the spirits. We only traveled to the island in the day time to mine copper but no Ojibwa lived there. This old man sounds like the real thing. It is definitely intriguing. Could you give me his phone number and address? I'd like to check him out myself."

Karen complied with David's request and the two left the AFN more captivated than ever. They were determined to seek Mr. Nanabush out themselves. Brad called his number on his cell phone but only got a recorded message, "The number you are dialing is no longer in service." They determined to go directly to the address he listed on his application.

When they arrived they were shocked to discover Mr. Nanabush had listed a vacant lot as his address. Where did he live? Better yet, who was he really? Was David Root right about the return of Nana'b'oozoo?